LONELY GODS

Shivani Singh grew up in Ranchi, in Jharkhand. She abandoned a doctorate in philosophy to take up film-making and subsequently abandoned that, too, to become a full-time novelist. Her first book, the widely acclaimed *The Secret of Sirikot,* was published in 2006. She lives in Gurgaon with her husband and twin sons. This is her second novel.

Lonely Gods

SHIVANI SINGH

hachette
INDIA

First published in 2011 by Hachette India
(Registered name: Hachette Book Publishing India Pvt. Ltd)
An Hachette UK company
www.hachetteindia.com

SRD

ISBN 978-93-5009-254-5

Hachette Book Publishing India Pvt. Ltd
612/614 (6th Floor), Time Tower,
M.G. Road, Sector 28, Gurgaon 122001, India

Typeset in Bembo 10.5/13
by InoSoft Systems, Noida

Printed and bound in India
by Manipal Press Limited, Manipal

FSC
www.fsc.org
MIX
Paper from responsible sources
FSC™ C104740

Think not you can direct the course of love, for love, if it finds you worthy, directs your course.

—*The Prophet*, Khalil Gibran

For GM, always.

Prologue

The twilight was powder-blue but edged with the metallic grey of certainty because the forms that shifted before them were strikingly solid. They watched them, rooted next to each other, centred in each other's eternity.

'This is a bad plan.' He sounded seriously worried, because she was seriously determined. 'I am not going to stand by and watch you burn to ashes.'

'Not even if all that remains is you?' she replied, trying not to look at him; because when they looked at each other the universe did not exist.

Nothing else existed.

Not even time.

That's how it was, how it is, and how it would be – a painful creation and dissolution of worlds just by looking, and then looking away. It was the sweetest pain of all. In some worlds they knew this pain as love.

She sighed. 'That is the way it is supposed to be,' she said.

He recognized the tone – chiselled in stone – and experienced an anxiety he had known before.

Then, taking a moment to steel herself, she turned around to see where they were this time. Her breath caught in her throat when she saw, in the twilit distance, a single crow flying off a palace turret.

'It's not going to be easy,' she said to fill the long pause as they watched the crow fly.

'Attempting to succeed, where six billion people routinely fail, isn't easy.' And after a pause, an afterthought: 'I would imagine,' added drily.

A temple spire loomed over the palace, darkening the horizon, and she shaded her eyes with her hands to closely look at the far images.

'Is that a gargoyle?' she peered at the palace ramparts.

'No,' he said. 'That would be a stone lion.' He was patient. She was curious, and he was always patient when she was curious.

'And that is not a church, because that is not a crucifix,' she exclaimed.

'That would be correct.' He wanted to plunge his hands into the pockets of his jeans when he realized it would be a long time before he would be wearing a pair of jeans again.

'This is not Europe.' Her eyes shone, feeling she was getting into the spirit of the game.

'That would be correct again,' he sighed. 'This is India. A very remote corner of India, actually.'

'I want to go see,' she twinkled and had already flown off before he could mutter, 'Be careful.'

The palace itself was like any other palace, magnificently darkened by its own particular atrocious history, yet there was a golden shimmer around it, as if it knew and was waiting to be redeemed. The only disturbance was the crows; there were two of them, then three, spreading like dark blotches into the twilight.

'So this is where our story unfolds,' she whispered by his side.

And in a flash she saw a series of visions.

Archers lined in a row, heads beautifully glanced, all symmetrically poised to release their arrows from their bows.

Surging swelling oceans where the shores never met.

Waterfalls.

Green meadows spread like a carpet before undulating inky blue mountains.

A lonely child running through an empty palace corridor.

A group of sleeping forms holding hands, clothed in white, levitating together.

A cosmic drum rolling out its thunder.

Lightning.

In its sodium flash, a face smiling its mocking smile at her, its teeth the whitest that could be imagined.

And a wail rose up from deep within the bowels of the palace, a wail without beginning, without end.

She shuddered. 'What if we don't find each other? What if we get lost? What if we are never together again?'

'Evil is only what you fear,' he said, drawing her close to him. The air around them spread out in curlicues, bursting into yellow butterflies and warm flushed flowers.

'I will find you,' he promised.

In that infinite moment of briefness, somewhere in the manifested world, she saw an artist walking towards an empty canvas, brush dripping in golden liquid, finally knowing exactly what he wanted to paint.

'What's his name?' she smiled.

'Klimt,' he said, always ready with his answers. 'And he is going to call his painting of us "The Garden of Life".'

1.

As Uma slammed the car door shut and gestured *chalo* to the driver, the mobile rang out *Kill Bill*'s signature whistle. Immediately her breathing turned shallow. She felt as if everybody and everything had suddenly decided to hold their collective breath – the pedestrians, the guard at the school gate, the drivers lounging by the cars, the children and mothers going home, the trees, the school emblem fixed on wrought iron, the unblinking headlights of her black, monstrous-looking Scorpio – all frozen in a quiet, impeccable hush. And the thought sprang into her head: *Something is going to happen.*

It was her sister calling from Calcutta; oh all right, Kolkata, but she felt old enough to be old-fashioned. Ishita's voice sounded strained. She was bedridden with a precious pregnancy. Uma winced every time she thought of her sister's tailbone tied to her cervix, stretching every time the baby grew.

'Looks like he is sinking,' Ishita said. Uma was surprised that her sister had taken the trouble to call her to give her an update on their uncle's illness, considering how antagonistic she was not only towards

Raj Mamu but also to Uma's intense interest and involvement in their uncle's life.

'But I spoke to Ma this morning,' Uma protested. 'She said that his condition was improving.' It was almost as if she was protesting against that black, snake-like coil slowly raising its hood over her heart. Protesting against the new density in the air, like coagulating syrup.

'Well,' Ishita said, sounding as if she had invested enough already in this tedious topic, 'thought I'd let you know – since Ma's in hospi with him. And Dodo's in office.'

Meaning, I wouldn't normally have bothered to call, but since there were no other takers... Uma took a deep breath, stifling the rise of an old bile. No time for that.

Her car was turning behemoth-like into the slow-moving spate of Gurgaon traffic. She was lost in thought, aware somewhere in her fringe consciousness that sitting beside her was her seven-year-old son, his schoolbag still fixed to his back, staring out of the biggest eyes she had ever known. A blank slate waiting to be written on.

'Who is not well, Mamma?' Large brown pupils, irises showing, like spokes in a cosmic wheel.

'Raj Mamu, beta.'

Her thoughts were already spinning out of control.

'Which Mamu is that?' he wanted to know.

Uma was thinking of her husband's plans for the weekend trip ahead. The servants, the dry-cleaning, the last-minute shopping.

'You mean Tuntuni Mamu?'

'"Tuntuni" Mamu? Oh yes,' Uma said and started laughing at the image that came up in her head – her mother's brother armed with a pair of scissors, a picture of mock menace, threatening to cut off Vir's little penis. Passing on, like an heirloom, the traditional family joke: 'I'm going to cut off your tuntuni!' The etymological roots of the word 'tuntuni' unknown yet instinctively understood by many generations of her clan's uncles, nephews and grand-nephews, in the cryptic language of those bonding with other males of their tribe. All done in the not-subtle, filial way of acknowledging that thing between their legs.

Half an hour later, when she reached home, Uma was surprised to find herself staring outside the window of her son's room for a brief moment, registering in her peripheral vision a miserable pigeon ruffling its feathers against the Delhi winter and then sitting down on the side of Vir's bed and bursting into tears.

Vir came inside and stared at her. She saw new sentences, maybe even a whole paragraph, being inscribed in the blank slate of his eyes.

'Why are you crying?' was the obvious question.

Yes, why *am* I crying? she wondered. Raj Mamu has been ill before. In fact he has been regularly hopping in and out of hospital the last few years. It was just one of the things he did. They were all used to it. Only this time – and she could see the words written in front of her in Times New Roman, bold – HE'S NOT GOING TO MAKE IT. *How do I know that?*

'Go take a bath,' she sniffed at Vir.

'But why are you crying?'

'I'm not crying.' Any more.

'Yes, you are. Your eyes are red, your cheeks are wet.'

Uma knew better than to get into an argument with a seven-year-old.

'Raj Mamu is not well.' She wished he'd stop staring at her in that intelligent, petrified way. 'Ghamalu, *baksa nikalo*,' she yelled in the direction of the help.

'Where are you going?'

'To Raj Mamu. He's very very ill...' For a moment she contemplated crying on Vir's puny shoulder, but it looked too puny. Not yet; too young.

'Will he die?'

'I don't know.'

'He's not dead yet, is he?'

'Go take a bath.'

Ghamalu appeared, face curious but a study in blankness.

'Should I cut the carrots round or long?'

'I am saddened by the fact that Tuntuni Mamu is dead –'

The doorbell rang its sweet tinkle. She shouted at the cook to get the door.

'– though it's not nice to cut off anybody's tuntuni. Especially young children's.'

The cook appeared, controlling the urgency of his emergency.

'The gardener wants an advance.'

Uma could sense her tenuous control on reality begin to slip.

'He's not dead yet,' she admonished Vir.

'What should I tell the gardener?' The cook was losing his patience.

'Go take a bath,' she hollered.

2.

As she sat, riveted in her white plastic vinyl chair through her first VNP lecture, Kamini felt the initial stirrings again, and this time about, an excitement, an anticipation of something that was going to happen. What was especially exciting was that she didn't have a clue what it was. 'Bull!' the sceptic in her said. 'I'm just excited because VNP is a secret Delhi society, and so half the time I'm expecting Shah Rukh Khan to suddenly walk in and give a lecture on tantric sex and the rest of the time I'm imagining that this is what the Freemason Lodge must be like. Well, kind of...' And so she let the voice from the podium come into focus:

'The purpose of human existence,' the voice from the podium was saying, 'is to find the Meaning of Love.' Gaurav was peering over his rimless reading glasses in that sheepish way of his, as if embarrassed that he needed reading glasses in the first place. He loomed over the podium. There were only fifteen people in attendance and the podium and the mike were really quite unnecessary even though Mira's basement was not small. Yet, they were there, and so was somebody manning the sound system on the side of the room, from the 'Audio-Visual Department'.

The fifteen others in attendance, of varying shapes, ages and dispositions, sat in the plastic chairs either scribbling vehemently into their spurious-looking notebooks or staring dreamily about, as if on the cusp of some great revelation. That, too, in just an introductory lecture, Kamini thought disparagingly, for the completely uninitiated.

'Whichever way we approach the sacred four-letter word LOVE – whether we peel it like an onion, or crack it like a coconut or a code...' Gaurav's eyes shone with the perspicacity of his own wit as he spoke on while Kamini doodled in her notebook, eyebrows knitted in fierce and very fake concentration.

'Is love the recipe for a salad?' she thought. 'Am I not only the youngest but also the *smartest* person in this room?'

Her landlady, Mira, sitting across from her, hands folded, a picture of rapt attention, looked at her with proprietary suspicion – as if she were her mother. Once again, Kamini experienced the feeling that she knew her landlady much better than she had reason to. She tried to shake off the thought, but it *was* odd that, though she had only met her landlady a month ago, she could not stop herself from offering to pay the landlady's mobile bills, or watering the plants in her garden, or seeking her advice on how to tackle her pesky colleagues at her new – and first-ever – job in an advertising firm; odd that she had been so effortlessly inveigled into attending these mysterious 'VNP' sessions in the basement of her house.

'I'm just badly brought up...' Her thoughts trailed off to her mother's voice, which seemed to be saying, 'You mean you are *too* well brought up, don't you?' And Kamini answered back her mother in her thoughts: 'Maybe it's just some stupid Freudian guilt complex for leaving you and Jaipur and your sadness-riddled existence.' That shut her mother up. Kamini shook herself out of her reverie and straightened up on the vinyl-backed chair.

'Please do not get scared by the esoteric sound of the words "Heart Chakra",' Gaurav was saying, flashing a reassuring smile at his audience, who did not look scared at all. 'Because whichever way we approach it, we all, eventually, reach the Heart Chakra.' His voice swelled to impress the import of his words.

'By the Heart Chakra, I think the ancients meant one's centre of being-ness, where the conflict of duality ceases to persist; where the centre is both spontaneously motionless and effortlessly moving, where the ego of resistance no longer torments. It is here that one is really walking the talk, where one has shed off every emotional and mental vestment, peeled away every intellectual conceit. And it is in this centre, this *Heart*' – Gaurav gesticulated again, seeming to try and clutch it in his hand – 'of things, of life, of *your* life, *your* world, this nucleus of the energy of your sorry existence, where everything you know and feel and experience is digested... from where nectar flows and your being lights up. And it is this light – the light of the heart – that shows one the way back home...'

As Gaurav tried to finish speaking his body began to tremble from an unconscionable coldness. A whisper hushed through the room like a cool and very light breath. In that frozen moment he and every one present knew he would not be able to move even if he tried. The crowd around him sat still. Not an eyelid batted, not a finger moved. And for no reason at all the skin on Kamini's arms rose in goosebumps and her eyes misted over.

'...And...uh...it is this light, the light of the heart that shows us the way back home,' Gaurav struggled to a close, stupefied, because the words were not his.

Kamini shivered. The only movement she could make was to look down at her notebook. She realized that she had doodled a huge 'Om' symbol on the open page. When she looked up again she had a sensation of having lost time somewhere. She gathered her thoughts as Gaurav said, this time clear-eyed, more in control: 'Negativity is ignorance. Negativity is lack of knowledge.'

Oh shoot, she thought. I missed that part about love, and the Heart Chakra. For a moment she felt a pang of guilt at the oddness of her acute interest in the lecture. She could hear her friends laughing at her: '*You should be discovering love in the backseat of a car in a parking lot. Not in this uncle's quotes from the scriptures.*'

To which she mentally scorned their lack of refinement and subtlety: *'But think of the advantages of having an affair in the subtle plane,'* she told them. *'You don't have to wax your legs.'*

And inspired by this new dimension of motivation, she squared her shoulders and focused once again on Gaurav's blinking rimless glasses.

'A lot of work needs to be done...' Gaurav was concluding his talk, gripping the edges of the podium, knuckles whitened by his vehemence.

'After all, 2012 is just a year away.'

3.

In the nineteen seventies, Calcutta was not called Kolkata but looked exactly like it does today. The same crowded streets, like a river in spate – 'Where do all these people come from?' was a common grumble of Raj's clan, quite oblivious to the fact that they too were part of the 'people'.

There were no malls then, only New Market, unscathed – still waiting to be burnt down in the 1985 fire. No cyber cafés, only PCO booths, with a list of city STD codes pasted on the walls next to telephones that had no push buttons, but dials where index fingers were exercised in vigorous turning and crooking motions.

In the nineteen seventies, people were still expected to entertain themselves by conventional methods like hanging out of balconies and watching the streaming masses, playing whist, or musical games like antakshari, or going to the 'cinema' as Raj's mother called the movies.

That's what Raj, then in his mid-twenties, and his cousin Manik decided to do that fateful May Saturday. *The Exorcist* was running at the Ritz across the road from their neighbouring Chowringhee flats. But in a large family like theirs the tricky question, of who was going to see the film, and when and why, started looking like an almost insurmountable hurdle as the day wore on. The sisters threatened them with dire consequences if they went without them; the mothers and aunts thought the movie was in bad taste.

'Why you want to waste your time watching a girl rotate her head and regurgitate her lunch escapes me!' Raj's mother's opinion came accompanied with her patented snorts and nose crinkles. It also prompted such a rash of vomiting imitations and head rotations from the rest of the family that any objective bystander having witnessed it, would have come to the very logical conclusion that the sanity of the family was in question. A nephew came up with the spurious news that an ambulance was on call at the Ritz, because, apparently, people were fainting and having heart attacks during the showing. This triggered such a volatile and serious discussion on the mortality rate of the film that it lasted till late evening.

Raj and Manik met in the corridor that interconnected their two flats and hatched a plan. They would sneak out and watch the 'night show' without their sisters. Both agreed that the responsibility of a gaggle of fainting female cousins while watching a film as mortifying as *The Exorcist*, and that too, during the excruciatingly dangerous time of a 'night show' would be too much to bear at their young and tender age.

They were not that young really, they were all in their twenties, but those were slower times, as they would sometimes philosophize. 'Those days' – 'those' here presumably some nebulous magical past – they said when they were much older, 'people took their time growing up.'

Their sisters' wrath would have to be withstood the next morning, but tomorrow was another day, as they had famously learnt from another film.

'What film was that?'

'The one with the two intervals.'

'Name, dunce, name...'

'You, dunce, you. You should know, considering you've been trying to copy the actor's handlebar moustache, and not getting it right since all of last year...'

'*Gone with the Wind.*' It came out like a relieved belch, and with that their daring evening tryst without their sisters was sealed.

Around one o' clock, in the dead of night, when they ejected out of the cinema-hall into the deathly quiet alley of Chowringhee, clinging to each other so tightly that they were tripping over each other's feet, they both agreed the film had been a bad idea from the word go.

Black cats were overturning trash in the alleyways. The shops that had looked so friendly during their usual frenetic activities in the daytime seemed to have deliberately put their shutters down in malice. Hooded, shrouded things, with only the faintest of human shapes decipherable, slept in rows on the pavement.

Their apartment building was just across the usually busy but now silent road. Their apartments were above the never-dusted, paper-encrusted offices of the Life Insurance Corporation of India and the Bank of Travancore, strange and mysterious worlds that Manik and Raj visited often. They knew the peon and the General Manager of the bank in exactly the same way, referring to them both with the cloying 'Babu moshai' – spoken like some intimate endearment. But there was nothing cloyingly intimate about the office building now. Linda Blair's malevolent gaze stared at them from every shadowy corner.

The lift in their apartment block was a wrought iron monster clanging like the nemesis of some inevitable destination. At any given point, it was always more expedient to take the stairs, and that night they both agreed that it would be easier to confront Linda Blair on the stairs rather than have her rotating head drop on them from the ceiling of the lift. At least on the stairs they could run away from her; in the lift they would be doomed to the eternal perdition of her projectile vomit gushing from the roof. The stairs were endless, as they actually were 'those days'. It was quite a waste, really; you could have built an entire flat in the hallway.

The servant who was in on their plan and who had been instructed to open the door went by the name 'Bearer'. Nobody quite knew why he had such a ridiculous name and only Manik's father enunciated his hollers for him in the Queen's English. The rest of them called him 'Bairah' because that's what the other servants called him, and that's how he referred to himself. Now Bairah had been given strict instructions not to have any ganja that night, not to sleep a wink, and to open the door on the third knock.

After the twenty-fifth time they gave up knocking, and the gentle hammering gave way to desperate banging. 'Ganja,' Manik was close to sobbing now, feeling Linda's hot breath on his neck.

Watching Manik reduced to such a slathering mass gave Raj a measure of comic relief, and he felt a surge of courage-based rationality course through him. Bringing his mouth close to Manik's ear he suddenly hissed, 'Stop it!' and noticed with satisfaction how his skin prickled at the back of his neck. At least somebody was a bigger coward than he was. 'If your father opens the door, my friend,' he sniggered, 'you are chopped liver.'

Manik collapsed beside the huge oaken doors of his apartment, seemingly shut forever for him. 'What do we do now?' He was desperate, sensing the silence of the deepening night closing in on them.

That's when Raj saw her. Actually, Manik saw her first, and it was his sudden dumb, hangdog expression that made Raj look in her direction.

She was peering down from the landing upstairs, in a white dressing-gown, her hair streaming down the banister. Slightly bemused, slightly frightened, but curious enough to find out what the commotion was about. It's not that she was a light sleeper, but her baby was, and he had just dropped off when the commotion below her had begun.

'Must be the rowdy men of the Singh-Deo clan,' she'd thought, grabbing and girdling her dressing-gown tight, firmly resolved to sound off the Singh-Deo boys in no uncertain terms. Phrases like 'civilized behaviour', 'newborn babies', and 'the dead of night' came to her mind but as she left the flat and reached the landing she was suddenly swept by a totally irrational wave of elation. A thrill coursed through her body.

She did not know whether the cool breeze that swept over her came from within her or without.

Unbeknownst to her, that's exactly what Raj had felt, and when he looked up at her face looking down at him from the landing the words 'Oh shit' popped inanely into his head. When he finally exhaled, his breath was so long and deep that he was acutely aware of how long he had held it. It was not that he hadn't seen attractive women before – his own family was full of them – but right there she appeared like a tremendous moment of such excruciating beauty that he had to steady himself. The moment passed, leaving him confused and disoriented, especially because his head was telling him that there was nothing really beautiful about a dishevelled woman in a voluminous dressing-gown staring at him in cross-eyed curiosity.

'Is there a problem?' she asked as politely and graciously as she could.

Between Manik and Raj it took fifteen minutes to relate the sequence of events and the magnitude of their distress accurately to her. She looked from person to person as if watching a tennis match and solved the problem with the simple practical wisdom of a woman who had given birth to another person. 'I have the keys to an unused terrace that connects with one of your servants' quarter balconies. You can return the keys to me tomorrow morning.'

She decided to focus her attention on Manik, because Raj had that unfocused look of one going into a pleasant daze. It took all her patience to make him understand that her apartment was above his, and that the building architect, in prophetic omniscience of exactly such an eventuality, had actually connected their flats in some way. He finally got it. She made a mental note that the Singh-Deo boys, while distractingly charming, were not very bright.

She led Manik, who was now looking curiously over his shoulder at Raj and who in turn led him, upstairs through her apartments to her unused terrace. Raj, used to opulence, could see the signs of financial struggle in her apartment: the cheap pieces of decoration; the faded upholstery; the lack of servants. He had an insane desire to protect her, to buy her an expensive gift. He experienced a sharp vision of how she would smile when she saw it. For no seeming reason, he shivered.

Embarrassedly, they crossed her bedroom. The sudden smell of baby formula, curdled milk and unwashed cloth diapers assaulted Raj's senses. It was an alien antagonistic smell, increasing Raj's confusion. All three politely and painfully craned their necks away from the rumpled bedclothes, even though it was fairly plain that her husband was not around. They concentrated on moving towards the terrace door.

As Raj filed past her after Manik into the balcony it seemed as if the moon had suddenly turned up its light. She caught a scent – male, clean, powerful – and reeled against the doorjamb.

Outside, somewhere between shades of moonlight and darkness, two figures were waving her goodnight.

'When can I come tomorrow to return the keys?' Raj was asking.

'Anytime,' she said.

And there it was.

Later, they both wondered whether the light had changed. Because they had exchanged an expression of such intimacy that it lit up and pierced through the night, shocking them both into silence.

The apartment seemed desolate, desperately empty after he left.

As Raj shimmied down the water pipe outside the servants' quarter balcony he thought he saw Linda Blair smiling at him. A nudge-nudge wink-wink kind of smile.

Neither Aparajita nor Raj slept that night.

The moon babysat them.

At dawn a gentle sun put them to sleep at exactly the same time.

4.

Even though she did not want to be sitting there, rooted to the chair like a nail to a cross, she knew that the choice was not hers to make. Kamini knew that she would keep coming back to this basement, to this house with its Punjabi baroque railings, and she would be captivated each time.

Her life was not going to be the same again, and she sighed in strange, bewildered relief. All decisions were movements, progressions to the inevitable, the irresistible, the irresistibly inevitable – her leaving her perpetually morose mother in Jaipur just a month ago; her new job in the advertising firm; the strange look in her landlady's eyes when she first saw her; the strange look in her boss Rita's eyes as if she knew something about her that Kamini didn't; the strange exchange of looks that Rita and Mira shared when Kamini caught them sipping tea together in Mira's living room when she stepped in to pay her rent:

'My boss and my landlady *know* each other! What are the odds of *that* happening?' she had Tweeted and immediately updated on Facebook.

'There is no such thing as coincidence,' her landlady Mira had remarked in answer over a thoughtful sip of her own excellently brewed Darjeeling tea.

Kamini thought it had been so clever of her to roll her eyes and retort: 'So you are in cahoots! I'm seriously flattered.'

'Darling, what if you came to know that the whole universe was in cahoots?' her boss Rita had said, in that way of hers that Kamini thought of as so 'advertisingly' cool.

Not to be intimidated by her boss's perfectly chiselled collarbones shown to perfection by her off-shoulder Chanel business suit, Kamini had had the presence of mind to reply: 'That would be flattery of cosmic proportions.'

The three women had tittered in a collective sorority at her remark and for a daring moment Kamini had wondered whether it was a good time to ask for an extra set of keys to the main gate, but remembering what her mother always said – that she was too well-brought-up for such cheapness – she desisted.

That had been around the time that Kamini had first felt the stirrings of restlessness, of the need for a search, of a desire to find answers to painful questions, for redemption, for resolution, for closure to a life that had never really opened. It was a spark that had been lit by the casual conversation Mira and Rita had struck up about this strange new phenomenon they called VNP. All sessions, they told her, were conducted right there, in Mira's house. Intrigued by their encouragement to search for existential answers in VNP's programmes she had found herself quickly enrolling for them.

Kamini had noticed Hari at the first VNP meet. She had frowned at him during Gaurav's lecture, gesturing at him to turn up the light faders. He had shrugged his shoulders from behind his audio-visual equipment suggesting anything and nothing.

Moron, Kamini had thought briefly and it had showed on her face. *Rock chick,* Hari had thought, and not a muscle had moved on his.

Now he was walking up to her again: ''Scuse me, Kamini, right?'

'Right.'

'They are looking for you.'

Eyes round as saucers she asked, 'Who?'

'They.'

'*They?* Could you specify, please? So as not to make this is sound like an alien abduction?'

Hari sensed her irritation. 'The Forum. Inside the Manager's office.'

'The Forum?' Suddenly unsure, her next question bore the air of a peace offering: 'Would you be knowing why?'

That was the moment he was waiting for. 'Find out for yourself,' he shrugged and sauntered off.

When Kamini let herself into the Manager's room it felt eerily as if she had shifted dimensions. There was a heavy sobriety within the room, making her feel immediately out of place. Gaurav and a few other worthies of whose augustness she had been informed in hushed whispers by Mira, sat around a table, exuding various degrees of hallowed luminosity. Her eyes popped when she saw Mira among the chosen – a picture of serene studiousness, not like a simple housewife at all.

The moron has sent me to the wrong room, Kamini panicked. She was about to turn tail and bolt before her landlady could see her, when a Voice – she didn't know what else to call it – stopped her: 'It's all right, Kamini, we want you to join us.'

She froze and turned to face a sombre circle of unblinking eyes, not knowing to whom the Voice belonged. Her landlady was looking at her as if she didn't know her. Stricken, she scraped a chair away from the table and took what she felt was an interminable amount of time smoothing down her dress and settling into her seat.

'We would like you to take the minutes of the meeting,' someone said.

Kamini nodded mutely and picked up the journal and pen lying on the table, praying to her Convent Christ to make the rest of the people gathered around the desk stop staring at her. Soon she realized that they were staring at her because they were waiting. So, with her pen poised and her scribble pad open, she waited too.

When Hari walked in a few minutes later, she immediately sensed the heightened gravity of his demeanour and the rush of anticipation in the room. He sat down and came straight to the point:

'I know we are all waiting for news of the Twin Flame project. But I have just heard from VNP that the project has been deemed classified and highly hierarchized. I am afraid there are some people here who, unfortunately, cannot, for undisclosed reasons, be part of this project.'

Kamini realized that she was staring at him and stopped. Not only was he speaking with an authority that took her breath away, there were bodies, persons, sane people, who were hanging on to his words. She shook her mane in disbelief and raised her pen.

'You don't have to write that,' he said without looking at her.

'Of course,' she responded with military promptness and put her pen down.

'Any reasons for the confidentiality?'

Kamini realized that the man asking the question was the one whom she had mentally labelled the 'Caucasian swami' because he wore a perfectly starched orange robe. At her first VNP meeting he had told her he was Spanish, and she had idly wondered what he would be like to flirt with – a thought it looked as if he had caught, because he had blushed to the roots of his blond hair.

'None given,' Hari was short but not impolite.

There was an awkward silence before Hari spoke again, trying not to look at anybody: 'I'm sorry, but I'll have to ask some very senior people in this room to leave.'

Another frozen silence. Kamini would have felt sorry for Hari if he hadn't looked so unfazed by his situation.

While everybody except Kamini braced themselves, Hari turned to Gaurav, 'Sir, I'm sorry but...'

'Oh, no problem, Hari,' Gaurav got up with alacrity. 'VNP always has a good reason.' He gathered his things trying not to look embarrassed. Then Kamini realized that an elderly aunty type too had started getting up from her chair, a few seconds before Hari turned to her. 'No offence, Auntie,' he said without looking at her.

'None taken, dear,' she smiled sweetly, and turned

to everybody with enviable poise: 'I'll be outside supervising the tea and samosas for later.' A few more people stood up on their own and left with her.

That graceful exchange over, Hari waited for everybody to settle down again and for Kamini to resume her pen-poised position.

'Friends, as you know the Twin Flame project is a new programme initiated by the global perspective. It came to VNP last month and is already functioning in France, Australia and Mexico. The project comprises of 6000 cases or files across the world, over fifty countries. Strangely, 1000 cases are from India alone, and thirty cases are from Delhi. Before I go into any further detail I have to inform you that there are six people assigned to our case, and that would include all of us in the room at the moment.'

He surveyed those in attendance, carefully ignoring Kamini, thus promptly cuing her to blurt: 'But I'm only here to take the minutes of the meeting!'

'You are also part of the project.'

Again, no eye contact. And before she could say *wowbutthat'socool* he had moved on.

'Before I can divulge any further details we will first introduce ourselves and participate in the secrecy ritual to seal the energies of the project. Those unfamiliar with the secrecy ritual can please speak to Swamiji for an orientation. Rudra, Gaurav's son, is also part of the project. Till I get a clear brief about what to do about Rudra, he will not be a part of our meetings. But he is definitely giving his energies to the project. And um, yes,' he added with a wry smile. 'I shall be the facilitator for the project.'

After the meeting, the members of the select group joined the others for tea and samosas in the hall, where a white tablecloth had been laid out on a vast table and everybody bravely attempted to balance a plate of samosas in one hand and a cup of tea in the other as they gesticulated about the brilliance of the programme.

Kamini was in no mood to socialize. So she hung back by the door, carefully maintaining the right-hand samosa and left-hand tea balance. A boy of about eight, slouching on one of the lobby sofas, stared at her. His expression said, 'I know what you're thinking.'

Flustered, she looked away and walked up to the Caucasian swami, who smiled at her and extended his hand. 'Hi, Kamini. We haven't been properly introduced. My name is Carlos.'

'Who is that kid sitting on the sofa?' she asked him.

'That would be Rudra, Gaurav's son, who is part of the project?'

'Him?' she said, a little shocked at how young the kid was.

'The kid can't talk,' Carlos said casually before turning back to the flask of tea for a refill.

She jerked her head back at the boy who hadn't stopped staring at her. There was an amused 'got you there' expression on his face this time.

'Why?' she asked, deciding to stare the kid down. He was beginning to smile at her now, an extremely unnerving, all-knowing kind of smile.

The swami shrugged. 'A virus, I was told.'

Kamini was incredulous. '*Viruses* can do that?'

'AIDS is a virus, remember?' The swami put down his cup of tea. 'And so what are you doing here?' he asked looking keenly at her for the first time, like an assayer surveying prospects.

She knew that look. 'Not much,' she said in a way she knew the nuns in her convent school would have approved of and excusing herself, walked up to Rudra. Who, had he been fifteen years older, she thought, would have done a good job of turning her into gooseflesh with his piercing look.

'Can you read minds?' she asked the child in all seriousness.

Rudra's eyes shone in momentary brilliance and then he laughed.

'I presume that's a yes,' she smiled too, trying not to feel foolish.

'We've tried everything –'

Kamini turned around and saw that it was Gaurav, who gesticulated as much even when he was not giving a lecture. 'Neurologists, bio-medicines, shrinks, homeopathy, alternative therapy, even fasting. Nothing helps. The harder we try, the worse he gets...'

Rudra immediately turned sullen, clapping his hands over his ears.

Gaurav gave a short hard laugh. 'That means he does not like what I said. Maybe I should make myself scarce.' Before she could stop him, Gaurav had swerved away.

The tension became worse when she realized that the little boy disconcerted her.

5.

When Uma landed in Kolkata, well into midnight, her mother and aunt were waiting for her at the exit of the Departure Lounge. Like much of the rest of the city, the airport looked unkempt, indifferent to orderliness. The floor smelt of too much disinfectant. Still, despite the corrosive indolence that always hit her when she reached Kolkata, she felt welcomed and included as always in its irrational bustle.

Her mother hadn't combed her hair and looked not only more dumpy than usual but also as if she needed to sit down. She glared at Uma abjectly. 'Why have you put on weight?'

'I think there are more important things right now to worry about,' Uma answered her mother, then smiled at her aunt and touched both the sisters' feet.

'That's an awful haircut. You look like a cabaret dancer,' her mother continued.

Her aunt, around the same age as her mother, and exactly the same build, giggled.

'Mamma, they don't have cabaret dancers anymore. You might mean a pole dancer. How have you been, Mausi?'

'Don't ask, Uma. It's very difficult to see Raj Dada like this.'

'Can I see him before going to Dodo's house?'

'It's very late now. They've moved Raj to the ICU,' her mother said. 'If we are going back to the hospital, I'll wait at the reception. I can't bear to see my younger brother in a coma.'

Uma gave her aunt a searching look. Her aunt shook her head. This was not good. Uma surveyed the situation. Her mother had, as usual, anesthetized herself into a pleasant daze. She had that preoccupied expression of a wedding guest wondering whether she had worn the wrong sari to the event. Her aunt looked dazed too, after all, she was on the periphery of the family crisis.

Uma's sister had her cervix tied to her tailbone like a stake. Dodo, her brother, was a software programmer, for God's sake. Meaning, *his* tailbone was tied to the office computer. That left her uncle's daughter Indira who had arrived in Kolkata the day before. She did not know what to expect from her – considering she had not yet visited her father in hospital, and that for the last six months Uma's mother had been pleading with her to visit him and she had refused. 'There's nothing wrong with him, Bua. Just ask him to drink tomato soup instead of alcohol for dinner,' had been the gist of their endless negotiations over his health.

In the taxi she could sense that her aunt and mother were relinquishing their uneasy burden onto her already.

'Let Uma handle this,' her mother told her aunt, as if she were passing out a ministry portfolio. 'She is so good with medical terms.'

'What do you mean, let her handle it?' Uma protested. The streets of Kolkata were dark, its movements slow. A sleeping Bengali, breathing deeply, stirring only once in a while. 'Isn't that what Indira should be doing? He's her dad, for God's sake.'

For a moment there was silence in the taxi, the only movement was the shifting of the Ambassador's gears, like bones creaking.

'Uma,' her aunt finally said, 'This time Raj Dada came to Kolkata with 888 rupees in his pocket. He...'

'888?' Uma was piqued.

'Yes,' her mother said, comfortably sinking into the torn car seat, as if getting ready for a nap. 'He handed a bunch of notes and coins in my hand, said "888" and passed out.'

'Where did you find him?'

Her mother had tried to explain this earlier to her on the phone but thanks to a failing network and her mad rush to the airport she hadn't got the story straight.

Between her mother and her aunt she finally understood that he had been found at the door of an apartment in Chowringhee just above where her mother, uncle and cousins had lived some thirty odd years ago.

'Why had he gone there?' Uma was intrigued.

Her mother shrugged, sinking deeper into the torn sweaty Rexine of the taxi. 'Maybe he had gone to visit Manik in the apartment below. He's the only one living there, since our apartments were sold. But how could he have forgotten the address to the apartment? Why had he gone instead to the apartment upstairs? Has alcohol scrambled his brains to such an extent, that he can't find the location of such a familiar address as his cousin's flat?'

Her mother was mumbling now, her eyes drooping.

'Don't you dare go off to sleep on me,' Uma raised her voice. 'I can't carry you up to Dodo's apartment.'

Her mother grunted thoughtfully.

'Who lives upstairs?' Uma couldn't shake off the image of the unyielding door, her uncle collapsed in a heap before it. Uma remembered the Chowringhee doors as white, chipped, and really large.

'Nobody knows,' her aunt said. 'It's been empty for years.'

The taxi stopped at a bylane in Ultadanga. In front was a small private nursing home of dubious credentials, like so many others around it. Knowing how hard up her mother was for cash Uma did not chide her for the obvious stinginess that had governed her choice of hospital, but she immediately panicked over her uncle's welfare. *Some nincompoop with a degree from an Institute very much like this one was treating her uncle with spurious medicines.* She looked up at the overly bright neon lighting on the roof of the building pretending to be a hospital. Saraswati Nursing Home, it said. She's the goddess of knowledge, thought Uma sarcastically, not healing – unless you are looking at your patients like a multiple-choice quiz.

In the tubelit, deserted lobby of the hospital her mother ensconced herself in one of those seats that are nailed to the floor, and looked as if she was not moving much, either. There was an orderly with an empty bed-stretcher waiting for its chance at the lift, so Uma took the stairs.

There were slippers and shoes scattered outside the ICU. Their incongruousness immediately irritated Uma. The ICU was crowded, every real-estate inch consumed by beeping instruments, or doctors and nurses jostling for space. The starched white stretch of hospital bed seemed to be the only obligation to luxury conferred to the patient. She saw her uncle slam bang in the middle of the ICU. His space was cordoned off from the rest by the sort of cheap green curtains that Uma always associated with dirty government hospitals.

There was something truly existential, Uma thought, of being sick and uncomfortable in a hospital at night, administered by healthy young Malayali nurses who talked above your head in a language you didn't understand, and who would rather be asleep than checking your blood pressure.

She walked up to her uncle's bed, her heart in a vice, and steeled herself for a better look. Immediately, she understood why her mother had refused to come up. Every ounce of her uncle's emaciated body looked diseased. This is what alcohol does to you, she cringed, thinking of her pre-dinner glass of wine. His feet were swollen, his breathing laboured, unnatural, his eyes sewn shut with mucus, his mouth slack and tortured.

'Oh God, Raj Mamu,' she thought. 'Are you going to die?'

'*Not if you help me,*' he seemed to say to her, his mouth shut, his eyes closed.

She took a deep breath and said, 'Raj Mamu, it's me, Uma. I've come from Delhi to see you.'

His eyes still shut like a new-born baby's, a guttural sound originated from somewhere in his throat.

'He said something...' Uma looked around her at nobody in particular. There was a skinny nurse in hospital greens flitting from bed to bed. She looked bored, listless.

Again that sound.

'Ughnnh.'

'Nurse,' Uma cried out. 'He's trying to say something.'

The nurse's face finally animated with an expression that said 'your point being?'

Uma realized that translating *unghnnh* sounds probably did not fall under the purview of the nurse's job description. *Fair enough,* Uma thought, and concentrated her attention on her uncle's shrivelled throat. In a moment she felt it throb with sound again.

'What is it, Mamu? Do you want water?'

'Ughghnn.'

She felt his terror at not being able to speak.

'Are you in pain?' she anguished.

He nodded. Victorious at getting somewhere she leaned closer, 'What do you want me to do?'

And there, she heard it. Like a ghost voice reaching out from the static of the cosmos. The words – '*Find her.*'

With a pang of jealousy she presumed her uncle meant Indira, his daughter. Never mind, she thought, that I left my home and family at a moment's notice to be by your side. Never mind, that your daughter is in town but has been avoiding you as if you were a dirty disease, which you actually are. It is she and not I who is your daughter, and it's good to establish the pecking order right off, thank you very much.

She leaned closer to his ear and said, 'I'll get her first thing tomorrow morning.'

She noticed, not without bitterness, that the lines of his face had miraculously smoothed out. The corners of his mouth turned up in an almost boyish smile.

Must be the old man saying thank you, she thought.

6.

Around the time the sun rose over the Calcutta skyline Aparajita finally went to sleep dreaming that Raj was making love to her. She felt his hands running over her body and when they reached between her legs she woke with the sensation of having exploded into a million points of light. Startled, she realized she was sitting upright on her bed and the sky outside the window was a teasing, liquid blue. The persistent vision of Raj kissing her neck forced her to the bathroom mirror where she brushed aside her hair from behind her right ear.

Just at the midpoint of her collarbone and the turn of her jaw line was the beginning of a love bite. It was the colour purple and she staggered back at the force of eroticism at the sheer sight of it.

It was a slow shaking walk back to her bed. She sat cross-legged at the edge of it beside her infant son and stared into the lightening darkness around, wondering what was happening to her. *Why* was it happening to her? Then another image came, like a pop-up: Raj lying in his own bed, a pillow between his legs, as bewildered as she was.

She smiled. At least she was not alone in this.

Indeed, she wasn't.

Raj had woken up at the same time as she had, wondering for the first time in his adult life how he had ended up in someone else's wet dream. He had been semi-conscious when he had started making love to her, and could not quite comprehend whether it was a deliberate attempt at self-arousal or simply a process beyond his control. He could taste her skin, feel her body move beneath him, her every curve pliant in his hands. In his dream, he was pleasantly surprised at his own expertise, and how much pleasure he was capable of. It was the strangest sensation. As if all of him, from bone to muscle to blood, was melting in droplets, only to solidify to fill the empty spaces of her curves. He awoke with a pillow between his legs, in the sweetest pain he had ever known, and the bemused feeling that life was outside his control from now on, and he hated it, and really, really loved it.

He propped up the pillows, put on his glasses and picked up a book from his bedside. It was the directory of the building. Absent-mindedly he flipped through it till his eyes rested on her name – Aparajita Ghosh. 7B. Astrologer.

Aparajita Ghosh. Just Aparajita sounded better. No Ghosh, no husband. *Astrologer?* Hmm.

And just as he was thinking of her, wondering why this erotic dream was not about being in control but losing it, she saw him in a flash. As she sat cross-legged on a bed that seemed suspended between the lightening Calcutta skyline and eternity, she saw him.

Propped up in bed, looking amused, reading a book, wearing glasses.

She frowned, uncertain about the magic of the situation. She didn't remember him wearing glasses.

She gave out a long deep sigh and settled back into her pillow, into a sleep she understood; into a lack of understanding she understood.

There was no happily ever after. No Romeo and Juliet. Everybody, even her three-year-old nephew, knew that there was no Santa Claus.

She did not know that Raj wore glasses only when he did not wear contact lenses, which was most of the time, vain that he was. They were not available in Calcutta then, and he had had a special pair of hard contact lenses fitted out for him in London.

Around mid-morning Raj told Manik he was going upstairs to return the terrace key.

'You look bright-eyed and bushy-tailed this morning,' Manik said, looking the worse for wear himself.

Really? thought Raj, bewildered by this since he had spent the entire night tossing around in his bed. 'Well, you look as if you spent the night with Linda Blair.'

'And who,' Manik asked, scratching his unshaven stubble insouciantly, 'did *you* spend the night with? The terrace key?'

Raj had an insane desire to smash his cousin's nose. Instead he laughed, pointed the key at him – now a burnished gleaming instrument in his hands – and said, 'Funny man.' He paused at the door as a flush rose over his face, turned and repeated, 'Very, very funny man,' then loped off up the winding stairs.

When her doorbell shrieked he expected his beating heart to drum up to a crescendo, and as expected, it did. But she did not open the door. A maidservant, a middle-aged woman with a broom, stood before him, surly, and in a hurry. Taken aback, Raj did not know what to say or do. He had not planned their meeting. The key still in his hand, not knowing exactly how to react, he brandished it before her feeling utterly defeated. 'I have to return this key to your memsahib,' he said.

Without a word, the maid plucked the shining key out of his hand and shut the door. Raj stood in front of the closed door for a long time before returning to his cousin's flat to regroup and strategize.

In his cousin's apartment, breakfast was a daily celebratory event that started around ten in the morning. Today it was in full swing, replete with its mandatory ritual bedlam.

Around twenty-thirty members of the blueblooded Singh-Deo clan would converge, as if by some unseen force, to any one of the apartments during mealtimes, to play out the daily fracas of eating. The cheerful noise of the breakfast tableau before him seemed more chaotic than the forces in his own head, so he went to his cousin's balcony for a surreptitious smoke and to clear his mind.

He could not understand why he was feeling so shattered by the fact that she hadn't answered the door. As if it were a pre-meditated attempt to ignore him. He leaned over the balcony, confused by the utter irrationality of his emotions, and tried to steady himself by thinking, '*This is just a crush. It happens to me every week. It will pass. Her image will fade away.*'

He took a deep pull on his cigarette and clearly heard her voice say –'I wish you wouldn't smoke. The smell bothers me.' Choking, coughing, he stubbed out his cigarette and flipped it into the busy Calcutta pavement below. It was a wonder that it landed on unpopulated concrete and not on somebody's head.

This time it was Manik's voice that said, 'How can you steal my dad's Dunhills and not smoke all of it? It's criminal.'

Raj wheeled around towards his cousin and couldn't stop blurting his question: 'The terrace key upstairs, do you think she's a witch?'

'Why?' Manik's smile was slow and sleazy. 'Has she cast a spell on you?'

Raj ignored the question. 'Do you know that she is listed in the directory as an astrologer?'

Manik looked at him closely. 'No.'

Raj heard what he did not say: *You are taking a lot of interest in her.* 'She obviously dabbles in the occult,' he said, nonchalantly. 'And you know that Bengal is the hotbed of the occult, especially the tantras.'

'Hmmm,' Manik was warming to the subject. 'Maybe the "Astrologer" sign is to lure handsome eligible bachelors like us into her web of deceit. Maybe her husband is poor, alcoholic, or worse, a partner in crime. Maybe he prepares secret tantric yantras to lure unsuspecting innocents to his house.'

For a moment, Raj contemplated trying to explain to Manik all the strange occurrences that had followed his meeting with her, and then thought – *Nah! He's too dumb.*

'But why would she do all that?'

'For control, for money.'

'Hmmm.'

'She's an extremely attractive woman. Maybe she's a dakini. And she uses her sexual control over hapless men like us for her tantric rituals.'

Raj gave his cousin a searching look. Why was Manik cutting so close to the bone, especially when he did not know what had happened last night? Why was he taking thoughts from his own head and giving them form? *What did he know?* 'It's not for nothing that our families are protected by the gods and saints,' Raj said. 'No dakini-sakini can control me. All the more reason for me to find out a little more about her.'

They looked at each other, and both knew Raj's reason was not investigative; he wanted to find out more about her. Period. It amused Manik and scared Raj.

'Time to get my birth-chart read,' Raj said, looking away.

'If she starts devouring you, just stick your head out the window and holler for help. I'll come rescue you,' Manik taunted him as Raj walked away, intrigued by the bizarre turn of their conversation.

It was not that Raj and Manik did not discuss 'girls'. They discussed 'girls' all the time. In fact 'girls' were a predominant part of their conversation. 'Girls' here referred to women who were not Rajput. Because Rajput women were either related to them in some way, or potentially marriageable, and hence had to be mentioned with a note of caution.

'Girls' were either friends of sisters, or sisters of friends, or those considered 'fast and loose'. Fast and loose fell in two categories: the first, of hot friend of sister/hot sister of friend; the other of the type who peddled herself in Park Street, where they regularly went to do what the entire clan called 'feast their eyes'. There was a third category in which fell the 'crush girls'. Crush girls were girls who made them stammer and their hearts skip a beat. Girls whom they watched from far, and who elicited cold deep sighs from them. In this category fell many actresses like Sharmila Tagore and Raquel Welch, and also one particular girl who stood at the bus-stop at five every evening (she had the most innocent face they had ever seen). Maybe because they could not categorize Aparajita, they were throwing this dakini witch business at her.

We also have a sexy neighbour category, but I just can't make her fit into it, Raj thought, sinking deeper into the mire of confusion; unsettled even more by the unnatural and overpowering need he felt to see her again.

When Raj returned to the flat he found Bairah sitting on his haunches in the servants' alley, smoking a beedi and grumbling about Manik's mother. He cut short his rant with a command:

'The upstairs memsahib in 7B does not have a telephone. Go to her *personally*' – and here he stared at Bairah to emphasize this point – 'and tell her that Raj Singh from 6B downstairs wants his birth-chart read. Then come back and tell me exactly what she said.'

'Huzur.' Bairah's face was expressionless.

Does he know, Raj thought wildly, the effect she has on me? 'Go immediately!'

'Huzur.' Bairah got off his haunches and threw away his beedi.

'Bairah, wait,' Raj called after him.

'Huzur?'

'Remember, tell me *exactly* what she says.'

And then Raj saw it, that expression similar to Manik's. The expression that said – *Buster, this time you've got it bad.*

7.

By the third VNP meeting, Kamini had become used to the air of otherworldliness in Mira's house, rather strangely called Machu Picchu. Later, she would wonder whether there was a connection between the VNP centre in Delhi named Machu Picchu and the Mayan prophesy about 2012.

The air around the house, she was sure, was rarefied and dense at the same time. And those who walked into Mira's house also came into its space time cloud, where light changed, as if dimensions had shifted.

What a find, Kamini congratulated herself once again for chancing upon it. Just ten thousand bucks for a room in this piece of heaven.

The secrecy ritual that Hari had spoken of at her first closed-door session of the anointed six of the VNP had turned out to be a fire havan in Mira's backyard. In keeping with Kamini's theme of shifting space time dimensions, Mira's overgrown modest backyard next to the colony's service lane, really did seem to all a wide expanse of lush greenery, like some mythological grove.

As the project members gathered around the makeshift fire-pit square in the middle of the backyard, Kamini could not shake off the absurd feeling that even if a hundred people were to descend on the cramped little backyard, there would be room to accommodate more.

Mira was the VNP pandit for the purpose, and she presided over the Vedic chants like some ancient high priestess. The authority with which she threw oblations into the fire made the short hairs rise on the back of Kamini's neck. Mira was dressed in orange silk robes that flowed over her portly body with an unlikely sinuousness and the bright red vermilion on her forehead gave her a strikingly different identity from that which Kamini had seen in her short acquaintance with her landlady.

Only once during the ceremony did Mira look disconcerted. When Kamini followed her distracted gaze she noticed that it had gone to three crows sitting on the backyard wall like three attentive and very important witnesses. But that was only for a moment. Mira's voice rose with a renewed strength as she proclaimed: 'A havan is a sacrifice of the lower to the higher. So surrender your energies here and let the fire purify them and lift them to the highest goal.'

And so the gods were invoked and a red cotton thread was consecrated, broken into seven (Rudra also attended the ceremony) lengths that were then tied to everybody's right wrist. Project members solemnized the ceremony by throwing naivedyam into the fire and made a sankalpa, a vow, to work together and keep their intentions pure.

Kamini looked around her. The chosen ones were a ragtag crew of different ages and dispositions. An outsider, unaware of what they were actually doing, may have even considered them a bunch of cranks and weirdos.

After the ceremony, the group sat gratefully under a spring sun that warmed them and lit them up in just the way they wanted. Chomping on VNP's ubiquitous samosas, a formal introduction of the team members finally took place.

Because of Rudra's lack of speech he was absent for this part of the session, whisked away by an attendant to a mysterious destination.

The group sat in a circle under a garden umbrella on throne-like, white, wrought iron garden chairs that sank into the ground with such unremitting force that tufts of Mira's garden grass were instantly uprooted.

Mellowed by the sunshine and a descending silence so different from the bark and snap of traffic just beyond the garden wall, Hari introduced himself first.

He was a property broker.

Hah! Kamini thought. *I knew it!*

The gemstones on his fingers to ward off the evil planets; the thick gold chain around his neck; his trouser pockets bulging with different mobiles. *Of course* he was a property broker. His flatly accented English, the careful side parting in his hair, all added up. Sitting around the stainless steel flask of the now tepid tea, Kamini imagined a sticker on the windshield of his presumably golden-coloured Mitsubishi Lancer that said 'Jai Mata Di'.

Interrupting Kamini's mental caricature sketch Hari briefly explained how he would be the clairvoyant and psychic of the project.

Her landlady Mira, after her magestic panditry, had once again become the silver-haired lady of indeterminate age, between sixty-five and seventy-five, who introduced herself as Mira, homemaker, grandmother, saying it was an important qualification these days. She had intricate knowledge of the Hindu scriptures and could quote verbatim from esoteric texts of which nobody in the gathering had even heard. She was also considered a good channeller and said she was an excellent astro-palmist. Some said her powers of prediction were fairly accurate. Maybe because of her great mane of silver hair she was also affectionately called 'the fountainhead'. Besides, Kamini thought, she *looked* like Ayn Rand.

Not counting Rudra – the 'honorary freak' of the project – the genders were evenly spaced. There were three females to the three males in the project. All ages were also covered in the spectrum. Carlos, the Caucasian swami was a handsome middle-aged man. The Spaniard was an expert in ashtanga yoga, and though the rumours were unverified, they said his supernatural powers ranged from being able to change himself into a crow, to becoming invisible. On the other hand, there *was* evidence that he could levitate. (Kamini would share with Hari later that he reminded her of Casteneda, to which Hari would pithily ask, Casteneda who? making Kamini snort in disgust.)

Carlos had taken direct discipleship from Babaji – a saint purported to reside in the general direction of the Himalayas, who assumed a human form to communicate with his devotees. (Kamini told Hari that all that she really cared about Carlos was that he was extremely good-looking, which was Hari's cue to snort in disgust. Nor did his retort that Carlos' good looks were evenly balanced by Rita's, do much for Kamini's self-esteem.)

But Kamini had to admit that her boss, Rita, though middle-aged like Carlos, was not only drop-dead gorgeous, but the brightest person she had ever met. A prospective grandmother at fifty, she looked twenty-four. It was rumoured that in her heydays she had been mistress to the prime minister, till a corporate magnate had fallen prey to her charms. Found always in her natural attire of Prada and Gucci, she headed a strange and new but popular department in VNP called Quantum Mythology. When, later, Kamini had quipped how different it was from what she was heading in the advertising firm – the Cola account – Rita had quoted Walt Whitman to her: *Well then,* she had said. *I contradict myself. I am large. I contain multitudes.*

She and other team members of the 'Quanti Mytho' department were involved in converting all the mythologies of the world into the language of Quantum Mechanics. They believed that every mythological figure – from Apollo to Krishna to Dionysus – were energies embodied as sub-atomic particles, and their stories or lilas were episodes, 'horizon events' in quanti parlance. They were descriptions of the play of energies during a sub-atomic process. For example, the story of Sati immolating herself because her husband Shiva was insulted by her father Daksha could be translated into a series of symbolic equations that made the myth look to the lay eye like a Pythagorean proof of a geometrical theorem.

Kamini found her area of specialization fascinating and would have tried to approach Rita to discuss her work with her had she not been so utterly overwhelmed by the entire package of beauty and genius wrapped in a Hermes scarf and served with a rocksure Punjabi confidence that made her entirely unapproachable.

If Rita and Carlos were the goddess and god of the project then Ali was the brat.

All of eighteen, with a straggly beard and a tattoo of the Yin Yang symbol on his waist – always on display because of his low hipster jeans and conspicuously visible Calvin Klein underwear – Ali was the sorcerer, the magic expert.

Call it the black arts, or tantra, his knowledge, he said, had begun to unfold at a very young age before the aghast eyes of parents who had never picked up a religious book in their lives. His father was a famous Muslim filmstar, his mother was a Hindu who called herself (in the film magazines) 'secular'. In Kamini's dictionary that meant that she thought religion was politically incorrect and worse, unfashionable. But Ali's predilection for the tantras had done a good job of ripping apart his mother's carefully Botoxed veneer. He had even briefly been considered a manifestation of the next Dalai Llama incarnation and had been interviewed behind closed doors for several days. Unfortunately, a little nugget of information he had accidentally let slip, went against his favour.

For once, his mother, excited by the prospect of her son becoming the next Dalai Llama, had tried to intervene but to no avail. The little nugget of information that Ali had rather gleefully disclosed was that his girlfriend had got herself a heart-shaped bikini wax.

Controversy raged behind oaken monastery doors for days, wherein his mother's contention that a heart-shaped bikini wax was merely a fashion accessory did not help at all. These days, Ali smiled cheekily, she had to content herself with his excellent grades and the fact that he was captain of the soccer team. He was also an alchemy adept and had done extensive research on medieval western and Indian texts on turning base metal into gold.

Hari, it was fairly obvious, was the Keeper of the Flame, in other words, the mid-wife, matron, the chief coordinator, and general dogsbody. Looking at Ali, Hari said, he was maybe even pimp and drug-peddler.

Blushing to the roots of her hair when it came to her turn to explain herself, Kamini said that she had no psychic skills or mediumistic talents. She was not a scholar or a channel or an adept. She was very new to VNP, more of a curious bystander. 'I am currently working with Rita in an ad agency and I've never even taken the minutes of a meeting before,' she confessed. And then, not looking at anybody in particular she stared at her hands and said: 'I'm very honoured to be a part of this project, but I don't know why I am here.'

And when nobody interrupted the silence that followed she added – 'You can call me the spare part of the project.'

To which Hari replied, with that special deadpan expression he reserved only for her, 'You'll find out your role soon enough. All that I can say is that there is a very good reason why you are here.'

Both noticed that the others were watching them and turned away, embarrassed. She to stare at her hands and he to fiddle with his perpetual folder of flying notes. The silence of the others watching them only deepened their discomfort and intensified Kamini's sudden sense of foreboding.

Everybody stared at the dying embers of the sanctifying fire and felt the impending weight of events to come.

Unwittingly, Kamini turned her head to the backyard wall. The three crows had become six.

After the secrecy ritual, the group trooped back to the basement where Mira opened the door to a large chrome and glass conference room that Kamini after two months of living in the house didn't even know existed. 'But,' she blustered, 'how, where…? This room was not there the last time I was here,' she exclaimed, quite tired by her own confusion.

Mira smiled indulgently as the group started pulling out chairs around the projector. Carlos ruffled her hair affectionately and sat down next to her. 'There's a lot of magic in VNP but –'

'– this room is not magic,' Hari was curt and very much in control.

'It's architecture.'

'I wasn't suggesting that this is Narnia,' Kamini withered at Hari.

'Oh, but it is,' Ali brightened from where he sat at the conference table. 'You see that mirror?' He pointed at a glass skylight in the direction of Mira's backyard. Kamini turned to look up at it, bewildered.

'Oh shut up, Ali,' Hari said before turning to Kamini. 'It's good to have a sense of wonder, but it's not good to be naïve.'

'Yes, Bwana,' Kamini muttered, sensing a hot flush rising up hcr facc.

And that was the exchange that the history of VNP would later remember as the one that henceforth labelled the conference room the Narnia Room.

When they had all quietened down Hari connected his computer to the projector and started his power point presentation. Kamini was riveted by the sheer audacity and weirdness of its nature. She looked around and could not understand how everybody, including Ali, could be so blasé about the presentation – as if Hari were reading out the weather report! How come, she frowned suspiciously, I am the only one whose jaw is dropping?

Twin Flames, Hari explained the bottomline, are two energies vibrating to the same frequency. The two genders, male and female, are the polarities of vibrational frequency, and their coming together unleashes a huge quantum of energy, much like nuclear fusion. This energy was called UCL – unconditional love – by VNP.

UCL – the highest and most refined energy in the universe – was necessary to balance out the destruction, the cataclysms of apocalyptic proportions that 2012 was starting to release.

'What are these Twin Flames?' Kamini asked.

Hari thought long and hard about it. 'People, actually,' he finally replied.

Kamini burst out laughing. 'This is the most unromantic love story I have ever heard,' she roared, wishing she didn't sound so hysterical.

'All love stories don't come with pink accessories.' Hari's admonishment was unnaturally gentle.

Mira was staring hard at her hands splayed flat on the glass conference table and did Kamini imagine it, or was there a catch in her voice, when she said:

'Kamini dear, you meet your Twin Flame after thousands of painful lifetimes. It is the end of the hardest road imaginable, the completion of a journey that started at the beginning of time. Of six billion, there are six thousand Twin Flames uniting in our time. I don't think even union with God can be more powerful than two halves finding each other after millions of years.'

Almost as if to ignore the sneaking suspicion that Mira's eyes were misting up – she was definitely leaving sweat prints on the glass table – Hari started to explain the specifics of their project. Their project involved reuniting two people, entirely unrelated and unaware of the project and VNP. Very strictly, at all times, they were to be referred to only as XX and XY, the genetic notation for the female and male gender respectively. Here, of course, XX and XY were not generalizations but two actual people who were living out their existences somewhere at an undisclosed location on the planet.

It was Rita who finally rose out of her reverie to raise her finger and ask a question. Thank you, Kamini thought, sighing in relief.

'Why the secrecy?' Rita said pouting her bee-stung lips. Only she, Kamini thought enviously, could carry off such an ostentatious shade of orange lipstick. 'Why don't you just give us their names?'

Hari replied in that deferential way that most men have only for extremely good looking women: 'Because, ma'am, at no time does VNP want us to forget that this is a project. It is about the energies, not the people concerned. At no time must we compromise our detachment to the subjects. We will be spending a lot of time studying them, watching their actions, their intentions...'

'Are we a spiritual organization or a detective agency?' Mira was frowning, clearly ill-at-ease with the human-subject-under-observation idea.

'Can we hurry this up?' Ali said. 'I have a tutorial in the evening.'

Kamini noticed with satisfaction that Hari was struggling to harness the burst of individualistic temperaments in the room. 'This is highly irregular...' Kamini, muttered under her breath, joining in the discontent.

'Trust me,' Hari said, raising his voice a little. 'This is only temporary. As we move deeper into the project it will all unfold, you will see. 'The first step is to create an energy profile for XX and XY. Here every skill base in the room will be required. Aura scans, past-life histories, karmic databases and detailed energy grids have to be created from ground up. Mira Aunty will be making the karmic database, Rita Ma'am, we will be requiring your expertise in energy profiling and morphogenetic fingerprinting. Carlos Sir, you will be required for their aura scan, and their co-ordinates in the hierarchical grid. Maybe you and Rita Ma'am could work together for this. Ali, you will be working with Mira Aunty and Carlos Sir on past-life reconstruction. I need a minimum of seven past-life reconstructions. And…'

'And me?' came a small voice from the corner. 'Do I continue to lend atmosphere?' Kamini laughed self-consciously.

'Yes, you…' Hari said, as if he had only just noticed her presence, 'you continue to take minutes.'

Next time bring some candy to keep me occupied, she thought, wondering whether the psychics in the room could see the smoke wafting out of her ears.

'And,' Hari said sternly, 'I want all of this by the end of this month.

'Impossible…' Carlos said.

'You've got to be kidding me…' Ali piped in.

'Oh come on,' Hari said. 'All this is a day's work for you guys.'

Amongst the grunts and groans that ensued came an interjection from the swami: 'We are to do this with absolutely zero information about the identity of the two subjects? No name, no photograph, no address, no history? How does VNP expect this to be even possible?'

'It is possible, Carlos Sir, and you know it,' Hari turned towards the Spaniard. 'I give you two words and a number: Twin Flames are the two words and 2012 is the number. Let the recent Japanese earthquake keep reminding you of the urgency of the crisis. VNP knows this is enough for you to crack the code. It's not for nothing that they have ladled out the cream of VNP for this project.'

'Will you stop talking as if I don't exist,' Kamini said.

A twitter riffled through the room breaking the serious mood.

Rock chick, Hari thought, carefully putting on his unimpressed expression.

'Flattery, darling,' Rita winked at Hari, 'will get you everywhere.'

'Will it get me my energy profile on time?' he flirted back.

Rita wagged her pen at him. 'That is not included in my definition of everywhere.'

They laughed. And Kamini noticed that Hari had a perfect set of white teeth.

'Cho chweet...' Ali said tapping his TAG Heuer watch, 'but can we please move on?'

'We meet again,' Hari cleared his throat, 'in a fortnight, for a status update, and to iron out issues, if any. Meantime, it would be a good idea to remain in touch with each other. The reason no information is being divulged about the two subjects is to keep the slate clean, free of preconditioned impressions. Ground zero. And please be very careful with the sketches you create. It is fairly important that they be accurate. The world depends on it.'

'I'm afraid I'll have to save the world after my tute. I really gotta go,' Ali said, gathering his Blackberry and Ramada Inn stationery.

'This meeting is adjourned,' Hari said.

As Ali, Hari and Kamini jostled each other in their hurry to get out, Mira, Rita and Carlos hung back in the conference room, watching them leave.

'Youth,' Mira smiled.

Carlos sighed in the direction of Kamini's receding rear end. 'Do you mean chronological youth or youthfulness?' he said.

'Carlos!' Rita simpered. 'Do you have to be so technical?'

And all three lapsed into a thoughtful interlude that they felt necessary before the question on all their minds could be verbalized.

Carlos finally voiced it. 'Do you think she knows?' he asked, staring out of the conference room window.

Mira had taken out her knitting from her purse, and Rita tried not to show her concern, because she knew that for Mira this was symptomatic of an uncontrollable anxiety.

'I don't think so,' Mira said. What she liked best about knitting was that she didn't need to look at anybody.

'Well, she was asking me who the VNP chief was,' Carlos said.

'Really?' Mira's knitting was picking up speed.

'Oh, so what?' Rita gesticulated. 'Many among us do not know who the VNP chief is.'

'So what did you say?' Reading glasses had mysteriously appeared on the bridge of Mira's nose and she peered over them now to stare intently at Carlos.

'I said that only a rare handful in VNP have had the privilege of direct instructions from the chief's physical form.'

What Rita and Mira loved about Carlos was how open his face was; how direct his gaze. 'I told her that most instructions were given in dreams. And that even if you did not see a person the VNP symbol was a sign of his presence.'

'Have you ever seen the chief?' Rita was curious.

'I think,' Carlos admitted. 'A day before I got the call to join the Twin Flame project, I saw an old man sitting on a wall, holding a VNP pamphlet in his hand.'

Mira nodded sagely as her needles clicked away.

'Yes, the pamphlet and the wall are his symbols.'

Carlos thought a while in silent camaraderie before blurting out, 'Does the chief exist?'

'What do you mean, exist?' Rita accused.

'I mean does he have a physical form?' the swami elaborated.

Mira let out a short laugh. 'Yes, he does.' And then frowning critically at the long length of what she had knitted she said, 'I have a more immediate concern.' And when Carlos and Rita waited for her to reply to her own concern Mira said, 'The energies of the meetings are becoming too intense for Kamini. We need to depersonalize them…'

'Let's ground them on a more neutral, intellectual plane,' Carlos said swivelling in his chair,

'Good idea,' Rita agreed. 'I'll ask Hari to throw in a few more presentations.'

'Ali could do one on Yin-Yang energies,' Mira suggested.

'Speaking of which,' Rita added – and when the other two turned to look at her she finished – 'I don't know whether it's a good idea for them to fall in love like this.'

'Not good at all,' Mira shook her silver head. 'Not good at all. Not only is it bad protocol, but the Keeper of the Flame has to be celibate at all costs, at least through the duration of the project.'

'Boy, am I glad *I'm* not the Keeper of the Flame.'

And when laughter burst out around him the Spaniard blushed in the way the project women had grown to adore. 'Uff,' he said. 'I didn't mean it like *that*.'

Outside Mira's house it was already getting to be dusk. It had rained recently and for a change the Delhi sky was a brilliant blue punctuated by shocking pink clouds. The moon had made an early appearance, like a slice of cheese cut in a hurry. The narrow alley outside the building was chocolate slush jammed with cars in every conceivable nook and cranny. Hari walking ahead of Kamini, looked up at the sun's last gold bursting through a cloud above them. Taking his car keys from his pocket, he said, with a degree of affectation: 'Ah,

Nature has mopped up.' He stood for a moment with his nose in the air and his eyes closed.

'God's light...' Kamini agreed, looking up at the dramatic gold and silver embroidery in the sky.'Like God's gaudy Punjabi upholstery has finally been dry-cleaned.'

Hari's car parked directly opposite her Santro was a silver-coloured Opel Astra. There was no Jai Mata Di sticker on his windshield but the goddess's ceremonial cloth was definitely tied around his rear-view mirror. *Close,* she thought. *I was so close.*

Hari unlocked his car thoughtfully and said, 'I'm Punjabi, you know.'

'You look it.'

'Now why did that sound like an insult?' he said.

'I wonder,' she smiled.

As she fiddled for her Santro keys, Ali came right up from behind her and asked, 'Are you Bengali?'

'No,' she said.

'Do you know in Bengal there is a term for an elder woman who initiates boys into the joys of sex?'

'Of course,' Kamini said, unfazed. 'And the initiation ritual comprises a good spanking with a hairbrush.'

'I love it,' Ali whispered into her ear, 'when you talk dirty to me.' He had moved out of reach as she swirled to face him.

'Ali,' Kamini grinned after him. 'You frusto! Just because your father is a famous actor does not mean you can say anything to anybody.'

Ali slipped into the driving seat of his Range Rover and rolled down the window to shout out at her: 'Tch. So incurious. Prude!'

'Do you have a licence to drive that thing?' she exclaimed, suddenly terror-stricken to see his car looming behind hers.

'Nope,' he leered, and almost backed into a lamp-post. 'Ta-da. Late for my flight.'

'Flight?'

He rolled his eyes. 'Children of famous actors can't possibly be living in Delhi now can they?'

'Oh.'

'Duh. Bye beautiful, we still have some serious R and D to do. Entirely in the interest of the spiritual sciences, of course. Later, then.'

And she suddenly felt very puny in her little car as she watched his Range Rover kick up a wake of Delhi dust.

Hari, who was watching her exchange with Ali in his car behind her, rested his head on the steering wheel for a moment and thought, 'Why me, God? Why do I get all the psychos?' And at that precise moment his cell phone rang out its Jai Mata Di caller tune.

'Yes?' Hari cut short the devotional bhajan in mid-rapture and listened with complete attention to the voice on the phone displaying his adeptness by turning down the FM radio and negotiating the steering wheel to reverse out of the slush without removing the mobile grafted to his ear. 'But why?' His interjection didn't have much conviction in it, and there was an almost secret grin playing at the corner of his lips.

He was soon calling Kamini's number, watching with satisfaction when her car, only a few yards ahead of his, pulled up to the kerb to take the call.

But his excitement gave way to chagrin when faced with Kamini's incessant questions. Questions that others – like Carlos – would have interpreted as maidenly resistance but to Hari seemed like good old-fashioned bloody-mindedness.

Yes, they had to go out that evening, preferably for dinner. No, it was not a date, it was a VNP order. Yes, it had come from the VNP chief, and no, it was not delivered personally. Yes, the reason was to dispel the energy disturbance their interaction was creating in the group. Yes, omigod, the VNP chief did seem to be watching them. No, this was not his idea, but he would go anyway. No, it's not that he didn't want to go out with her, well yes, he did, well no, well yes, maybe… hey, why don't we just go out and be done with it?

Fine.

Fine.

See you at eight.

8.

When Uma finally reached her brother's flat in the early hours of the morning with her aunt and mother in tow, Raj's daughter and Uma's first cousin, Indira, was waiting at the door with outstretched arms. She wrapped her arms around Uma and Uma thought she did a fine job of shuddering and shivering down her neck. If she tried harder, Uma thought, she might even squeeze out a few tears.

'Thank God you are here,' Indira said not looking at anybody in particular. She had the same incredibly large eyes and long eyelashes that her son Vir had inherited. The softness of her entirely circular face, so typical of Eastern India, belied a coldness that Uma couldn't help marvel at.

Uma smiled tightly at her cousin and thought, *Of course you are glad I am here. Somebody needs to pay the bills.*

'Your father has been asking for you,' Uma said as they walked inside, but Indira pretended not to hear.

'I can't take it anymore,' Uma's mother sank heavily into the only comfortable armchair in her son Dodo's flat. The sofa protested with a gentle 'poof' against her heaviness.

Uma's sister, Ishita, waddled up to her, painstakingly pregnant, a banana in her hand, and hugging Uma she addressed her cousin, 'Why doesn't your dad do my mother and everybody else a favour by dying without all this fuss?'

Uma stared at her aunt over Ishita's shoulder and read her aunt's exaggerated lip-reading: 'Hormones.'

'I *know*...' Indira agreed with Ishita.

Uma now turned to stare at her. *This* was the daughter Raj Mamu was hanging by a thread to see, she mentally noted.

'That's what alcoholics should do,' Ishita gritted her teeth. 'Just die without a fuss.'

'Maybe you are taking your first trimester aversions a bit too far,' Uma laughed.

'Oh God...' Uma's mother moaned, sensing an impending battle.

'No, but she's right,' Indira said. 'I don't owe any responsibility to an alcoholic father.'

'Then why are you here?' The long flight, the visit to the hospital, and the high-strung atmosphere in the flat had finally put Uma on edge.

'To get the property papers signed by her dad before he cops it,' Ishita said, carefully peeling her banana.

'For God's sake,' Uma exclaimed. 'He's in a coma.'

'I can always get a thumb impression,' Indira said calmly.

Uma looked at her as if she had gone mad.

'Thousands of acres of arable land, and ten acres of a three-hundred-year-old palace full of artefacts waiting to be sold, you think I am going to let all of that go?'

'You have a mother and a sister too, you know?' Uma inadvertently said, fighting hard to steer away from her cousin's sordid machinations.

'Really? Those people who did not even bother to *be* at my wedding?'

'Those people you didn't even bother to *invite* to your wedding?'

'Have you ever heard of a mother and sister needing invitations to be at your wedding?'

'You would in a family as polarized as yours.'

'After I get his thumb impression on the will bequeathing everything to me, I will not let them enter Vishnupur.'

Uma shook her head and looked around her. 'Is this woman for real?'

'It's called unmitigated greed,' Ishita explained, her mouth full of banana.

'I don't remember any truth serum hormones during my pregnancy,' Uma laughed with her sister, a momentary gang-up against the cousin.

'I'm just being honest,' Indira said, her eyes widening, clouding over.

'Stop it, all of you.' Uma's mother rose dramatically from her armchair. 'My brother is not dead yet!

'Oh, shut up, Ma,' Uma said feeling herself thinning, pulled in too many directions. 'Just go to sleep.'

'Drama queen,' her sister Ishita said, exiting equally dramatically, her voluminous nightdress billowing behind her.

'Helloo ladies.'

Uma turned in relief to see her brother standing at the door, night shift over, motorbike keys in his hand, the company dog-tag still around his neck.

'Dodo!' Uma said, brightening at his presence. 'It's so nice to see someone who is not in some stage of menopause.'

He reached out to hug her, smelling of the winter night, sweat and city taxis. 'One of these days you've got to stop calling me that.'

'Shut up,' Uma said. 'It's your name that made you the smart young man that you are today. And where have you been?'

'Organizing blood for our dying, alcoholic uncle.'

'Am I the only one who feels sorry for the bloke?' Uma looked around her.

'The one and only,' went the chorus.

'Well, you and the oh-god lady in the bedroom,' Indira said, pointing in the general direction of Uma's mother.

It was after they had all filed into Dodo's bedroom where, not knowing any better, they took to teasing and ribbing the aunt and mother who lay supine, that Dodo finally remembered. 'Oh, I forgot to mention, I met Manik Mamu on my way out of the hospital.'

'Manik?' His mother raised her head, decided not to bother, and went back to lying horizontal.

'He said to return this to Raj Mamu.' They all watched in utter amazement as Dodo fished out from his pocket an exquisite, velvet blue Cartier jewellery case.

Indira snatched it away with an automatic 'show me' and snapped it open. A diamond solitaire ring winked blue and violet in Dodo's bedroom light.

'This is worth lakhs,' Indira whispered, reverentially.

'What is going on?' Uma said. Her mother and aunt were now sitting bolt upright on the bed.

'Now, everybody stay calm,' Dodo said as Ishita jostled for a better vantage point.

'The theory is that it dropped out of Raj Mamu's pocket when he passed out on the doorstep of the flat above Manik Mamu's.'

'But who found it?' Uma's mother said. 'I was told that nobody stays there any more.'

'Apparently, they do,' Dodo said, trying to recollect the rest of the story. 'An old couple lives there. They returned from the US yesterday. The husband found this at the doorstep and discovered that some weirdo had been carted off from his floor by Manik Mamu in an ambulance. Presuming this to be his, he personally visited Manik Mamu yesterday and handed it over.'

A thoughtful haze descended on the gathering.

'It lay undiscovered all these days,' Uma's aunt was mesmerized by the light beckoning her from the stone.

'If the building municipal sweeper had found it you would never even have heard this story.'

Ishita was making gusty inroads on an apple now. 'If it was meant to come back to the owner, the municipal sweeper too would have returned it,' she said.

Another thoughtful silence ensued while longing looks were cast on the solitaire.

'That is deep, Ishita, *if* Raj Mamu is the owner,' Uma noted.

'Obviously, he is the owner. The ring was for me,' Indira concluded decisively. 'Dad had promised me one last year. It's nice to see him finally getting around to buying it.'

Uma and Ishita exchanged a quick look that said 'she's lying again'. 'I'm sure that's exactly what happened,' Ishita said with exaggerated sweetness.

'That's fine,' Uma's mother said. 'But who is this for? Is it even Raj's? He has been living in such penury for the last ten years, it's almost as if he were punishing himself. His pancreas has shrivelled to a prune. His liver is pickled in alcohol. Even his brain has swollen up. Now that explains his erratic behaviour, his abusiveness, his solitariness, his insistence on living alone in the Vishnupur palace, so far from civilization, when he could so easily have lived in Calcutta, close to Manik and Dodo, his friends and family.'

'I have heard,' the aunt said, 'that he had become so abusive that the villagers refused to work in the palace. He would sweep the palace corridors himself and when he could no longer bear the physical strain of cooking he took a kilo of rice to the grass-cutter's wife and begged her to cook it for him.'

Uma and Ishita exchanged glances. Malicious gossip spread fastest among relations.

But Uma's mother shamefacedly corroborated the story. 'It's true. So many times I have told Indira, call him to Bangalore, make him live with you, but she never listened. So many times I told him to come and live with me, or at least live in the Calcutta flat, but he never listened. Now it may be too late. I have failed him. Indira, you have failed your father,' she sighed and focused again on remaining horizontal.

Indira put the ring back in its satin smooth case. 'It's not my fault. He has been so abusive to my husband that my husband refuses to be in the same room as him. An alcoholic father is not my responsibility.'

'Property...' Ishita sang soulfully, in a tune similar to Billy Joel's song 'Honesty'.

Indira looked up sharply as Dodo said, 'Oh good. Now we can finally have a catfight...'

'I have decided not to oblige you,' Indira said to Dodo, and glaring at Ishita, added, 'and I refuse to dignify that with a response.'

Unrelenting, Ishita broke into a squeakier rendition of Billy Joel's song. '*Property* is *such* a lonely word...' she sang. 'Isn't that your signature tune?'

Before Indira could respond, Uma snapped the jewellery case closed and said, 'This stays in Ma's suitcase till we decide what to do with it. I'll ask Raj Mamu tomorrow whether it belongs to him.'

'As if he is fit enough to reply.'

Uma could tell that Indira was beginning to feel surly and besieged. 'If he is fit enough to make thumb impressions on your will, he is fit enough to indicate yes and no,' she could not help respond as she walked off to the adjoining room with her booty. There she found Raj's battered VIP suitcase lying next to her mother's luggage.

She opened it uncertainly. Two shirts and a pair of trousers. A towel reeking of the sweet stench of stale alcohol, a gun licence but no gun, a toothbrush worn down to the stub, a bar of soap wrapped in newspaper. The pathetic remains of an imminently dead man?

No, you can't die, Raj Mamu. You are going to come back from the edge of whatever hell you are looking down at and pull yourself together. You were a stylish, sophisticated man. This is not who you are. A decaying thing, dying in obscurity.

She felt the self-indulgent softness of the velvet jewellery case in her hands and realized the incongruity of associating it with Raj Mamu's decrepitude. Could it really have slipped out of his pocket? How extremely well-bred of the gentleman who returned it on the basis of a presumption. She opened the case to look at the solitaire one last time and noticed a rip in its satin edge. On an impulse, she probed beneath it. There was a piece of paper folded and secreted away in the mysteries wrapped around the diamond. With heightening curiosity she unfolded the piece of paper, and it surrendered its message to her like a profound and lofty truth.

She read the missive with interest, stunned by the content of its words and the incongruity of the situation.

What was this? Was it a reply to a question? Did the question expect a reply? Was it even a question? It was her uncle's handwriting, all right. So the diamond was his. But who was it for? This was definitely not for his daughter. The handwritten piece of paper sounded more like a lover's message, written by a crazed man ripped asunder by the agony of separation. Could it be that Raj Mamu had a secret mistress? She could not imagine her uncle – a bitter, angry old man – in love. She couldn't even imagine him capable of it.

She shut the case and put it in her purse. Tomorrow, she resolved, I will go to the apartment upstairs in Chowringhee and find out whether the old couple knows anything about the diamond.

9.

They met at Olive. It was her first time in its whitewashed, Mediterranean hacienda sophistication with the Qutb Minar as a backdrop, and she tried not to show that she was impressed. Especially because he was courteously on time; especially because she liked the smell of his aftershave.

He tried not to notice that the light was doing flattering things to her skin, or be ruffled by the easy poise with which she sat on her chair, her hair swinging just so across her shoulders. He coughed and looked away.

'That's the worst pick-up line ever,' she started.

'What is?'

'"The chief says we have to go out for dinner".'

Hari looked at Kamini with so much disinterest that she immediately regretted her words, and choosing to wear a top that showed too much.

'Look, Kamini. I'm not here to flirt with you. I have a project to finish, and if there is any animosity building up between us the sooner we dispel it, the better.'

It was when he saw the slow flush creep up her downcast face that he realized how acutely embarrassed she was. With a faint premonition that he had gone too far, he resorted to an old technique, one that always worked on his mother. 'I know!' he said, trying his best to sound cheerful.

'What?' she said in voice so small it was barely audible.

'How about I give you all the gossip you want on all of us in the VNP group?'

'Really?' she brightened.

He shook his head in genuine amusement. 'I don't believe it. Works every time.'

'Okay,' Kamini said, immediately businesslike. 'Rita.'

'Hmmm, Rita.' He took a delicate sip of his Chardonnay. 'She's not as rich as she looks,' he said.

'That's so typically Punjabi,' Kamini retorted and then clapped her mouth in horror at her own words.

'I'll let that pass,' he sighed, and gestured across her shoulder for a refill of his glass. 'She's led an unhappy life, actually,' he continued. 'Two divorces. The last spouse ran off with a Malay twenty-five years his junior. Left her without a penny. She's working to see her daughter through college.'

'Really?' Kamini was wide-eyed. 'She's always bursting with so much confidence. I would never have guessed.'

When she knew that that was all Hari was going to divulge, whether out of deference to Rita Ma'am or because of a lack of knowledge, or both, Kamini said, 'Mira?'

'You probably know Mira better than I do.'

'I know,' Kamini said. 'It's as if I've known her for ever. We have the strangest connection, but I don't know much about her history.'

'Not much history,' Hari fiddled with his artichokes. It made Kamini suddenly suspicious that he would rather be downing butter chicken masala with a large whisky. 'She's old-Delhi rich,' he said. She noticed with relief that his mouth was not full. 'Born into money, married into money, the foundation on which VNP India rests. She's the fuel that keeps it going. A tireless worker.'

'Boring,' Kamini commented. 'Considering that she's widowed. Even her grandchildren don't visit her in that huge property. I would imagine that VNP is as good a pastime as her knitting.'

Hari did not know whether he knew her well enough to say that she was being spiteful, so he kept shut. Besides, they seemed to have hit a smooth patch, so why risk it?

'Carlos,' she announced next, as if he had won the lottery.

'Ah!' Hari said, and Kamini stiffened because it sounded close to a belch. And then she saw it – the gold chain peeping from under his collar. Her fork froze, and then quivered in distaste over her ravioli.

'Now there's a swami with a history,' he said.

That got the ravioli a smooth transition to her mouth.

'He was ostracized from his community, you know.'

'Really?' The food was tasting good. 'Why?'

'He broke his vows of celibacy.'

He noticed that this prompted some thoughtful chewing. 'I could believe that,' she finally said.

'And I, as I have many of your other comments, shall let that one pass.'

Kamini giggled.

'The interesting part is that the woman he broke his vows for was also a swami from his order' – and here Hari paused, momentarily petrified, because there was a sliver of prawn stuck in his front teeth and he knew his companion was of delicate temperament.

'And...?' she prompted, impatient for more.

'He never gave up on her. He stuck to her all along.' Thankfully, the prawn had released its grip, and he continued, grateful for being allowed his moment of dignity. 'Finally they were both reinstated as swamis... together.'

They both lapsed into a contemplative, and for once companionable, silence.

'So much for the vows,' he said.

'Or true love.'

They both raised their glasses in a toast.

'Ali?' she asked after a longish silence.

'Oh,' he said, downing the last of his wine, feeling full, satiated, grateful even, for her company. The mandolin music had soothed his nerves to the right tensility. 'Just your regular, psychotic Bollywood spawn.'

She noticed his unusual, almost literary choice of words, not like a property-broker at all. 'He's just so high strung, so precariously balanced... as if at the edge of a cliff...' she observed.

'Don't be taken in by appearances,' he warned. 'He's a yogi. He wouldn't turn a hair if his entire family died and he was reduced to penury.' When she had absorbed this, he continued, 'A very expensive psychiatrist might say that his detachment is symptomatic of a deep-seated neuroses, but VNP knows the high level of advancement he operates from.'

'What a bunch of oddballs,' she said, wondering whether it would be impolite to order dessert.

'Yes, they are,' he agreed. 'You need to be an oddball to be on this path. It's not for the herd, for those with a weak stomach for experience. It's for the risk-takers, for the seekers of the real. Most people know reality as an experience. At VNP we know that experience is the *only* reality.'

He looked at her as if he were challenging her. She was not going to take the bait. She was going to challenge him back. She leaned forward on the white table linen, and cupping her chin artfully in her hands, her hair streaming down her back, she asked, 'And what about you? You don't seem like a classified VNP oddball. In fact, I doubt anyone could get more regular than you.'

He leaned back on his very comfortable Olive chair and sighed once more. He realized he did a lot of sighing when Kamini was around. 'I believe you are trying to insult me again.'

She was, but she wasn't going to admit it. Not realizing that her lipstick had worn off with the passing of the evening, and that she wasn't looking quite the femme fatale she presumed, she teased him, 'Let's say I'm challenging you.'

That's when he felt it, that constriction in his heart, as if reacting against the sudden intensity in the air. 'I have my share of complexes,' he admitted.

'Oh, tell me more,' she beamed like Mata Hari after a successful act of seduction.

'Well, I have a brother I would willingly kill given half a chance.'

'Oh,' she was crushed with disappointment. 'How boring. I have a sister I could kill given half a chance.'

He looked at her, deep in a strange quietness.

'Isn't that normal?' she said, thinking she should have that chocolate mousse after all.

'I don't know,' he shrugged. 'I didn't attend his wedding.'

'Nor I, hers,' Kamini looked up, startled at the coincidence.

'Great,' he said. 'We finally have something in common.'

The unease in him, around him, was growing thicker, more sinister. He knew he needed to get out of there fast. He felt an unseen presence in their midst, breathing heavily. It did not help that she was getting into a convivial mood.

'I have a secret,' she said. 'I don't understand what's going on. You know this whole 2012 thing?' She was hesitant, quizzical.

'Tch,' he said. And repeated the next part by rote, as if he had done it several times before: 'With the shift in magnetic poles, the energy matrix of the planet is changing, bringing about transformation at every possible level. Some people call the tsunamis a disaster, we call it a cleansing. People will be forced to align with the light, or with the darkness. There is a collective ascension and descent happening at the same time; the proverbial churning of the ocean, in our *das avatar* myth. Those who align with the light are going to be the leaders of the future.'

'Christ said the meek shall inherit the earth,' she concluded.

'So he did,' Hari agreed, glad to see the last of the chocolate mousse disappearing into her mouth. A very delectable mouth, he decided, focusing on folding his napkin very carefully.

'I still don't get the big picture,' she lingered, realizing that she was actually having a good time and didn't want the evening to end. 'Why is this project so important? What is with these Twin Flames?'

Hari knew he had to get out of there quickly, because something was terribly amiss. His throat was constricting again, as if something heavy sat astride his chest. 'They are necessary to raise the threshold of the earth's energy matrix to the next level. Think Noah's Ark,' Hari said, all the while trying to reduce the anxiety of the moment by breathing deeply. 'When the deluge happened, all the twos were taken to higher ground. VNP is the Ark. And we have to get all the Twin Flames together, so that their union can release the energies of unconditional love, and the earth can heal from the trauma of the great energetic purge.'

'I'm sorry, that sounds really corny,' she offered.

'Have you ever seen satellite images of the earth?' Hari shifted in his chair.

She was quiet for a while. 'I'm presuming that's a rhetorical question.'

'As night progresses you see little sparkling dots, like a string of bulbs lighting up the earth.'

'So?'

'That's what twin unions are like – a string of lights illuminating the energy matrix of the earth.'

'Oh, give me break!' she said loudly, the wine finally settling in.

And just as she was getting ready for a good argument he got up and holding her by the elbow said as calmly as he could, 'We really should be going now.'

It was in the car, while he was driving her back, that he realized what was happening. Her hands folded demurely on her lap, the scent of her sitting next to him, was so overpowering that his head started to swim. It seemed as if her mouth had gathered a life of its own, and the only reasonable act left for him was to take her in his arms and kiss it.

'Kiss me,' she seemed to be saying, but she wasn't saying that. She was talking incessantly about how unreal and mystifying the whole VNP part of her life was, and how it was addling her brain.

I have to kiss her. I must kiss her. I am meant to kiss her.

He was deeply relieved when he pulled up outside Mira's house, the VNP headquarters, at the end of a dead alley.

The silence of his acute desire magnified the sound of the gravel crunching under his newly-treaded tyres, the sound of a lone street dog barking out its territory, the sound of cars whizzing far across the highway. He could hear the depths of Mira's sleepless night, but he could not hear a word of what Kamini was saying, sitting close, so close, to him. He could only see her mouth move.

He must not kiss her.

He knew then that the sabotage of the project had begun. His uncontrollable desire to kiss Kamini was being manipulated to make the Keeper of the Flame break his vow.

The bugle had been sounded. The invisible battle had begun. Already.

But her mouth. *How can that motor mouth have so much power over me?* Hari could have wept with frustration.

'Shhh,' he turned to her and placed his finger on her mouth. Eyes limpid in the moonlight she looked at him, stunned momentarily. 'Just shut up for a moment will you?'

That was his cue, as good as it would ever get. It couldn't have gotten better than that, because she had nodded dumb-mute, entirely awed by the intensity of the moment.

Later, other project members would wonder whether the history of their mission would have been different if, in that nano second when Hari's head had bent towards a more-than-willing Kamini, a sharp knock had not ricocheted off the car window, deep into the night.

In a daze, Hari rolled down the window and found Mira smiling at them with all the false sweetness of a hostel matron.

'Oh, it's only you two! I was wondering who it was!'

10.

When Aparajita saw the terrace key glistening in her maid's hand the sudden sensation of Raj touching the key forced her to take a deep breath to steady herself. She immediately understood what had occurred and had an insane desire to fly down the stairs and tell him that she was feeding her baby and could he please come back to the door again, this time she would answer on the first bell. She looked at her maid's sullen face and contemplated taking the broom and beating her with it.

What is wrong with me? She shook her head, trying to shake off the currents and counter-currents of something – she didn't know what – surging through her body, clouding her brain, hazing her judgement. *What is this?* she asked herself again. Why is this happening? Have I been possessed by some evil spirit? Is Ma Durga punishing me for not loving my husband enough? Are the gods testing my fidelity? *What in the name of God is this?*

For the next few hours she went through her daily chores of chopping vegetables, folding the clothes, and giving her baby a bath in a sweet daze of intoxication, surrounded in a cloud of Raj. The tilt of his face, his voice, his carefree laugh, the touch of his hand, what it would feel like if it ever came in contact with hers, the smell of his body. With a shock she realized that she knew his body intimately, in a way that was no business of hers. She dropped the clothes she was folding in exasperation. As she did so, she caught a sudden whiff of his overpowering male scent and turned to face her maid who was scowling at the door.

'Man from downstairs flat. Wants an appointment.'

Aparajita inhaled sharply and counselled herself to stay calm. 'Who has come? The sahib or his servant?'

'Bairah, cook,' the maid said, obviously knowing him well.

Aparajita was relieved to find herself moving slowly to meet Bairah who stood in the hall with a patience that came from practised experience; as a long-time abettor of Raj's shenanigans.

Aparajita had to stop herself from giving him a hero's welcome but could not prevent herself from asking him two questions three times in the space of their brief conversation. 'Who sent you? Where have you come from?' Then, with a great deal of imperiousness, she instructed Bairah, 'Tell your sahib that I can see him at the earliest at three o'clock this afternoon.' She made it sound as if it was the only, distant date in her very crowded appointment diary, when it was barely four hours away.

'Huzur.' Bairah turned and left without ceremony, but Aparajita imagined trumpets blaring as he left.

It seemed as if the cosmos was watching and colluding when Raj and Aparajita met for the second time in their lives. The Chowringhee apartment building was drugged in the stupor of a Calcuttan siesta. The baby was asleep. The maid was gone. The chores were finished. As the minute hand of the grandfather clock in her sitting room reached twelve, a split second before the bell rang, she had already risen from the sofa to meet her destiny.

When they said hello to each other both were relieved to notice the facility of casualness between them, as if nothing were going on at all. It helped raise the doubt in both their minds that maybe the intensity they saw in the other was imagined. But the comfort was a bit too casual, like an oil slick between them, and every once in a while they would slide and slip on it, momentarily overwhelmed by the heady sensation of freefall.

'Would you like some lemonade?' She glided across the room with the practised ease of a busy astro-palmist very used to asking this question, when in reality she managed a client only once or twice a month. She headed towards the dumpy Allwyn fridge in the kitchen, he watching her, she watching him watching her. He knew that she had a jar of lemonade prepared just for him in the kitchen. That he knew this shocked and stilled him.

'Nothing, thank you. I've just had lunch.'

She was disappointed. He knew she had laboured over the lemonade. Her disappointment caused him pain, but it was excruciatingly sweet. Every easy movement she made, every smile, every casual laugh, revealed to him an innocence and vulnerability that cleaved his heart into two.

She was remarkably accurate with his birth-chart. It confused both of them. She, because she was aware of her natural gift for predictions but not to such levels of precision, and he because he could not tell how much of her accuracy was because of her talent and how much an awareness of their past history that had mysteriously backed up on them – like a FedEx package with an unknown forwarding address and no instructions on how to open it.

But when she told him that he had three mango trees growing in a triangle in the garden of his ancestral palace, they both looked at each other in now-familiar astonishment. And since by now both had understood that astonishment was pointless, they looked away.

'You are not yet married.' The verb lay between them like the intimacy of unbearable sensuality. 'But soon…' she said in small voice, and saw images of his life without her, a woman in his life who was not her, and the pain of the thought was as sharp as the sweetness of his presence. He looked at her lowered face, her eyes cast down on his horoscope, and could sense his power over her life, her thoughts, her breath. He had a vague premonition that he was a victim of the same affliction, and for the first time since they had met he felt a pang of fear.

Many years later, he would quiz his children on what the opposite of love was.

'Hate,' one said.

'Anger,' the other said, with long exposure to her father's philosophical proclivities.

'Clever,' Raj said. 'But no.'

'Indifference,' his wife said, acclimatized to her own bitterness.

'No,' the husband said, acclimatized to his own guilt, which he had carried for more time than he cared to remember. 'The opposite of love is fear. Unconditional love is the most difficult thing in the world because it requires a superhuman amount of courage. One of the most common misconceptions is that unconditional love is self-sacrificing masochism. No it's not, because that would make it an act of cowardice. Unconditional love is the capacity to love without fear of loving selflessly.'

But that was many years later.

At that moment they sat opposite each other, a glass centre-table between them, a grandfather clock behind them, acutely aware that the hours were flying faster than either of them wanted, that there was so much to catch up on.

Catch up on. Neither questioned the strangeness of the catching up of total strangers. They did not suspect it because of the ease with which they had slipped into the ancient intimacy between them.

He told her of his palace in Vishnupur, she of the mangoes in her grandmother's orchard. He spoke of his closeness to his cousins and she of hers. He said that he had fractured his skull in a car accident when he was eight. She had, too, when she had fallen off a swing when she was seven. They had both lost their fathers a couple of years ago. They both loved history and hated bananas.

When she started laughing he did too, at exactly the same time. The mirth was hers, the depth of it, his.

When she finished sighing he would exhale, long and deep, as surprised as she was, a little more frightened each time. The line of a song flashed in her mind, 'I am the sun, you are the moon, I am the song, you are the tune,' and Raj heard the unfamiliar lyrics play in his own head.

She wanted to lay her head on his shoulder and ask him where he had been all these thousands of years. The image conjured itself in front of Raj and though hesitant at first, he became more and more sexually explicit with the moving picture they were creating between them, totally oblivious of the other's awareness of it, though they each felt the sparkling energy swirl between them, like a gentle typhoon made of sugar syrup. It made Aparajita giddy and Raj physically ache from the tension of not snatching her into his arms.

'Do you like ghazals?' he asked.

'Yes, I do,' she said. 'Though I don't have much exposure to the part of the country they come from.'

And he recited to her a couplet that rose to the surface of his consciousness like a long suppressed memory: 'Her lips were bruised,' he said. 'But I had kissed only her photograph in my dreams.'

He looked at her then, full of mischief, obviously referring to the sexual scenes he suspected she too was fooling around with in her mind.

Aparajita experienced a wrenching coyness that wanted to make her laugh. *But I am a woman who has given birth to a child. I am not exactly a stranger to sexual experience or the male gender.* She did not realize that her coyness cast an expression on her face that Raj had only seen in the faces of goddesses in calendar art.

Like the cue for some divine comedy, the edge of her sari slipped and Raj was completely thrown by the sudden sight of her cleavage. The gods are taunting me, he thought. When she realized what had happened she quickly adjusted her sari, her blush deepening till she started to feel faint.

'Do you mind if I go into the kitchen now? My husband will be home any minute,' she said, desperately picking up the strands of their social conversation, putting on her veil, covering her modesty.

'I should go,' he said, unable to stop looking at her, unable to move.

It was she who got up first.

When he moved away from her door it felt like glue being unstuck. 'I can't tell time when I am with you,' he blurted.

I know, she thought.

He heard.

'I still have a few more questions about my birth-chart. Can I come back later?'

She felt little joy birds fly at the desperation in his voice. 'Of course,' she replied. 'Tomorrow, same time, we will have to meet again. You still have to pay me.'

'Of course. Tomorrow then,' he said, backing away from her.

'Tomorrow,' she whispered, shutting the door.

Then the fear that had already visited Raj paid her a visit, and she braced against it, sitting down heavily on her sofa, looking blankly about her.

Only an hour had passed. But the world was not the same.

11.

'Dudes,' Ali said, pointing to the slide on the wall screen of his power point presentation. 'I thought I would make this presentation about concept clarification, just so we are all on the same page.'

Hari was twirling a pen in staccato rhythm over his spider web scribblings. 'That's fine,' he said. 'But you will have to hurry up. I've called this emergency meeting for a reason.' He seemed restless, pent up.

It's obviously not just the oily parathas his mother fed him this morning, Kamini thought. There were dark rings under his eyes. It was something else. She placed her hand over his and stopped his turbine-like movements.

He turned to her, rattled by her touch. *What?* his expression seemed to say.

'It's called the devil's tattoo,' she said.

And even though he responded with blankness, she knew there was something else behind his eyes.

She was right, because last night Hari had dreamt of her. In his dream he was attending her wedding *to his brother.* His brother was the only person Hari would hate till he died. And in his dream his brother sat next to his bride looking exactly like the grim reaper: tall, hooded in a black cowl, his sickle in place. Hari shifted away from Kamini.

Kamini sighed. Why did I dream I was getting married to Hari last night? she thought. Why *Hari* of all people? His mother will make me fast on Tuesdays and I will have to eat parathas for breakfast all my life. As if getting married to Hari in a dream wasn't bad enough, why did that man in a black cowl snatch me away from Hari? It's not that she *wanted* to get married to Hari, but in principle, it was just the wrong thing to do. And in her dream when she, screaming, had tried to pull his black cowl from his face, a hundred crows had flown out of his hood. *Terrible,* she couldn't stop her sighing, *truly terrible...*

'I'll keep it short,' Ali was saying. 'Just want to sort out some gender issues.'

The first slide in Ali's presentation carried the Yin Yang symbol. Black and white, with two eyes, black in white, white in black, like a panda melted into a ball. He held a similar black and white sphere in his hand, the Yin Yang in three dimensions, the spaces of two contrasting halves merged into a whole.

'We first need to define male and female; understand the meaning of the two terms. If I separate out the male and female in this sphere' – and he managed to do so with a little click; the sphere was made of some malleable polymer – 'it becomes like this...'

Ali held up a three-dimensional infinity symbol, a horizontal figure of eight. It became evident to his audience that if the two petals of the horizontal eight symbol of infinity were rolled into its centre it became a sphere.

'The sphere,' Ali said, 'is the most perfect geometrical shape in the universe. It is also the shape of a fertilized egg. In the case of the yin and yang, when they merge like this' – he rolled them back into a sphere again – 'they are what the scriptures call "in divine union". They form the cosmic egg.' Turning to Mira he cued her with: 'We have several names for the cosmic egg in Indian scriptures…' And she nodded her silver mane taking it from him:

'Brahm-anda, Brahma's egg, *hiranyagarbha*, golden egg, but its most common and accurate definition is in a symbol we are all familiar with,' Mira said.

'And the symbol? asked Ali, thoroughly enjoying his role as the freaky conductor of a crazy orchestra.

His band responded to his imaginary baton.

'Om,' they chorused.

'Correct,' he said. 'In the beginning was the word. And the word was...'

'Om.' Hari said. 'Not, "damn, eggs for breakfast again".'

Ali drew the symbol on a whiteboard. 'Notice the two halves meeting in the centre? These symbols are the actual movements of energy patterns.'

It was Rita's turn to start nodding violently.

'It is from this point,' Ali ignored her as he pointed at the centre of the two halves where the symbol spouted out a weave, 'that the energy of the union starts rolling out, like a dragon's tail.'

'Exactly depicted in the Ocean of Nectar mythology and the churning of the Ocean,' Rita muttered.

'Which you will be talking of in *your* presentation, right?' Ali said pointedly.

'Right.'

'Then let me come back to my small unilateral depiction of Om. Om is also the seed syllable. When I say seed I use it in the most literal way possible, from which everything, and I mean everything, ladies and gentlemen, is created.

'If I were to start deconstructing Om,' Ali continued, 'I would find many ways. It is also the horizontal trishul of Shiva, his three-pronged fork; apparently, Satan also has one of these. The three-pronged fork; the trinity of Brahma, Vishnu, Mahesh; Shiva, Shakti and Ardhnareshwar; the son, the father, and the holy ghost; the male, the female, the fertilized egg – good things and bad, it seems, come in threes.'

'When you talk about Shiva and Shakti and the cosmic egg, you are talking,' Carlos contributed, 'of the creative principle that is also the cause; the agent of every known and unknown "thing" in this universe.'

'"Thing", of course, being a very accurate generalization of that mysterious entity that takes a lot of theorizing in Quantum Mechanics,' Rita said solemnly.

'That, basically, was Einstein's unified field theory. A theory of everything, now incarnated as string theory,' Hari said.

'Einstein died trying.' Ali, insecure about losing his audience, impatiently veered them all back to his point. 'Yin is female, yang is male. Yin is black, yang is white. They are also symbolized as mountains. Yin, the female, is the shadowy side of the mountain. Yang, the male, is the sunny side of the mountain. Mountain – because again, they are like two sides of an equilateral triangle, reaching for the pinnacle, the apex.'

'In the language of Quantum Mechanics,' Rita said in her pronounced accent, 'male and female are the positive and negative poles. Female is dark because she is a magnetic energy; male is white because he is electric.'

'Can you please explain that in your presentation?' Ali whined.

'Sure, darling,' Rita smiled at him. 'Didn't mean to rain on your parade.'

'As the mirror workers of VNP teach us, the microcosm reflects the macrocosm. Let's see, then,' Ali said, clearly happy to get back his space, 'how these universal principles manifest in the chakra system of the human body.'

Kamini noticed that for all his cleverness Ali had a childish immaturity that no amount of spiritual power could conceal. He may be a superhero, Kamini thought, but he's still only eighteen.

A downloaded scan of the Kundalini chakras slipped into the next slide. The beatific face of a man whose body was a maze of energy patterns designed as lotus petals presented itself for exhibition.

'Next to the central channel or *sushumna* run two energy channels invisible to the naked eye, but visible to the clairvoyant. The ida and the pingala. The ida is the female channel, the pingala is the male channel. The moon channel and the sun channel. The moon channel is powered by inhalation, the sun channel is powered by exhalation.'

Rita and Mira started breathing in and out thoughtfully.

Ali smiled, feeling confident again. 'If you notice carefully, inhalations are cool, exhalations are warm. Female – cool, male – hot. Funny, isn't it, how much "hot" and "cool" are part of our daily lingo? Inhalation also makes the sound "ham", a lower frequency sound, a female sound because she is denoted by the passive darker sound. Exhalation makes the higher frequency, lighter sound of "so" or "sa". "Ham" also means "I am"; "sa" means "that"; "I" is the smaller individual ; "that" is the Absolute. Together they are "sohamso". When they merge they lose their ends and become Om. I am that. The individual self merges with the higher self. Divine union. And just like the formation of the Western Union, that's the time to start cashing in.'

'This is getting more and more sexist,' Kamini complained.

'How?' Ali was confused.

'She is passive. She is dark, she is the smaller individual with a lower frequency. She lives in his reflected glory. The moon's light is borrowed from the sun, it has no light of its own, while he is the sun, radiant with light, vibrating at a higher frequency, the Absolute Truth. Sheesh, even the goddesses have a glass ceiling, there's only so much of the chakra system available to them.'

Kamini turned to appeal to the women in the room. 'This has to be a lot of bunkum.'

When Rita looked shifty, Kamini turned incredulously at Ali who was already looking at her.

'When Rita Ma'am translates all this into physics equations you will see how far from the truth you are. It's not like that at all,' he said. 'Kamini, she is Shakti, she is the play. She is every known and unknown manifestation we can conceive, perceive, or decipher. All he does is be Shiva. He just sits there, being the Absolute, doing nothing.'

'Great,' Kamini grumbled. 'Now she is the one who has to do everything. He is the guy who leaves his dirty socks on the floor expecting her to pick up after him.'

'No...' Ali moaned, frustrated at not getting across. 'It's not like that at all. How can Shiva and Shakti be sexist? What a sacrilegious idea. He is *Shiva*.' Ali seemed in genuine pain, needing resolution. 'Is the sex act sexist? He is the phallus, she the receptacle, the vijayjay...' he smiled then and gave her his cute charming look. 'You watch too much Oprah.'

Kamini would not be placated. 'Well, I don't know about sexist, but that is definitely gross.'

'I am sorry,' Hari said loudly, 'to interrupt the bedroom conversation. Not that,' he turned to Ali, 'they were not great pick-up lines,' and turning back to the group, 'but we just don't have the time. Need I remind you that I received a code red on our project, and need I remind you again that that means that our XX and XY are up shit's creek? Without our intervention, they might even die. So all this intellectualizing is all very well, but we need to get down to real work – very, very soon.'

'I'm wrapping up,' Ali said, disconcerted.

'This intellectualizing, O Keeper of the Project Flame,' Kamini said, 'may be necessary for everybody to get a grip on the situation.'

Hari opened his mouth to retort and shut it when Rita and Mira mumbled 'I agree,' and Carlos nodded.

'Just keep your presentations short,' Hari retreated. 'Ali, just cut to the chase, man.'

'Aye aye, Cap'n.' Ali clicked on the last slide. 'So to recap, let's just go over all that you wanted to know after reading *Men are from Mars, Women are from Venus*, but didn't know whom to ask.'

The two columns on his next slide were captioned XX and XY. 'Female. Passive, moon, cool, dark. Low frequency. Heavy. Gross. Black. Ham. Ida. Inhalation. Shakti, receptacle.' He looked around to see whether everybody was digesting the information. 'Male. Active, sun, hot, light, high frequency, light, fine, white, sa, pingala, exhalation, Shiva, phallus.'

And then turning to Hari, Ali pleaded: 'I wanted to finish with a presentation on Adam and Eve.'

'Are you mad?' Hari exclaimed. 'That could go on forever.'

'Okay,' Ali said, preoccupied, fidgeting. 'But I had to talk about something really important.'

'Regarding?' Hari asked with exaggerated patience.

'Our subjects, XX and XY.'

'And...?'

'Well, you see, they...'

'Oh come on, kid,' Hari burst out impatiently. 'Just spit it out.'

'They are greening.'

'Greening?'

'It's an alchemical term, mostly found in medieval European texts...'

'Just tell me whether it's good news or bad news.' Hari cut him short, his own nervousness finally finding a breach.

Ali raised his hands as if warding off an onslaught and said, 'It's very, very bad.'

☯

Afterwards, Carlos found Kamini in the basement, at the samosa table, scribbling in her notebook, brow furrowed, a picture of perplexed concentration. He pulled up a chair next to her and throwing his orange duffel bag on the wobbly table, sat down.

'Let me try and simplify it for you. The universal energy or 1, breaks into two polarized energies, 2. Male, female, positive, negative, whatever, whatever, and when the two energies achieve union, as in 2 becomes 1, then the third, 3, or the creative energy, comes into being. 1,2,3 is also an ancient and sacred Fibonacci sequence.'

Kamini dropped her pen and stared at him.

'Voila,' Carlos finished with a flourish. 'It's easy as 1,2,3...'

'Then what is love?' Kamini asked, her pencil poised in mid-air in a perfect balance.

'Love is the irresistible power of union,' Carlos said. 'It is the power that creates all the worlds.'

12.

When Uma pressed the doorbell on the left side of the Ghosh's gigantic white door, the Cartier jewellery case bulging in the pocket of her jeans, there was the germ of an idea in her struggling to find creation, like a bubble rising to the surface.

Mr Ghosh answered the door. A very kindly-old-gentleman kind of guy, was the thought that immediately popped into her head.

'Is Mrs Ghosh at home?' she asked, not sure why she asked for her.

'Yes, she is,' he said peering over his glasses, trying to place her; to peg a label on her.

She quickly introduced herself as his neighbour Manik's niece, and said that her visit was regarding the diamond he had handed over.

'Oh!' he said, his grey hair only slightly uncombed, his shorts olive green, a much-read newspaper tucked under his arm. 'Oh, I see.' Ushering her in he said, 'Mrs Ghosh is in the sitting room.' His English was impeccable with only the slightest trace of a Bengali accent. 'But I must warn you that she can't speak, and is bound to the wheelchair. She has Alzheimer's you see…' he said the name of the disease as if it was a dreaded word, and she nodded in empathy, signifying that she understood the dread.

The room was well decorated with beautifully mounted Jamini Roy paintings and Chinese blue pottery urns. Uma noticed that the carpet was not faux Persian but genuinely expensive. Yet there was poverty in the room and the dankness of disease. Uma sensed the helpless struggle against decay and all kinds of death. She looked around, taking in her surroundings and that is when she saw her, sitting in her wheelchair by the window, staring at her with an intentness that made Uma's hair stand on end.

'She has not been keeping well these past few days,' Mr Ghosh was saying apologetically, and gestured to a maid lurking in the kitchen to make some tea. You could tell that he was pleased to have company and would have loved a good chat. 'Sit down, dear, and unwind, it's really humid outside.'

But his pleasant prattle registered only vaguely in Uma's subconscious because Aparajita's intense stare was cutting across the room with a laser sharpness that stopped Uma from walking. The bubble found the surface, the suppressed thought its form:

'*It was she, Raj Mamu had meant when he said, find her, not his daughter, Indira.*'

Though the thought now had a body there was still very little logic to support it, so it hung in the air, suspended in disbelief. But so knowing was Aparajita's stare, so full of awareness, that as Uma's skin rose in gooseflesh, so also came the certainty that something beyond her wildest imagination was going on.

'She is saying something,' Mr Ghosh uttered in surprise, and was instantly by his wife's side, listening to the rustling sounds her breath was making. He was self-conscious in the presence of a stranger, a self-consciousness heightened by the sudden speech of his wife. It muddled him, because she hadn't spoken in years. Besides, her sensorium usually worsened after an epileptic attack, which she had suffered only a week ago. This was highly irregular, and Mr Ghosh was not very comfortable with irregularity.

'She is saying,' his eyes blinking behind his glasses in astonishment, 'she is saying – "you have come".'

Mrs Ghosh was still an extraordinarily beautiful woman. Her eyes shiny with trapped brilliance, her skin clear as alabaster, she sat upright in her chair, as if it were a throne. Though her skin was unnaturally stretched because of muscular dystrophy she smiled at Uma as if she were a long-lost friend. It pierced Uma to the heart and brought her down on her knees, as she grasped her outstretched hand.

'There is an explanation for this.' Mr Ghosh was embarrassed by this show of familiarity. 'She has mistaken you for somebody else, maybe one of her nieces,' he said with a great deal of relief as the thought struck him, still embarrassed at putting a young stranger through the idiosyncrasies of old age.

'But that's fine,' Uma was saying, her eyes filling with tears for no reason, holding the old woman's hand even tighter, in total disregard of the old man's discomfiture. She continued to stare at Aparajita so hard that it seemed that it was because of this pain that a teardrop wound an uneasy course down the older woman's frozen cheek.

Aparajita shook her head in anguish and shut her eyes for a moment.

'Maybe she wants to say something.' Uma looked up at Mr Ghosh but his blinking bewilderment was of no help. Then Uma had a sudden brainwave. 'Maybe it's about the diamond.'

She fished out the jewellery case from her pocket.

'Are you trying to say something about the diamond? Does this belong to you?' She snapped the box open and held it in front of Mrs Ghosh. In infinitesimally slow movements Mrs Ghosh turned to look at it. The sight of it seemed to rip her apart. Choking, sobbing, the old lady's head fell back and rivulets of tears started splashing her blouse.

'Oh, I'm so sorry.' Confounded, hand on her heart, Uma turned to Mr Ghosh and said, 'I think I've upset her. It must be something I said.'

When she got up from the floor Uma's head was reeling. The maid, now silently by Mrs Ghosh's side, wheeled her away.

After a while Uma turned to Mr Ghosh who was still standing in the middle of the room, his lips pursed, his newspaper dangling by his side.

'She obviously knows this ring, Mr Ghosh.' Uma sat down on the sofa uninvited. She needed to sit. 'Maybe it belongs to her. Maybe she should keep it.'

Mr Ghosh lowered himself onto the edge of an armchair opposite her.

Uma remembered the note inside the box written in her uncle's hand and couldn't help saying, 'I think something very strange is going on here.'

'Nothing strange about it.' By the simple act of sitting down in a chair Mr Ghosh seemed to have regained his lost composure. He handed her a cup of tea and settled back into the armchair. 'Have your tea, young lady, such are the ravages of disease.'

'So you mean?' Uma took a sip of perfectly brewed Darjeeling tea made just the way she liked it and her heart warmed towards Mr Ghosh.

'She is delusional,' he explained. 'Every effect in this universe has a logical cause. She is in the second stage of her disease. Since the faculty of short-term memory is now mostly wiped out, the brain dredges up long suppressed memories to filter sensory input to process any situation. The sight of the ring, I think, has brought up the memory of her sister's wedding. In her mind she may have gone back to that time and mistaken you for her sister. At this moment she might be mentally preparing for her sister's wedding farewell, hence the tears. Or she might be anguishing over her own spinster status thinking she is eighteen years old! She was unmarried during her sister's wedding. She might come out now and not recognize me. She might even think I am an intruder in her house and order her maid to throw me out.'

Uma looked up from her tea at him with deep sympathy. 'Does this happen often?'

'Almost every day.' Relaxed now, feeling himself again, he crossed his legs. 'Once she got up in the middle of the night screaming "corpse, corpse". I realized that the white duvet I had wrapped myself in must have looked like a shroud.'

'I don't know, Mr Ghosh,' Uma said as gently as she could. 'I know this sounds presumptuous, and I am nobody to judge, but her eyes shine with an almost unearthly intelligence.'

In the way that people who spend too much time brooding over things without talking do, Mr Ghosh ignored what she said, continuing to speak as if Uma had not said a word: 'A year ago, when she could still walk, the maid was returning from the fish market and found her roaming the streets in her nightdress. The maid – thank her dear heart, I have survived my wife's disease only because of her efficiency – calmly held her hand and asked where she was going. You know what my wife said?'

Uma sipped her tea thoughtfully.

'She said, "I have to go and open the gates to the Vishnupur palace."'

For a moment the room became silent for Uma. The only sound she heard was that of her cup loudly finding the saucer.

'Hey,' he said.

'Hey,' she said.

'How grey your hair is.'

'How puny you look.'

'Ha ha. But isn't that how it works?'

'True,' she said solemnly. 'You have so much physical growing up to do, you poor thing.'

He looked around him. 'Why do you keep coming back here?'

She looked around her too. The ornateness of the balcony they hung out of could have been Byzantine. There were only grey shadowy shapes ahead in the distance; only the faintest hint of a green ground below them.

'Because this is where it is all going to happen.'

'What?'

'What they call 2012. The apocalypse. The end of the world or whatever.'

'Are you prepared?'

'Getting there,' she said. 'And you?'

'Work in progress,' he said.

She turned to leave.

'Wait,' he said. 'I believe you have found the place of unconditional love?'

'Not yet,' she laughed. 'But quite close now.'

'Is it any fun?' he asked. 'Love without the ego? Without the pain, the longing, the fights, the kissing and making up, the poetry, the stuff ballads and epics are made of?'

Her laughter was gay abandon. 'Of course it's fun. It's a different kind of fun.' She struggled for words. 'It's a place a lot like this. You just have to be there.'

He smiled. 'One day, hopefully.'

'One day, surely.'

'Bye for now, then.'

'Bye.'

'Grandmother.'

'Grandson.'

They both cracked up with mirth.

13.

There had been a sudden death in the family so Raj sent a message through Bairah saying that he would see her after a couple of weeks. Sweet poison infused the languor of the two weeks that went by. In a house of tragedy, Raj's feet should not have moved with such inappropriate elation.

Upstairs, Aparajita spent hours folding all the clothes in her cupboard not realizing the speed with which time was progressing towards some foregone destination. It was in the nights that the strange laws of a different world took over. They tossed unruly on their beds, waking up from dreams of such profound eroticism that she was shocked by her own extreme licentiousness. In all her years of marriage and youth she had considered herself to be sexually staid. She could not understand what part of her Freudian psyche was secreting so much wantonness.

She had the uneasy feeling that somewhere far from Calcutta, Raj was enjoying her permissiveness, and was the gleeful recipient of her uncontrollable sensuality.

They would wake in the middle of the night to the sensation of lips against their skin, of hands clutching their hair, of hip against hip. The sensation would be followed by extreme physical pain, as if their bodies were stretching to be with the other. Soon after, it would start raining. As if the sky and the clouds and the private parts of Nature were conspiring and participating in the wetness of their thighs, their nights, precipitating their union almost like the grand partner in a ménage a trois.

In the morning, on Raj's bedroom window, two mynahs would stare wide-eyed at him, chiding him for his nocturnal promiscuities while around the same time, but sometimes with a time lag, depending on how the Universe was feeling that morning, a pair of ripe green parrots would fly by Aparajita's window.

The languishing flowerpots on Aparajita's terrace burst into bloom, and friends and family started commenting on her motherhood glow, deepening her guilt every time.

Each passing day also settled in her fear at the strangeness of the processes that were unfolding within and without her. Sometimes, for no apparent reason, a bolt of lightning would pass through her body followed by an excruciating longing for Raj. It would make her head reel and force her into an autoerotic fantasy that she acted out like a pornographic actress being blackmailed by a corrupt producer. She noticed that at these times – when she was having sex with an imaginary Raj – strange occurrences solidified her unholy act: the baby would never cry, the maid would leave at the right time, the milk would finish boiling and the chores would get done. After, she invariably saw two pigeons mating or flying across her apartment, or it would drizzle, or an electrical appliance, usually her table fan, would short circuit and restart spontaneously with a whirring noise.

Numbers jumped at her, and they all had something to do with the number eleven. Clouds, spoons, flight patterns of birds, clocks, streets and car licence plates, road signs, bus numbers – all pointed to the number eleven. The more confounded all this made her, the more she longed for Raj, just so she could put her head on his shoulder and weep her confusion; as if that would stop the energy currents swirling within her body night and day.

And even as she tore off the pages of her kitchen calendar, two days before Raj was supposed to return on the 11th of July, she suddenly huffed to her bedroom cupboard, grabbed her purse, put on her kolhapuri slippers and told the maid loudly to mind the baby, she was going out for an hour.

Kalighat during mid-day was fairly deserted. She got a good view of the black goddess, and then feeling weak in the knees, sank back behind the pavilion. Weeping bitterly, she chided Goddess Kali for trying to ruin her life: 'Why, Mother, do you test me like this? What past sins are backing up on me? Have I not led a virtuous life so far? I have tried my best to be a good daughter, wife, mother. What obscene challenge is this? Who is this man you have sent to wreck my peaceful life? My thoughts become polluted, I start behaving like a harlot even when a remote thought crosses my mind. Is he a monster in disguise sent by you to test me? Why do I hunger for his touch? What madness is this?'

She sat cross-legged on the floor at the back of the temple courtyard, gazing at the bronze, vermilion-smeared eyes of the goddess. Slowly, the lunatic tides within her body stilled, her eyes closed, her back straightened, and she slipped into a trancelike meditative state as a beautiful blue light switched on in the middle of Kali's eyebrows and spread out and into her. A cool breeze caressed her skin and again that familiar feeling – of not knowing whether it came from within her, or without. The light ebbed and flowed, ebbed and flowed, changing patterns, changing hues, making intricate geometric designs that she did not understand. Her breath stilled, and from the stillness of that breath, came words:

'Holy. All Holy.'

She opened her eyes to gaze again at the red-tongued visage staring at her steadily over the bobbing heads of the mid-morning faithful.

'Holy. All Holy.'

And peace pervaded her. She let out an amused laugh. What guiltless justification of a fallen woman must this be? As she got up from bowing over the goddess's kumkum-encrusted feet, two red hibiscus flowers fell into her lap. Aparajita looked up in surprise.

It seemed as if the goddess was smiling, in cahoots!

How ridiculous is that? She smiled all the way back on the rickshaw ride; the gods have finally gone crazy.

There was nothing to stop her from throwing herself into Raj's arms the next time he stopped by with his horoscope, besides, of course, the conditioned upbringing of a Hindu girl trained not to behave like a cheap slut.

So finally when Raj did ring her doorbell to the sound of kettledrums and cosmic thunder she received him with a casualness bordering on indifference, even though the sight of him stilled the perpetual state of restlessness she always seemed to be in.

Raj, too, when he finally saw her after two eternal, infernal, endless weeks – saw her actually, physically, standing in front of him, and not in his dreams or his imagination or his thoughts or fantasies – felt a calmness through his entire body, as if the world had finally stopped its damned moving. And when she smiled at him – a smile that could not hide the sweetness of their togetherness – he was seized by such an irrational gratitude for that smile that it frightened him. He knew that she could see the power she had over him. At that moment, it didn't matter; let her have that power, it's hers to have, he thought, but then, in his peripheral vision, he saw a framed photograph of her wedding and he contracted back into a closed space again. Fear was better, fear was familiar ground.

'Would you like some tea?' she said.

She was floating – a feather that had found a thermal in winter.

'Sure,' he said, his eyes following her, not insolent but proprietary, just knowing her every curve, owning her each loosened lock of hair. She was his. With her walk she lead his gaze, as if by the hand, to the kitchen where the water boiling in a beaten-down saucepan became sacred worship and the tea leaves, lending their colour to the colourlessness around, a gesture of complete surrender.

It had started raining again, and they sipped their tea and they talked inanely of inconsequential things that they went over and over, like a dog-eared book, for the rest of their lives. They watched the raindrops chase each other on her window sill and the water collect in the cracks of her panes, as if for a secret rendezvous. They finished each other's sentences, read each other's thoughts, laughed at exactly the same time and forgot where one ended and the other began. Nor, when that happened, did they feel the need to touch.

So when, perfectly, in the course of the flow of their conversation, he told her that in the highly-strung atmosphere of a family death, his mother and other relations had forced his consent for marriage to a girl from a neighbouring princely state, she very naturally told him it was the right thing to do.

He looked carefully at her for signs of pain, and did not see any. The incongruity of that in regard to his power over her bothered him. He could not tell whether she was hiding it well or wasn't feeling it at all. The uncertainty made him retreat back into the familiar territory of suspicion. Like an old shoe it comforted him. He did not realize that his presence had lulled her into such a state of wellness that nothing seemed to disturb her.

Of course she would feel pain, she told him in her reveries. Every time she was silent, or saw the sun lose its last ray of dusk light, or a duck swim alone, the pain would appear like a diseased patient she had to care for. She was condemned to carry that pain.

From his horoscope file he took out a Cartier catalogue, a glossy brochure for jewellery items like watches and wedding rings. The kind Audrey Hepburn and the King of Brunei wore casually and the rest of the world aspired toward.

'Which one do you think I should buy for my prospective wife?' he had asked her. 'I want a woman's perspective.'

She hesitated over the sample photographs titillating her, luxurious, brazenly unnecessary. Cartier, Carrion, Cruel, Cold, Calculating Carter of Corpses. Exquisite designs of double diamonds, baguettes, intertwined rings, twin hearts, ancient Maltese crosses and gothic knots.

'Oh, but don't ask me. I don't know what she would like.'

He looked at her direct open face and she knew he was saying that she would know because it was she he would see in the woman he married. It was she he saw in every woman he had met, would ever meet; loved, admired, respected, would love, would admire, would respect. She read his eyes but her own clouded over a moment later, almost as if the suspicion he had felt a moment ago had finally reached her after a time lag.

If he loved her, what was stopping him from telling her so? How did he know that she would not leave her husband and her child in a trice to be with him? She wouldn't, but he didn't know that. Or did he? Still, if he loved her he would have told her so by now. And if he hadn't it was obviously because he didn't. Surely she must be suffering from some kind of postpartum depression to be fantasizing about her neighbour like this.

'You would –' he began, and for the first time since they had met he struggled to find words. What he wanted to say was, 'You would, because even though she will be wearing the ring, I will be marrying you. I have to marry. I can't remain unmarried, thinking about your husband and family every day. And I can't marry you. I have to get married to equalize the injustice that when I met you, you were already taken.'

She saw him struggle for words and felt the first germ of anger against his cowardice. *It is a falsehood,* she thought, *that true love exists only between perfect people. This one is a dunce.* 'That one,' she said finally, not really interested, but pretending for his sake.

He sensed her anger and it fired his suspicion. *She is trying to trap me*, he couldn't stop himself from thinking. *She really is a witch, capable of leaving her husband and new-born baby over the prospects of a richer man.* The moment the thought rose like a stain on perfect marble, he wanted to pin her against the wall and crush her mouth with his, preventing any possibility of their separation.

'One diamond. A solitaire,' she said finally. 'Because one is not alone, one is two merged in union.'

He gasped. She looked up at him from the catalogue ever so slowly and tore him apart.

'One it is.'

'What will you tell your wife, Raj? That the ring was chosen not by your mother or sister but by some crazy horoscope lady upstairs?'

'I'll tell her...' he said, not being able to take his eyes away from her, 'I don't know what I'll tell her.'

Coward, she thought, and turned to look away. He knew that he had disappointed her but chose not to do anything about it. That was when she started hating him a little. And he didn't know how to stop it because he was hating her a little too.

Whether they would have hated each other more or less had they known that they would never meet again, is a question neither would have been able to answer at that point of time.

Outside, somewhere in a hyacinth-ridden lake in Calcutta, the ripples made by two pebbles finished intercrossing their tremors and the hyacinth began growing over it, covering up the spot.

14.

Kamini turned the door handle and was about to enter Rita's office cubicle when she froze, overhearing the words: 'Karmic peg'.

'All karmic pegs come with handle-with-care signs,' Rita's airy voice wafted out the door of her swanky office and Kamini knew she was talking to Mira on the telephone, and that it was related to the VNP project. She steeled herself, then pushed open Rita's door and walked in with a flourish. 'What's a karmic peg?'

Rita stiffened when she saw Kamini and her laughter was a touch strained. 'Oh, forget about that,' Rita said, 'and tell me what you think of this storyboard.'

Kamini knew then that she would not get anything more out of Rita. It was privilege enough to be in Rita's cubicle – nicknamed the Queen's chamber in the agency. To be sitting on one of her ostentatious, radical-chic Mackintosh chairs meant that she was already a chosen one, and to be asked to give an opinion on a senior's storyboard was more than she could ask for.

Trying not to show how upset she felt, Kamini pored over the storyboard quietly, lost in her own thoughts, and Rita relented a little: 'If you are going to start dating Hari, I hope you like men with disturbed psyches,' she said.

'Really?' Kamini fell for the bait, and instantly looked up at Rita, who had put up her feet on her own plush red leather chair with complete aplomb. '*Hari?*' She flicked away the storyboard, unimpressed. 'A disturbed psyche would actually make him interesting. He is so… '

'So?' Rita quirked a perfectly shaped eyebrow at her.

'So staid,' Kamini finished. 'And boring.'

'You'd be surprised,' Rita said.

'Everybody keeps saying that, in VNP,' Kamini complained. 'And it's true, I am always surprised. In fact every day seems to be a new mystery.'

'He has a troubled family history,' Rita offered, careful with her choice of words.

'Really?' Kamini said, wondering whether she was saying the word too often.

'A family feud with his brother, or something like that.'

Kamini shrugged. She was enjoying getting chummy with her boss while her colleagues stewed outside, in speculation of what they might be discussing. 'Who hasn't got a family feud running at some stage or the other?' she said, and then because Rita said nothing she felt pressed to add, 'I mean, I haven't spoken to *my* sister in years.' Then, because Rita's attention on her was so intent, she felt the need to confess: 'My parents were separated when I was very young.'

Silence.

'Not divorced. Separated.'

Silence.

'I live with my mother.' This time Kamini did not wait for any more silence to ensue. 'Why do I feel you know that?' she blurted.

That's when Rita lowered her gaze to fiddle with a Mont Blanc pen and deftly changed the course of the conversation. 'It's not like that with Hari.'

'What do you mean?' Kamini allowed the tactical shift in full awareness that somehow, somewhere she was being manoeuvred.

'His brother is evil, seriously evil, the antithesis of Hari.'

'How do you mean?' Hari was suddenly taking on larger-than-life proportions for Kamini.

'Let's say that his brother embodies all that VNP stands against.'

Kamini picked up her bag with smooth affectation and arched an eyebrow: 'How interesting,' she said getting up from her chair. And with one last look at her boss sitting perfectly silhouetted against a Mae West print said, 'Looks like I'll *have* to go on another date with him now.'

The statement was supposed to be a mischievous last word, but as Kamini walked out of Rita's door, it felt more like a foregone conclusion.

15.

'What the hell is greening?' Carlos said as soon as Ali's class resumed.

'And why the hell is it bad?' Rita wanted to know.

'Well, have you noticed that we are having solar eclipses far more frequently these days?' Ali asked, looking around his class.

'Sure,' Mira said. 'Every time there is a solar eclipse we are told we are not getting another one for a hundred years and lo and behold it turns up like a bad penny again in twelve months.'

'There's a reason for that. It's because of the galactic shift. It's causing a change in our space time continuum. The suns and moons are shifting position. The energy matrix of the earth is changing. A new age is dawning. The magnetic poles will shift their axis in 2012. 2012 is a process that started several years ago. Even now, the impending earthquake in Delhi, the famine in Kerala, the bankruptcies of the Fortune 500 companies are all par for the course. We all know that.' Hari's voice was grim.

'And our project's immediate concern is the cyclone build-up in Orissa, and the Naxalite conflict festering in that area. We all are aware that it is a direct effect of the dark energies building up there because of continuous Twin Flame activities. But you need to back up a little on your alchemy stuff,' Hari said, returning to Ali, 'because most people are unfamiliar with the subject. Unless of course, it's Kamini, who is new to everything.'

Everybody laughed politely, mostly because they needed a break. But Kamini found his joke particularly cruel. Hari was behaving as if they had never gone out for that date, never almost-kissed.

☯

She accosted him when they broke for ten minutes, following him into the washroom as he was drying his hands. 'You know I'm not as stupid as you think, Hari.'

'No?' he asked.

'You think I haven't noticed that Rudra's dad, a very senior practitioner in VNP, was asked to leave the project, while Rudra was picked up for no presumable reason? I, who really have no business to be here among such serious adepts, was picked up too.'

Hari started walking slowly out of the washroom. Kamini's instinct told her she was on the right track.

'So?' he said.

'So, how about you tell me what is really going on?'

And then she saw a flicker in his face, and she recognized it as pity. It scared her because it meant he had some knowledge about her that could make him feel that way. She stopped walking behind him.

'In time,' Hari said, stopping with her.

She touched his elbow, her vulnerability now compounded by fear. 'Hari, please,' she said.

'We are late,' Hari told her gently. 'The water break is over.'

Back in the room, she concentrated on the eighteen-year-old's valiant efforts to bring some order to his unwieldy mind. Watching the struggle between sagacity and youth was such a fascinating sight that it made her feel better.

The new-grown hair on his face making him look even more fledgling, Ali said: 'It's such a vast subject. I really don't know where to start.'

'Start at the beginning,' Rita said.

'Start with what comes off the top of your head.'

'Pick up from where we all understand.' Mira actually took out her knitting from her purse, and leaned back as if for a relaxing afternoon of TV watching.

This immediately put Ali at ease. He brightened, 'Bingo! Let me start with the ten effects of Cupid. We all know Cupid, right?'

A synchronized nod went up.

'The ten effects of Cupid,' he wrote on the white board. 'First, the attraction through the eyes. You can call it first contact. Second, intense attachment through the mind, then determination, then loss of sleep, then emaciation, then disinterest in external things, then shamelessness, madness, becoming stunned or comatose, then death.'

'Wow,' Kamini said. 'I had no idea falling in love could be so dangerous. Sounds like the symptoms for the plague.'

'Well, rest assured, darling,' Ali leered at her – leering at Kamini somehow always seemed to make him feel more adult – 'it doesn't happen to regular people like you and me. You see, with us it's more a case of hormones, of biochemistry, and though in a way the hormone-driven symptoms do mimic the ten effects, what is being described in this case is the genuine article. The real shebang.'

'What's that?' Hari snorted. 'True love?'

'Umm,' Ali hesitated. 'Well, yes, if you use the term in a very, very loose way. Like saying that a pentagram is a lucky charm.'

'Get to the point, love,' Rita said with the patience of many babysitting sessions.

'The point I am making,' Ali said, gathering his thoughts with one deep breath, 'is that the ten effects describe a process, very much the way alchemy does. Most people understand alchemy as the science of turning base metal into gold. If it were just that it would very much be the hokum that people think it is, and what the Church decried it to be. But that is a wrong definition. You don't just put lead in a beaker and light a Bunsen burner underneath and keep adding bat-tails till it turns to gold.'

'No?' Carlos smiled, smoothing the folds of his perfectly starched orange robes. 'Live and learn.'

'Pick up any secret mystical doctrine – now no longer secret thanks to the net – and look at all its symbols and emblems. The first step in deciphering the text is to understand that its figures and symbols are describing energies within the human body, its environment and the universe, and their differing conjugations in particular circumstances. Alchemy in its pure definition means the process of turning the gross into the subtle. In Rita Ma'am's quantum mechanical terms, it is the art and the science of making an electron make a quantum leap from one electronic orbit to the next.'

'Then whenceforth, dear one' – Carlos was in the mood to rib Ali – 'the apparatus, the beaker, the little alchemy kit, the secret labs in the cellar?'

'Because,' Ali said, warming to the subject, 'of the golden, pun intended, rule expounded by the greatest alchemist of all time, Hermes Thoth. He said, "As is above so is below".'

'"The microcosm reflects the macrocosm."' Mira turned to Carlos who was looking confused.

'The atom reflects the solar system,' Rita helped. 'So the energy principles in the subtlest realms react and conjugate in a particular manner. What the alchemists were doing was learning how to mimic the laws of the subtler realms in the material world.'

'The pimply teenager mimicking the ten effects of Cupid,' Ali added, as if it were the piece de resistance.

'Okay, can we have a little more explanation on that, professor?'

'Sure,' Ali said. 'The ten effects of Cupid talk about the principles of sexual alchemy. In the above, it manifests as the processes unfolding in divine union. Below, in any life process – the birds, the bees, the pollination of the hibiscus flower. It manifests in almost any interactive process known to us. In chemical, processes, in physical, biological, material, economic, spiritual – think of a category and it will manifest.'

'But why Cupid?' Kamini wanted to know.

'Cupid works with male and female energies. Male and female are also genetic versions of the two generic poles. All energy processes are bipolar. Just as computer languages speak in the language of one and zero, the language of the universe is spoken by male and female, yin and yang, Shiv and Shakti.'

'Okay,' Hari was finally impressed. 'I think I am getting it.'

'In us there is a very important X-factor, the human factor, I call it the H-factor. When these energies manifest in humans they cause emotion.'

'E-motion,' Rita said, tapping a perfectly manicured nail on the table. 'The motion caused when electrons collide in the human aura. The heat energy caused by this collision we better know as emotion.'

'Out of the different emotions causing the collision of electrons, the highest, most productive emotion that Cupid and we are concerned with is the four-letter word: LOVE.'

'Finally,' Mira's sigh was full of exaggerated longing. 'The L word.'

'Yes, ladies and dudes,' Ali gestured dramatically swishing his invisible cloak. 'I give to you the masterpiece of them all. None other than the one and only, the world famous, LOVE.'

'A little bit of interesting information...' Hari intervened. His team turned to look at him.

'Do you know how dolphins communicate?'

'No.'

'Their sound waves are very refined energy patterns that interfere to cause visual images that can be transmitted to other dolphins. It's also the principle of telepathy.'

'If telepathy can create mental images then it's possible to have telepathic sex?'

'Of course. It would be better than telephone sex.'

The men let out a collective sigh.

'Okay, darlings,' Mira said, switching to grandmother mode. 'This is where we return to relevance. Let's get back to first, XX and XY and second, what you were saying about greening.'

'Sure,' Ali said, in his element, centre-stage. 'Though the effects of alchemy physicalize in all known phenomena it is in two subjects with strong Shiva and Shakti energies or Yin Yang energies that it can manifest in the highest end of the spectrum. What in most religious texts is defined as divine.'

'And you call it?' Rita frowned in concentration.

'Spectrum High end. HSE,' Ali said.

'Okay, please carry on.'

'Fast,' said Hari, tapping his watch.

'Well,' Ali said, looking at Hari from the corner of his eye, 'I will go into a technical explanation later. Actually, Rita Ma'am will probably do a much better job of that. Suffice it for us to conclude for the moment that our two subjects XX and XY are Spectrum High Ends or HSEs. Through a series of processes they have reached a fairly dangerous phase of the energy conjunction called greening. It is also symbolized in alchemical texts as the Black Sun.'

He stopped, waiting for an interjection. None came.

'The black sun occurs when the sun and the moon, the Yin and the Yang are in coniunuctio, union. It causes an eclipse and lowering of consciousness to such an extent that medieval texts have called it the state of putrefaction. This is also a time in which, because of the eclipse, a lot of negative and dark energies are released. It is a time when the spirit is resisting the push towards manifestation in the physical. It is a time of decay and conflict. The ninth effect of Cupid before death occurs.'

'Madness and coma,' Carlos said. There was a hush in the room.

'Also, if I use Thoth's thumb rule of "As is above so is below" in the physical world, the reflection of greening would be the first appearance of chlorophyll. It is the first sign that the decomposition of the compost in the soil is now complete. It now requires sunlight for further progress. If there is no sunshine, the decay and decomposition will continue into total nothingness, dissolution.'

Ali walked up to the XX and XY symbols on the whiteboard and started crossing them out with a thick marker. Kamini shivered.

'This is the time that if a third agent, a catalyst – in medieval texts the white dove – is not introduced, it will cause the death of the subjects and the failure of the entire project.'

'What is the third agent in this case?' Hari asked.

'VNP,' Ali said.

16.

All through the taxi ride back to her brother's flat, Uma had the sensation that she was in an elevator and that it was taking her down into the bowels of the earth. How many levels to reach the centre, Uma wondered. 5000? She felt she was being tossed around, plucked out for some very important purpose she was clueless about. When the elevator halted with a sleep-awakening 'ping' she realized she was on the sixth floor of her brother's apartment complex.

The door of his flat was open. The maid had put the garbage out. Her mother was sitting in the armchair as usual, combing her thinning hair. Uma couldn't tell whether she had sunk deeper into the upholstery or her reverie. Her sister was trying to explain to the maid, in excruciatingly indecipherable Bengali, how to fry potatoes non-Bengali style. Uma could tell there was an entire sub-cultural bomb waiting to explode in the kitchen. Indira had shut the door to Dodo's bedroom and one could make out from the tone and agitation in her muffled voice that she was on her mobile phone. Her aunt had dropped in with home-made pickle and was organizing containers. Dodo was lounging about in his pyjamas because it was Sunday. He was watching *Diehard* for the eleventh time on Star Movies.

Uma threw her purse on an unoccupied armchair and, enervated by the Calcutta humidity, found a cushion to rest her head on before saying, 'Everybody gather up. We need to talk.'

Curling her finger around the pickle jar and licking off the mustard oil slick, her aunt obediently walked towards her.

'Okay, you do it your way,' Ishita finished her diatribe to the maid in shattering Bengali. Her mother did not move. Dodo switched off the TV.

Uma who had shut her eyes for a moment looked up to see all eyes on her, waiting, intent. She started laughing.

'What?' Ishita grumbled.

'Yes, what?' Dodo said.

'What did I do? Call out the zombies to rise from the dead?' Uma found herself laughing uncontrollably. 'If only you could see your own expressions,' she giggled.

'Hysteria,' Ishita declared and favouring her stitched tailbone started limping back to the kitchen.

'Hurry up and say what you have to say,' their mother hissed, brandishing her comb in the direction of Dodo's room, 'before *she* comes out. She's been talking non-stop – lawyers, accountants, estate managers and what not. Not a word about poor Raj in hospital.'

Suddenly calm, Uma said aloud what had been playing in her head like a mantra ever since she had set foot in Calcutta: 'Something strange is going on.'

Dodo's bedroom had been silent for a while. Now Indira walked out with an air of forced casualness. 'How is Dad? Are you coming from the hospital?'

'I'm on my way there,' Uma said. 'Came home for a breather.' She was curt, sensing a shift in the alliances in the room. 'I went to visit the Ghoshes upstairs in Chowringhee. I wanted to ask them about the ring.'

'And ?' said her mother.

'They are lovely people. I felt a weird attraction to Mrs Ghosh.' And not knowing how to frame it, added, 'I think Raj Mamu knows her.'

'Quite possible,' their mother said. 'They've been our neighbours for years. And even though we clannish Rajputs are not very social, it is quite possible that they bumped into each other now and then. Though chances of that are rare, because Raj put his flat up on rent soon after his wedding.'

Uma thought about the slip of paper in the jewellery case and some instinct stopped her from mentioning it. 'No, I mean *really* know each other.'

'What makes you say that?' Dodo said.

'She started weeping when she saw the ring,' Uma replied.

'That's weird,' Ishita commented.

'Is the ring hers?' Uma's mother asked.

'What would Mrs Ghosh know?' Indira said. 'She's got Alzheimer's.'

'Oh, that explains it. She's probably hallucinating,' the aunt said.

'Do they hallucinate in Alzheimer's?' Dodo puzzled.

'Where is the ring?' Indira asked.

But Uma was not listening to the question. She had turned squarely to face Indira, and eyes flashing the way they seldom did with her, she asked: 'How do *you* know she has Alzheimer's?'

Everybody turned to look at Indira in stunned bewilderment.

The tips of Indira's ears turned crimson. 'You said she had Alzheimer's,' she threw back.

'No, I didn't,' Uma said, not once taking her eyes off her.

'Yes, you did.'

'No, I didn't.'

'No, she didn't,' Dodo said.

Like one living organism everybody turned to face Indira. She took a step back. 'Is it not enough that I have a dad dying in hospital? Do you people have to pick on me too?' Her eyes welling up, she stepped back and retreating into Dodo's bedroom, slammed the door.

'Let me say for the millionth and seventeenth time,' Uma said. 'Something very, very strange is going on.'

'Very strange,' Ishita said.

'Very, very strange,' Dodo echoed.

'What is the neighbour like? And what is this strange strange you keep talking about?' Their mother, as usual the most clueless person in the group, wanted to know.

'When I was leaving the apartment,' Uma said, flicking on the AC remote, unable to get it to a temperature below 18 degrees that felt like twenty-five, 'Mrs Ghosh's maid caught up with me at the elevator. I think she has been with the family a long time. A woman called Jhunu.'

'They are all called Jhunu,' Ishita said with much affected sagacity. 'Even Dodo's maid is called Jhunu.'

'Jhinku,' Dodo corrected.

'Whatever,' Ishita said.

'Anyway, you know what Jhunu said to me?' Uma asked, as if she were disclosing the climax of a suspense novel.

'What?' her mother said, looking even more tired, if that were possible.

'She said, don't listen to the sahib. She said that her madam may be sick but she has special powers.'

'What do you mean special powers?' asked her mother, thoroughly exasperated.

'Apparently, she can heal. Dead birds fly off from her hands. Sick people become fine, mad people sane.'

'Meaning?' Dodo was cross-eyed in confusion.

'She made it sound as if Mrs Ghosh was some kind of a shaman – you know like the medicine women in African tribal societies.'

'What bullshit,' the mother said, and because she made such a modern swear word sound almost anachronistic, her children laughed.

'Also, I am red-flagging everybody,' Uma continued, 'about the huffy puffy lady in Dodo's room.' Uma lifted her eyes towards the bedroom then raised her feet up on Dodo's divan and prepared to lie down. 'She's definitely hiding something.'

'Not for long,' Dodo laughed, flicking on the TV remote. 'Not as long as my sisters are here.'

'Heh heh to that,' said Ishita, sitting down to a plate of hot fried potatoes.

17.

When she walked Raj to the door, she was unable to shut it, and he was unable to go for a full ten minutes. When he left it was as if she had been peeled away from him, like a second skin. He walked down the stairs shaking his head, wondering how he would fit this phenomenon into his life.

I can't, Raj thought. What will I tell my family? There is a married woman with a new-born baby upstairs, and when we look at each other a ray of white light passes between our pupils reminding us of an ancient beginning when we were together as one?

His head was reeling when he entered his flat and the chaos of his noisy, clannish existence. Where in all this, the thought wrenched him out, would she fit in?

And with a flash of anger he admonished himself, warning himself that he should not fall prey to this silly Bengali Devdas concept of unrequited love. *She obviously does not love me,* he thought. *She didn't bat an eyelid when I told her I was getting married.* This has to stop, he steeled himself. I will end up getting myself and her into trouble. She is a married woman, and if my family ever gets to know – well, perish the thought.

His rejection of the 'phenomenon' brought in its wake anger and a compelling need to hurt her. More so, because though he was sure that she was just a bored housewife passing time, he also sensed her pining for him. Neither of them realized at the time that, like a mirror image reflecting back, she was matching him resentment for resentment, and the more the hatred grew between them, like a well-maintained ward, the more their desire for each other deepened in the realm of their thoughts and fantasies.

Away from the cosy hullabaloo of kith and kin he locked himself in the only place he knew he would find peace – his uncle's private bathroom.

He sat on the edge of the enamel bathtub, took out a cigar from his uncle's secret drawer and smelt it. He inhaled the rich smell of lovingly cured tobacco, but with it also came the perfume of her hair. It swirled around him and he shut his eyes, sinking to his knees, because now she had her arms wrapped around him, and he surrendered his face up to her for her to kiss, and she did. His knees buckled. Within moments he could smell the perfume between her breasts and her legs, and finally when he exploded in ecstasy, he knew so had she.

When he tucked his shirt in, she asked him, 'Is this how it's going to be between us?'

'Looks like,' he said, kissing her face with a gentleness he never thought he was capable of.

'Why?'

'Why what?' He saw her in his arms, her face looking up at him.

'Why can't you come up to me and tell me how you feel? Between the two of us you are the only man around, aren't you?'

He looked down at her face. How could looking at someone's face fill you with so much peace? he wondered. Outside the bedroom, on the Binaca radio station, a Hindi film song that Jhunu downstairs had tuned into in the kitchen, was playing. It sang of their love, of being alone and never being alone.

'At least give me a sign, so I know that all this is happening,' she pleaded. 'And I haven't finally gone cuckoo.'

'And how do I do that?' he said, feeling the softness of her arms, hugging her closer to his chest.

'Send Bairah with a chit to me saying that you have chosen the solitaire. That's all. I'll know then that the solitaire was meant for me.'

He laughed. 'You'll think I've gone crazy.'

'No I won't,' she insisted. 'Okay, just one word – solitaire. I'll know.'

'Never, your husband might find it.' He was kissing the nape of her neck. When they were like this, he indulged her even when he refuted her, and she surrendered to him even when she was angry with him. How different reality feels, Raj sighed.

'You must do it, Raj.' Lifting her face closer to his, wrapping her arms around him a little more tightly, making his eyes roll to the back of his head. 'Don't you see that this is the only proof we have of our existence? There is nothing else.'

'I can't,' he said without anger.

'You must,' she said without resentment.

'I won't,' he said. She seemed to be fading now, his senses were shutting down.

'Doubt will kill us,' seemed to be the last thing she said.

'I doubt,' Raj smiled at her fading image as he buckled his belt, 'that anything can kill this. This doesn't feel like something that can die easily.'

Her absence filled him with doubt, just like she had said before leaving. A firm resolve of never seeing her again came with anguish at the mere thought of it, followed by the suspicion that he was all alone in this crazy fantasizing, which was followed by an inexplicable rage that she was not suffering the way he was.

Upstairs, Aparajita felt his rage as a heaviness in her heart. She sat down on the edge of her bed, a silver bowl of uneaten baby formula still in her hands, and started to sob.

As Raj shut the door to his uncle's bedroom, a wet drop appeared on his shirt front. When he looked down at it he sensed the warmth and saltiness of her tears. For a moment he leaned back against the wall behind him and rested his head against the wood panelling. If he died for her, would she please stop crying?

The next moment he was exhaling sharply and getting his head off the wall, walking towards the din in the family room.

Good, he thought, she is hurting too.

'Where *were* you?' Manik confronted him in a room full of family in various positions of extreme ennui and attempted relaxation.

'With the terrace key,' Raj gave him a faux conspiratorial wink.

Their cousins picked up the word, and many dirty allusions and puns were made on the word 'key' that Raj thoroughly enjoyed because it brought forth her filmy presence among them. More so, because his sister and cousins had no clue what they were talking about.

It took him a while to figure out that in the far corner of the fairly large room a stranger, a panditji, was looking at everybody's birth-chart. Raj laughed out loud.

'What is it with birth-charts these days?'

After much prodding and inane laughter his chart was produced before the extremely hairy and wrinkly fortune-teller.

The panditji looked up sharply from Raj's horoscope to stare at him. Then he looked around the large drawing room: colonial bric a brac, hunting trophies, ceremonial swords, an entire wall draped in tiger skins and Raja Ravi Verma paintings, all reflecting the dying glory of old Indian royalty. Then he turned to assess Raj again, as if trying to sniff out a scent like a dog, and only after Raj started fidgeting under his burning gaze and the silence became uncomfortable did the panditji say as cryptically as the dramatic pause demanded: 'The meaning of Yoga is union, my son.'

'Meaning?' Manik said.

'Yoga of what?' His sisters wanted to know.

In the commotion, during which the hirsute pandit didn't stop looking at him, Raj asked quietly, 'Will I achieve that union?'

'Too many indecipherables, too many unknowns, too many factors,' Panditji replied, not even looking at the horoscope.

'Still?' Raj insisted.

Everybody stopped talking, as if straining to listen to the hush that had pervaded the room.

'In the ripeness of the moment, in the fullness of time,' the soothsayer's low voice seemed loud in the sudden silence, 'if the world permits it –'

'– then Raj will become a saint.' Manik made his solemn declaration.

Raj's sisters hooted with laughter and there was much gesturing behind the soothsayer's head and lip-syncing of the word 'fraud'. In Raj's mind the whooshing sound of planets aligning themselves in the thick black syrup of time faded away. It was replaced with the determination that his well-being depended on his staying away from his voluptuous neighbour.

Stay away from me, you minx, he said, *and don't cry on my shirt.* And he made another observation that the moment he formed a hurtful thought he felt his gut ripping into two, formalizing the sensation of pain, but he was unable to locate the source of it, whether him or her.

'Bewitching charm of Bengali enchantresses,' he heard the words waft up to him, and even though he knew that they were spoken in a context unrelated to his, he read a message in them.

'Fine,' he thought. 'I am never seeing you again.'

'Not even if I throw myself at you and beg?' she asked.

'Oh, then, I'll definitely see you,' he smiled.

He saw her throw her head back and laugh. He saw the slightly crooked set of her teeth and her hair falling down to her shoulder.

'The bewitching charm of the Bengali enchantress,' she taunted.

'I don't care anymore. You've already driven me crazy. And I'm beginning to think resistance is useless where you are concerned.'

He felt a slim finger pull back the collar from his shirt. The softest of kisses against his chest miraculously shortened his breath and quickened his feet to his uncle's bedroom.

'Is there a way,' he asked panting now, locking the door after him, 'to actually meet in our dreams?'

'Go to the National Library in Tollygunje tomorrow and find a book on lucid dreaming,' she said.

Later, still glowing from the release she gave him, almost in preparation of his visit to the library for the book, he fell into a trancelike sleep right there in his uncle's bedroom, even as his uncle was having his post-dinner cigar. Breathing heavily, he found himself gliding into her bedroom. He tried not to bump against her dressing bureau. Thankfully the moon was full and he could decipher the sleeping forms of her husband and her infant son. He just hoped they didn't hear his heavy breathing. He had trouble walking. It was only the deep strength of his breath that provided some movement to his slow gliding legs. Legs that were not real, yet real enough to be able to be moved by his breath.

When he reached her, she awoke and half sat on her own sleeping body.

She saw him as a dark figure approaching her unsteadily, his gusty breath like a steam engine. She stretched her arms out to him and unable to release herself entirely from her prone body pulled him down to her and started to weep uncontrollably. He sat on her sleeping body and taking her half-sitting form in his arms started stroking her hair.

'Why are you crying?' he asked, shushing her, pressing his lips against her forehead.

'Don't leave me,' she said, an etheric drop of snot running down his pyjama front.

'Would you leave your husband and son for me?' he whispered in her ear.

'No,' she shook her head against his shirt.

'Then don't cry. Why do you cry so much?' He buried his head in her hair.

'I don't know. Just please don't leave me.'

'Shush,' he said, stroking her hair, holding her tight.

And they sat in the moonlight of the bedroom for a long time, sitting on her sleeping body, next to her husband and son. The light was darker, the air heavier, her sobbing unbearably sweet. But not once did he say that he would not leave her.

'I do not mean to send you away,' he said.

'You cannot keep me either,' she said.

18.

At any given moment an individual operates in four different dimensions. That means that not only are we using ten per cent of our brains, we are perceiving only ten per cent of reality as it can be perceived,' the disembodied voice said.

Kamini tossed in her bed.

As she twitched and fidgeted, somewhere there was the dim consciousness that she was sleeping, that the mattress was too hard against her muscles, that her body was numbed by its own shape, its own texture. Her senses were prickling and desensitizing at the same time and it made her thrash about in her sleep a little more.

In her dream she sat around the Narnia conference table, wide-eyed from the light shining through the skylight and in everybody's eyes.

And in her dream Kamini thought that if a dream is in such focus, in such Eastman Technicolor, and in such a logical sequence, it had to be very, very real.

'A human has four bodies,' Carlos began his presentation, and when he gestured this, Kamini noticed that his fingers were blurry with light.

Rudra was present for the meeting. The last time the team was together Hari had received an sms chiding him for not having Rudra present at the meetings. So now he was there, making their number an odd seven, presenting to each one of them the gift of his indefinable stare of black trapped light.

'This is all very basic stuff,' Hari grinned at Kamini, and like Alice's Cheshire cat, his smile lingered for too long. 'But for the benefit of the dunce of the class…'

Kamini blushed, feeling colour but no heat.

'Don't be so hard on yourself, Hari,' Carlos defended Kamini.

'Thank you, Carlos,' Kamini said, still embarrassed and noticing that in dreams fidgeting caused no physical discomfort.

'This inner voice that everybody talks about,' Carlos returned to the topic training his gentle blue eyes on her, 'not only has a voice but eyes and ears and nose and touch. Because the inner voice belongs to the second body. The first body, of course, is our gross physical body. Some reiki and praanic healers call the second body the energy body because it is the energy replica of the physical body.'

Must be the body with which we dream, Kamini thought, but held her silence, not wanting to disturb her dream friends with her dream theories.

'That, darling, means,' Mira bobbed her silver hair in Kamini's direction, clicking her needle points, half the front side of a baby's sweater already complete, 'that your liver and your kidneys all have replicas in the energy body. And the light of all this reflects in the aura that clairvoyants see.'

Does she know we are dreaming, Kamini thought. Is she dreaming too right now?

'Tibetans call it the mental body,' Mira was saying. 'All your memories and past-life impressions, your likes and dislikes, remain intact in this form. The mental body is powered by the breath, the way movement in the physical body is powered by the legs. Hindus see this body as a white flame in the region of the heart. They call it the subtle body, the body we use to travel in our dreams. Some schools call it the dream body.'

Instructions about reality in a dream, how cool is that? Kamini smiled in her sleep.

'If you notice,' Rita said to Kamini – everybody's ministrations seemed to be directed towards her – 'we don't walk in our dreams. We glide.'

'I thought dreams were caused by neurons firing wrongly when we slept,' Kamini said.

Carlos smiled: 'I wouldn't say that is wrong. I would say that it is a very gross approximation of what really happens. You see, science is not really wrong or contradictory or absolute, it is just inadequate, vaguely in the ball park, never in the bull's eye. It's a blind man's reality.'

'True,' Hari said. 'But after centuries of wandering about I would say science, or rather western science is blundering close to the truth.'

'He talks of Quantum Mechanics,' Rita informed Kamini who nodded wisely in understanding, she hoped.

The VNP chief, Kamini suddenly remembered. I am dreaming this because he is going to visit us. Kamini looked around her, shivering with excitement. Why isn't he here? Is it a he?

'Well, not just Quantum mechanics,' Carlos was countering across the glassy expanse of the Narnia table. 'All levels of science, whether the search for meta-materials or superconductivity, are breaking the glass ceiling, if I may mix my metaphors.'

'You may,' Rita smiled, happy for him.

Carlos continued, 'When they hit upon a meta or para concept, whether it is parapsychology, or metaphysics –'

'Have you noticed,' Mira interrupted, eyes and fingers flying on knit, purl, knit, 'how the prefix "para" means the same in English and Hindi, whose roots of course are Latin and Sanskrit?'

'And they both mean the transcendent, the beyond,' Hari finished thoughtfully.

Kamini brightened. 'Science and Spirituality are moving towards union. Yoga.'

Rudra gave her a knowing smile.

For once, Hari's look towards her was indulgent too. 'Eureka,' he completed for her.

'But, Carlos,' she returned to him. 'If there are as many bodies as you say, why does it sound like such an alien concept? Why is there no instinct of knowing about something that is supposed to exist within us? We are aware of our thoughts and feelings. So why not this?'

'Because, darling, though these identities exist, they are too refined to be perceived with our gross senses. Our senses need to be polished; much like a skill that needs to be honed,' Mira said, not looking up, ending a line of stitches with a flourish. Her knitting seemed to be focusing the group on its needle points.

Who knits these days? Kamini wondered. And Rudra flashed his knowing laser gaze at her again.

'We are all in various levels of not being in touch with ourselves. How would you define self-realization? Self-realization is the capability to realize and be aware of oneself, of who we are. That's what saints are. Just people who know who they are. Simply put, they are people who are always in complete touch with themselves,' Carlos said.

'But why is it so difficult?' Kamini could not give up her question. 'If that is our natural state, we should all be aware.'

Everybody gave her a collective, brightly-lit smile. The walls of the room expanded around them.

'Ah', said Rita pointing a bright neon red fingernail at her: 'We are all aware. We have just forgotten. We are all in different stages of forgetting. That's our karma. But we are also all progressing towards recognition, *pratyabhijnahridayam* – re-cognition, if you please – at our own pace and in our own way. Just as a caterpillar intrinsically moves towards becoming a butterfly,' she finished, rather pleased with her analogy.

And Hari said, 'Even as we speak there are those, the greater beings who walk this earth, pretending to be human.'

'Meaning?' Kaminin asked.

'There are those ' – Hari's voice sounded suddenly far off, making the short hairs of her neck rise, even in her dream – 'though most have actually forgotten, there are those who pretend they have forgotten. And there are some who know they have forgotten. A deep knowledge nags them.'

'Like a half-forgotten memory,' Mira said.

'Like snatches of an old love song,' Rita said.

'Coming back, then, to our third body,' Carlos abruptly steered the group back to his topic. 'The third body is the causal body.'

'Now we have really reached the meta level,' Rita whispered to Kamini, as if she were close to finding out that the butler was the murderer. She felt overwhelmed by all the attention she was getting.

Kamini shivered and looked around, waiting for the VNP chief. I don't think he is coming, she thought. Also, the room was getting dark. Not strictly dark, Kamini observed, it was a fluorescent inky-blue. It's a wonder we can see each other, but see each other we can.

'The causal body is an extremely refined energy state attained by very advanced practitioners. Let me see, how do I explain it?'

'A spectrum,' prompted Ali coming out of his shut-eyed, cross-legged meditative state, sitting in his chair.

Kamini noticed with a start that he was levitating.

'Aha! Ali is with us again. Welcome back and thank you, Ali,' Carlos said. Ali took a deep bow from six inches above his chair.

'Let's consider the spectrum VIBGYOR – the rainbow colours that light breaks up into. Red and violet are the extreme ends of the spectrum. These are all different bandwidths of light vibrating at different frequencies. And like sound, the higher the frequency, the more refined the vibrational energy. Red signifies the gross body here.'

'What do you mean "signifies"?' Kamini wanted to know.

Carlos sighed. 'You are making my life difficult now. Significance, correspondence, points of reference, all these are words whose definitions take on more and more refined aspects as we move up the spectrum.'

'Almost as if meaning, and therefore knowledge, was getting more and more refined as we move up the spectrum ladder,' Kamini offered. And in her dream, Kamini had a dream-thought she did not share with the others, like a secret: *We are in the causal level now, and so the chief can only manifest as a symbol or sign. Yoohoo, last call for Mr* VNP *chief.*

'She's a bright girl,' Rita confided to Mira, as if she were not there, 'I like that.'

Kamini felt as if Versace had just paid her a compliment.

Hari smiled all around, full of pride at her, as if the credit was all his, prompting Rudra to throw back his head and laugh at the now non-existent ceiling.

'Yes. So if the red and the gross body are at the bottom end of the spectrum of the low frequencies, the causal body corresponds to indigo, the middle order of refined energies, ' Carlos said.

'If I spoke in Hindu mythology-ese', Mira's needles clicked, 'I'd say we are in Krishna-land.'

Ah, yes, the light! This must be Krishna-land, Kamini mused. 'Krishna is blue or black. Bluish-black.'

'Yup,' Rita nodded. 'Depending on which side of the bed he got up from.'

'But what has this got to do with the causal body?' Kamini saw her thoughts as spinning electrons in orbit.

'There is a verse in the Bhagvad Gita,' Carlos offered, 'that describes his cosmic form. All known creations are absorbed in him. An individual's causal body is but an aspect of Krishna, one of his divine sparks. One ray of the blue-black light. Krishna means black.'

Inside Kamini, connections that the finest fingers of her mind could not quite grasp, seemed to be falling into place. 'But I always presumed black as negative energy, as the lack of energy.'

'No,' Carlos said. 'Black is shunya, nothingness, pure consciousness. Difficult for the mind to grasp.'

'Wittgenstein, the Austrian philosopher, had said about the mind, that it is the ladder that one throws *after* climbing the wall,' Kamini said.

'Huh?' Hari was impressed.

'Never mind,' Kamini said imperiously and was pleasantly surprised to observe that she was actually climbing a ladder, leading to the skylight in the conference room.

'She's right,' Carlos was gleeful. 'You have to leave behind the ladder of the mind when you jump off the wall of the subtle body into the blue nothingness of the causal body.'

'Is there a connection between Krishna Consciousness and Christ Consciousness?' Kamini stopped on the ladder, poised in thoughtful contemplation. Rita and Mira exchanged glances, like a couple who had just discovered that their three-year-old was not only a great adept at the monkey bars but a genius too.

'Yes,' Carlos indulged her. 'But that's a different story. Suffice it to say, as you yourself so eloquently put it, in the causal realm, or in the causal body, we are pure energy, without the petty encumbrances of the meat and potatoes mind, or the disturbances of our memories or the paltry conditioning of the intellect...'

'That thinks no end of itself,' Mira clucked.

'There's no gender here.'

'Or age.'

'Or parents.'

'Or psychotic spouses,' Rita sighed.

'Or disgust at schoolteachers who pick their noses,' Ali raised his hand.

'Or revulsion at men who scratch their balls,' Kamini added.

'I don't scratch my balls,' Hari instinctively defended himself. Only Rudra did not laugh because he didn't understand the joke.

'Also,' Hari sighed, regaining his composure, 'there are no VNP deadlines, no time constraints.' He stopped, thought for a minute, and couldn't resist asking, 'Is there time in Krishna-land? Or is that a dumb question?'

'Not at all, Hari,' Carlos returned to the whiteboard. 'Thank you for cueing me into the next part of my presentation. Coming back to the fourth body, the supra-causal body commonly generalized and bastardized as Gee Oh Dee, or Parabrahman or the Divine. I shall dwell on it only briefly given the superfine nature of its concept and principles. The reason for that is, as Hari prompted, we keep going up the ladder and or deeper down the well.'

'Within our own bodies,' Rita's red fingernail went up.

Kamini realized that she was still climbing the ladder, only the ladder was suspended, unsupported in a black space that was ink and powder and liquid all at once, if that were possible.

'We also start crossing space time dimensions as one layer is shed and another begins. There are as many as fourteen different dimensions –'

'Um… that varies,' Mira's needlepoints clicked across time, across space, like a cosmic metronome.

'Some say nine,' Ali went.

'Whatever, let's not split hairs. The fact remains that as we cross energy lines into the more refined energies of other dimensions –'

Suddenly the conference table disappeared and the entire VNP group floated around the base of the ladder, staring up at her –

'Where are these energy lines?' Kamini asked, looking down at them, feeling majestic, regal almost.

'These energy lines are portals,' Ali clarified, and his words hung in the air in reasonably-sized Times New Roman italics.

'Where are they?' Kamini cried.

'You make them sound like Jimmy Choo shoes,' Rita laughed. And Kamini saw that Rita was wearing the same red shoes she had worn to the office. Must be Jimmy Choo. But I must not be distracted, she thought, or the dream will change direction.

'But where are they?' Kamini repeated.

'When in doubt go back to first base,' Mira scratched her scalp with a knitting needle, and it made a sound across the universe.

'Inside the body,' Ali disclosed.

'*Inside* the body?' Kamini was so astounded she fell off the ladder. Across time, across space, down the universe.

'Inside the body,' Mira confirmed, watching her descent over her knitting. 'The nine chakras on the spinal column, remember? The body is the city of nine gates? The chakras are energy portals to other dimensions. But don't get impatient, sweetheart, I'll tell you when my turn comes to play presentation-presentation.'

'Thank you, Mira,' Carlos quickly intervened. 'For giving me back my turn. As I was saying, the space time continuum distorts and shifts and no longer maintains the familiar qualities that we know. When Einstein said that space is curved he was trying to say that matter is the condensation of space. Descent down the spectrum of space and time gets calibrated as different dimensions as time and space condense and distort. For example, when we die, that is leave our physical body and move into our subtle body, we follow different calibrations of time. They say that one day of their time in their dimension is equivalent to a year of our time.'

'Each change in dimension is a change in energy line, like an electron making a quantum leap into another orbit.' Mira's needles kept up their staccato rhythm.

'An electron jumping to another orbit is directly proportional and equivalent to a human jumping into another body,' Rita prompted.

'And these energy lines, or portals, are within our own body, as Mira, stealing my thunder, said. We don't need expensive spacecraft to travel in space and time, Mr HG Wells, you got it all wrong,' Carlos grinned.

'Ali can do it right here and now,' Rita said. 'Sitting on a chair whose upholstery desperately needs dry cleaning.'

'Like technology that desperately needs scriptural understanding,' Kamini said.

'Bravo,' Carlos and Rita clapped. Kamini was at last beginning to feel like one of them.

And their applause echoed through her dream, as they hoisted her on their shoulders and joshed with her and played and she said she was sorry that the chief never showed and they said never mind, there's always a next time.

And when Kamini woke she lay in bed for a long time, staring at the ceiling that did exist, trying to understand why she felt so rested, so sated, so full of answers, so simply happy.

☯

Kamini sat through the actual presentation the next morning in a daze, jolted in and out of scraping sensations of déjà vu that nobody seemed to notice. But what followed next she was very sure was completely original; the palpable fear it generated could not be a recreation:

'Okay,' Hari suddenly clapped his hands loudly, jarring them out of their reveries, making Mira drop a stitch: 'Sorry to bust the party but I have an important question to ask all of you.'

'But I haven't finished,' Carlos interjected, taking a sip of water from a glass.

(A glass, Kamini speculated, that was not condensed space time. It was a *real* glass, containing *real* water. She could use some herself, thank you very much.)

'Well, you should have finished by now.' Hari was curt, pulling rank, gathering up the forces of the group.

'The question I have to ask is, how many of you have been seeing a black man in your dreams these last few days?'

All at once, a darkness descended on the group. For a while nobody spoke. Even Mira's needles stopped clicking.

Kamini was stunned at the question.

Ali's hand went up tentatively. 'I saw the grim reaper,' he confessed. 'Cowl, sickle, et al.'

'When?'

'Two weeks ago. He's a really tall guy, no face, only cowl.'

'Anybody else?' Hari looked around.

'I saw a dark man last night,' Rita said. 'Good looking, very white teeth.'

Carlos said, 'I saw him too. He exudes a lot of power.'

'Yes,' Ali concurred. 'I seem to know him.'

'Me too. And I also see a lot of crows,' Mira confessed, though a bit grudgingly.

'And you?' Hari asked Kamini.

'I saw a black man a few nights ago,' Kamini was hesitant, still shocked at the turn of conversation. 'He seemed to be running through the corridors of a...'

'Of a?' Hari prompted, raising his eyebrows comically at her.

But Kamini couldn't have laughed, even if she tried. 'Of a palace?' she seemed to ask.

There was a sharp exchange of glances all around.

'Have you seen the palace before?' Hari's eyes bore down on her.

Kamini was quiet.

'I repeat,' Hari said, his tone almost belligerent. 'Have you seen that palace before?'

'Can't say,' Kamini finally muttered, her head lowered, not looking at anybody.

Hari knew she was lying. He glanced grimly at the others, who were watching the two of them like gallery spectators.

'The game, ladies and gentlemen,' he announced grimly, 'is definitely afoot.'

19.

Raj's doctor looked like a young pretty patient of a psychiatric ward getting treatment for a nervous disorder. She was making Uma more testy with every passing minute. Uma practised the breathing technique she had learnt during her son's early tantrums. It took all her restraint to stop her from flinging Raj's thick file at the doctor's face.

'This is a very difficult case.'

The doctor was fidgety, high-pitched, gesticulating. She's way too namby-pamby to be a doctor, Uma thought with contempt.

'I couldn't sleep last night.' The doctor tried to stroke an invisible ache from her forehead. 'So many complications, the sodium potassium levels are so imbalanced. So much swelling in the brain.'

Yours or his? Uma wondered. She crossed her legs and gave the doctor the predatory look her family always watched out for and feared. 'Maybe if you calmed down you'll figure something out,' *you moron*, Uma finished in her head.

'You do not understand. There seems to be no one reason for his coma. I've been trying to get this through to his daughter and explain it to her, but she just doesn't listen.'

Alarm bells rang off in Uma's head but she did not change her expression. She did not want to distract the doctor with juicy family gossip.

Her bird-like movements becoming more and more pronounced under Uma's piercing look, the doctor squeaked, 'There are too many toxins in his system coming from too many avenues.'

Stop making my uncle sound like Park Street during rush hour, Uma thought, but held her tongue.

'And now there is a chest infection.' The doctor looked guilty, shifty-eyed; as if she had personally infected him with it.

'Chest infection?' Uma pounced. 'Why did that happen?'

'I don't know,' the doctor wailed, sweating visibly now. 'Your caasin –' the doctor's affected American accent became thickly Bengali as her anxiety grew.

'– cousin,' Uma snapped,

'– that's what I said,' the doctor wailed some more, 'has been visiting every few hours since yesterday and feeds him stuff orally–'

'What?' Uma raised her voice,

'I repeatedly told her not to interfere with his treatment, but she does not listen.'

Uma thought that if she exhaled the flimsy walls of the doctor's minuscule cubicle would collapse. I've got to get out of here, she thought.

'I'll speak to you later, doctor,' she said, grabbing her purse and starting the difficult manoeuvres necessary to get out of the tiny cabin.

'But who will sign the consent form?'

'Consent form for what?' Uma was trying her best not to shout at the doctor.

The doctor's badly plucked eyebrows threatened to disappear into her hairline. 'We need to put him on a ventilator, or he will die.'

'And you told my caasin about this?' Uma asked coldly.

'Yes, I did,' the doctor wailed.

'And she did nothing?'

'Absolutely nothing.' The doctor in her panic switched to British cockney.

'Give me the damn form, I'll sign it right now,' Uma said. After signing the form she stood up once again. 'I'm going now. Don't you dare have a nervous breakdown till I get back.'

The doctor nodded obediently.

All through the rattling taxi ride, sweltering in Kolkata's unending humidity, Uma forged a plan on how to confront Indira. It was not just a burning curiosity that propelled her desire for disclosure of whatever seamy truth Uma was sure her cousin was hiding, but a growing sense of fear that a terrible outcome awaited if she did not prevent Indira from carrying out her fiendish schemes. From doing *what,* she did not know.

Uma got off the taxi wondering why so many crows had suddenly converged onto Calcutta. Two had sat on the doctor's window sill, while scores had wheeled in the sky, cawing menacingly outside the hospital. Now they were here as well, hanging like a rain cloud over Dodo's apartment.

She entered the apartment meaning to take her family and aunt aside and in very careful terms – keeping in view her total lack of faith in her family's intelligence – tell them about her concerns.

She will have to be quarantined; Uma thought of Indira as a virulence.

But the inside of the apartment presented a tableau that deepened her terror of the situation she knew impended on them. It was lunchtime and everybody had fitted themselves about Dodo's tiny dining table, like square pegs about a round hole. Indira was among them, too much pickle on her plate, frowning at some distasteful thought. Her mother looked contemplative, as she did when she did not understand something, which was often. Her brother and sister sat huddled together, not responding as she walked across the room. Her aunt gave her a malevolent glare.

Uma's steps slowed, as if the air before her had increased its resistance. She picked up a Melmoware plate and stainless steel spoon from the dining table hoping to dispel the dense silence as she spooned some rice onto her plate. 'What's wrong? You can cut the air with a knife.'

Silence.

There was egg curry and potatoes fried non-Bengali style – Ishita's north Indian triumph in Kolkata. Uma took a bite but the food stuck lumpily in her throat. She felt herself losing her grip. She turned towards Indira, who had not so much as lifted her eyes from her plate, and burst out: 'What's the matter with you? You look as if you've swallowed a lizard.'

'Ask your brother,' she said not looking up from her food. Her victory was clear to the both of them. *I've got your weak spot – your brother.*

'Okay, Dodo.' She faced her downcast brother squarely: 'Put me out of my misery. What is going on?'

Dodo looked up for the briefest second to ask in a tone so cold that even as it transferred its lack of heat to Uma, it seemed to warm Indira: 'Why are you here, Didi? Or do you even know?'

'What kind of a question is that?'

'No, answer me.'

No one was eating any more.

That's a tone he's never used on me, Uma thought dismayed, badly masticated rice refusing to slide down her throat. 'I'm here because my mother needs me,' she said, choking back her tears. 'I'm here because for some unfathomable reason I love that stupid alcoholic, wheezing around in a coma in that stupid hospital.'

'Why, then,' Ishita's lips twisted in a way that Uma neither knew nor recognized, 'are the doctors in the hospital complaining about your high-handed behaviour there?'

'What?' Uma had a sensation of something heavy falling on her head.

'You've been tampering with the treatment.' Dodo's coldness quotient had dropped even further.

'Uma, I fail to understand you,' her mother complained. 'Why are you preventing the signing of the consent form? If Raj is not put on the ventilator, he will die. I know you understand medical technical terms better than us, but any idiot can see that he needs the ventilator.'

'Who said I'm preventing the consent form from being signed?' Uma asked, sounding as astounded as she looked.

'Indira has been in constant touch with the doctors, Uma,' her mother said giving her the full benefit of her how-*could*-you look.

'And you believe her?' Uma exclaimed.

'Are you telling us that we should not believe a daughter's concerns about her dying father?'

Temperatures continued to drop in the subzero part of the room. At this rate it could start snowing in Cal, Uma thought.

'Are you telling us Indira has reason to lie?' Ishita looked at Uma in genuine wide-eyed disbelief.

'She was the one trying to get uncle's thumb imprints remember?' Uma reminded her sister, amazed at her complete volte-face.

'So?' Ishita asked, still wide-eyed, deepening Uma's suspicion of she didn't know what.

'Oh, go fry some potatoes,' Uma exploded, disgusted at her sister's naiveté.

'What did you say?' Ishita's nostrils flared, as did her hormones.

Indira looked up for the first time, with an air of satisfaction. There was a fight in the air. She could smell it.

'Now, now,' Dodo warned.

'Girls!' Their mother got up, imperiously raising herself to her full height of five feet nothing.

'I can't believe,' Uma said, 'that I left my son and husband –'

'What a little martyr you are,' Dodo said.

'Stop sounding like a witch at the stake –' Ishita added.

'– spent my time and money –' Uma continued her litany.

'Stop your emotional blackmail,' her mother said.

'– for this,' Uma finished. But then, when she saw Indira's smile, she knew that she was face to face with a power far superior than she had ever known. Utterly defeated, Uma turned on her heel and marched off to Dodo's bedroom, pausing before the ritual slam to declare to the mob baying for her blood: 'By the way I *have* signed the bloody consent form.'

'Oh thank God,' Indira said piously. 'Finally.'

Slam.

'I hope Raj Mamu gets better before that door comes off its hinges,' Dodo said.

'Dodo's patented dry humour,' Indira laughed in admiration.

He smiled back at her. 'I'm sorry about my sister,' he said. 'You are going through a lot. You should not be subjected to this.'

'This is only the half of it.' Indira looked up at him, warm in the glow of the new camaraderie between them, 'The rest is unmentionable.'

20.

'Coward, coward, coward!' muttered Aparajita, removing her breast from her son's mouth, scared that she would contaminate him with the bile rising in her.

Raj and Aparajita had not been in touch for several weeks now, filling her with an inexplicable fury that refused to abate. I was married when I met you, she told him during one of their eternal conversations. I can't change that truth, but you could have chosen to remain unmarried. You are marrying because you are weak and a coward, and you are going to ruin the lives of your wife and your children. I wouldn't have married, if I were you. And I asked you for a one-word message, an acknowledgement that one of the rarest and most profound phenomena possible is unfolding between us, but you couldn't even do that. All Bairah had to do was come to me and say, 'Sahib said solitaire.' But you couldn't do that because you are a coward, a coward a coward. And you are a coward because you are a man. It is a known fact that all men are cowards. You did not even go to the library, like I asked you to. Now we will not be able to meet in our dreams. And that's because you are not only a coward, but a lazy coward.

I did not go to the library, he shot back, because you are a bully. And if not obeying your commands means being a coward, so be it.

Fine, she thought.

Fine, he thought back.

And you haven't even paid me. Is asking for my money also an act of domination?

Oh come on, he replied, you know that far more was going on between us than you reading my horoscope. Maybe you should pay me! He was laughing now, teasing her.

Preposterous! She was beside herself with rage. But she could not help wondering why the anger she directed against Raj had no fire in it, no poison. Like a heated game of chequers; they could stop playing whenever they wanted.

You should pay me my ten rupees, she told him, and set her jaw in a pugnacious line when she felt the apartment building reverberate with his mocking laughter.

Here I am ready to lay down my life for you, and all you want is ten rupees?

That's the problem, a tear escaped from the corner of her eye. If I knew that for sure, I would not make another wish or have another desire as long as I lived.

At that point Raj's sister called him to settle her dispute with the pandit over one of the wedding rituals and like a broadcast signal, their conversation link that neither believed in, broke.

Theoretically speaking, Aparajita thought to herself, I am crazy. This is what crazy people do. Have imaginary conversations, hear sentences that have not been said, smell non-existent scents like his breath against her ear, taste what is not there like the salt on his skin after his shopping trip to New Market. These thoughts are delusional; they see what is not there, like the blue shirt with black stripes he is wearing today. I am a prized case study, a collector's item. And if I am alone in this, and none of this is happening to him like I think it is, I should be really sent away to the nuthouse.

But do crazy people love like I do? Are they insanely happy the moment they think of their beloved, the way I do? If they do, then maybe it's all right to be crazy. *There's a pleasure sure in being mad,* she remembered a quote, *that none but madmen know.* Now where did I pick that one up?

Needing to know, she moved to her husband's library, full of the musty smell of the jurisprudence and legislature that her husband practised, and kept in bound leather, in shelves that stood sentinel to his professional discipline. There was a section that he reserved for lighter reading, and with husbandly thoughtfulness, on the last two shelves, to the left of his rocking chair and behind his writing bureau, he had left space for her collection. There was a common shelf of Rabindranath Tagore and William Shakespeare and Sherlock Holmes and Guy de Maupassant that they both loved. Her collection comprised mostly books on spirituality – Vivekananda and Paul Brunton, and the writings of Annie Besant and Madam Blavatsky, Swami Yogananda's *Autobiography of a Yogi*, and many Bengali magazines and pamphlets of Rama Krishna Paramhansa and Anandamayee Ma. The last two shelves were her shelves, entirely hers, writings of and from her inner world and life that her husband had no interest in, and she was grateful for that.

Funnily, the Book of Quotations lay in their common shelf, between Agatha Christie and H.G.Well's *Time Machine*. She opened the book and found the quotation, one of Dryden's, from *The Spanish Friar*. She flipped a few pages. Another quote caught her eye. 'Ten Effects of Cupid'. She read it, all the while observing a new sensation that was giving birth deep within her being.

It was neither fear nor exhilaration, but both, neither despair nor hope, but both, neither courage nor cowardice but both, neither sexuality nor love, but both, and she knew that now she could lie down and rest her head, for she knew what was happening to her. She was merging, uniting, evolving, metamorphozing all at the same time. The higher with the lower, the positive with the negative, the horizontal with the vertical, they were all meeting within her, like galaxies falling into place, and if she stretched her arms across and out into the inky blue of the universe, the universe would hug her right back.

She heard a distinct hum resonate from deep within her body, like the first flutter of life in a new foetus, and as it grew louder, she heard it clearly. It sounded like 'Om' only when she strained to hear it, but otherwise it was like an ancient bee that has been from the beginning of time. Like the faint sound of bells coming from some buried mythological civilization deep in the sea, like the magical incantations whispered into the ear of a conch shell. She smiled and lay down on the bed, her hair fanning out on the pillow. It was fine, she was not alone. The universe was taking care of her.

But the next moment she was up again, determined to get the money owed to her.

Oh for God's sake, Raj said, it's only ten rupees.

No, it's not, she primly replied. It's the principle of the matter.

The next day when her maid came scurrying back from the flat downstairs, with ten rupees clutched in her hand, Aparajita's fury was apoplectic, making the petrified maid recount again and again what had happened.

'I was coming up to the apartment –'

'How?'

'From the stairs.'

'What time was it?'

'Around ten.'

'What time was it?'

'Ten minutes past ten,' the maid lied.

He was having breakfast, Aparajita thought, his three-egg omelette sliced eight times. (This was a real fact in the visible world, but not one she really believed to be true.)

'Then?'

'I met Bairah on the third step on the landing on the left of the main door to the apartment.' The reason for the maid's surgical precision was that given the frequency with which this question was asked she could now successfully give a trained response.

'Then?'

'Then what?' The maid was tired of the game. She also had to finish the dishes by noon. 'Then he gave me the money, and said sahib said to give it to your memsahib.'

'No, no,' Aparajita insisted. 'What *exactly* did he say?'

'That's what he said,' the maid gesticulated sharply. 'He said Raj sahib said give this to your memsahib.'

'See?' Aparajita pointed out the mistake with much assumed patience. 'You have already changed your statement twice. First you said sahib, then it became Raj sahib. Lord knows what other information you have forgotten to tell me.' Aparajita rolled her eyes to which the maid protested with a sullen silence.

'Is that all he said?' Aparajita was unable to stop herself.

'That's all he said,' the maid scowled.

'That horrible, horrible man,' Aparajita said and collapsing on the bed, dissolved into tears.

The maid couldn't believe the tortuous interview was over. 'Can I go back to the dishes now?'

'Go, just go,' came the dismissal in between muffled sobs.

You horrible, horrible person. You did not even have the decency to return the money personally. How dare you be so condescending? What do you think I am, a charity case? You think I am after your money? This arrogance is not good, my dear one, not good at all. You could not send a one-word message through Bairah, but you sent back ten measly rupees? What do you think, I want you to gift me diamond rings? And if you don't want to see me, why don't you say so. Oh, God, I've made such a fool of myself. I should just die.

Hair dishevelled, she raised her hands in prayer and said, Let the earth part now and swallow me whole.

Bengali melodrama, Raj scoffed.

Her nostrils flared. How dare you, you parochial little squire.

Squire? He looked confused.

No, make that illiterate, parochial little squire, she flashed.

I love it, he grinned, when you get angry.

And they made love, right there and then. But later, to prove to him that she was unfazed by his antics, she sent a message to him in the form of a folded piece of paper. 'Thank you for the money, you needn't have bothered.'

She got no reply.

And she did not know what the silence meant. It contained within its womb a hundred of her desperate questions of herself, of him, of the universe. It was full of a lack of understanding, and mysteries and secrets that only time would reveal. The silence hummed between them, whispering words in their hearts, of patience and longing and forgotten stories.

She stopped taking the lift. She walked an entire flight of stairs so she would cross his door. It took the time of three steps for a hidden portal to open and give her a glimpse of him. He was lounging in the balcony pining for her, or sitting with his mother, working out the wedding invitations. Now he was sitting across his lawyer, signing on some property papers. Now his sister was teasing him about how she knew he hid his fiancée's photograph under his pillow, and he smiled back his acknowledgement to his sister, saying, isn't that what they all wanted.

And Aparajita saw the face of the sweet unsuspecting woman who was to be Raj's wife and leaned against the corridor wall momentarily to shut her eyes.

You must love and respect her, she tried to make him swear, the way you could not love or respect me. Promise me that. But there was nothing. So he has forgotten me, she thought bitterly.

But he would come in the nights, making love to her in her dreams. Torturing her with his touch, assaulting her senses with his unbearable power. She would wake up several times realizing that she had climaxed in her sleep. The first thought when she awoke in the morning was always of him, followed by the memory that they had been together through the night.

Once, a wandering Kashmiri merchant spread his wares of embroidered pashmina shawls in her living room and, to tempt her, started telling her of all the purchases the people downstairs had made. Her secretive silence and sad melting eyes prodded him to say more than he wanted.

He told her about the number of shawls the gentleman downstairs had bought for his wife's trousseau. 'I sold him a pure shahtoosh stole,' the hook-nosed Kashmiri said, rolling his eyes and r's in the characteristic Pushtu way, 'for a thousand rupees! Some young bride in this country has been made truly fortunate. Now I can buy my fare home and rest the entire summer. He has asked me to come back again next year, in case his wife likes the stole and wants to make a few more purchases, may Allah be blessed.'

'Looks like there is going to be a wedding in the apartment downstairs,' Aparajita's words were cold, her smile wan. She pulled up her legs on the divan, needing to rest her head on her shaking knees because the Kashmiri by mentioning him, by putting him in words, was manifesting in reality what she secretly bore in her thoughts all the time.

'Wedding sounds like an understatement!' He exclaimed so loudly that she could see the pink of his palate. 'It is as if the Queen of England herself were coming! What hustle and bustle! Sarees and jewellery strewn everywhere! Money flowing like water!'

'Does he sound happy, this gentleman of yours?' she asked fingering the fineness of one of his shawls.

'See this madam, pure pashmina, you could run it through a finger ring. Do you have a finger ring? I will show it to you.'

'I don't wear finger rings. You didn't answer my question, Kashmiri bhaisahab. Did he look happy?'

Inky blue mountain eyes met hers for an instant, like two stones clicking. She looked away instantly, guilty, shamefaced.

'Everybody is happy before their wedding. Ask him the day after,' he smiled, then dismissed him, getting back to the business at hand: 'You don't believe my shawl is pashmina? I pulled this very same shawl through the ring he had bought his beloved.'

'How do you know it was the ring he had bought his beloved?' she asked, carefully casual.

'He said so. And the shawl flowed through it like water.'

'His beloved must be a wrestler with fat fingers,' she joked, sparkling briefly, enjoying her own spite.

'Oh, no,' the Kashmiri took affront. 'It was the smallest ring, for the slimmest of fingers, like yours.'

She raised desperate kohl-streaked eyes at him. 'What did the ring look like?'

'Are you going to buy my pashmina?' the Kashmiri huffed.

'What did the ring look like?' she repeated, brazen, beyond care.

A shrewd, knowing shadow passed over the Kashmiri's face. 'It had one brilliant solitaire diamond in it,' he said quietly.

Aparajita buried her face in her knees. All the Kashmiri could see was her black hair, like a dark cloud about to rain.

'Never mind, daughter.' The Kashmiri knew his young customer would not be making any purchases. 'Some flowers bloom only when the seasons change.'

'What?' she raised her head from her tangled mass of hair.

'Nothing, child,' he said, tying a knot in his bundle of hand-woven shawls. 'Maybe some other time you will buy a shawl. When there is a right occasion.'

'This is the right occasion,' she looked at him, as she would her father. 'I sense a very cold winter ahead.'

He hoisted his bundle on his shoulders and made for the door. 'Yes, but there is spring beyond that. I'll come again when the flowers in my valley are in bloom.

Raj experienced her like a haunting face, like goddess Durga in calendar art. He felt a wrench in his gut and reeled back to briefly rest his head against the wall. She is pining for me, he realized. Why can't I savour this moment without feeling what she feels?

21.

Many thousands of miles away, under the shade of a terrace awning, peering into his laptop, he made a shushing gesture at his wife sitting next to him, just as she was about to open her mouth to speak. On his laptop in front of him was Kamini's Facebook profile, and he was sifting through her friends list one by one. Not one of them was a VNP member.

'She's put on weight,' the wife insisted on finishing what she wanted to say.

The crows around him seemed blacker in the afternoon sun, shrivelled by the intense heat, and they seemed to hop closer towards him, for strength, for a little of his awe-inspiring magnetism maybe. He shut the laptop and closed his eyes. He loved the afternoon sun in rural India, so full of a slow sweet leisure, a luxury that even the poor could afford. He loved the warm feel of old stone beneath him, especially stone that had been cured over with three hundred years of history. History that whispered stories; stories of atrocities, stories of valour and human weakness, stories of love and betrayal.

His wife looked at him closely. He seemed to exude more power with his eyes closed than his eyes open. She knew what he was doing. He was listening to the voices in his head, and he was using his concentration to make the voices more audible, like fine-tuning into a frequency by cutting out the static. His wife had easily identified Kamini's Facebook profile picture and had helped him locate the co-ordinates of her whereabouts. Once he had found her, his faculties of clairaudience were enough to eavesdrop into every detail of the conversation she was having in the moment.

Sitting next to him, she did not know what her husband was listening in to, but was as usual, very impressed.

☯

Rudra sat impassive, his face vacant. Looking at him Kamini doubted whether he understood anything at all. Rita and Mira huddled together like two peasant women braving a storm. Hari had dark moons under his eyes and Carlos was as orange as ever. Only Ali, fresh and scented, oozed the special ease that came with the cockiness of youth, or perhaps that came with his father's superstar status, then again, perhaps, that came with his high level of spiritual attainment.

'The crucial question is' – Mira wrapped her knitting and put it away in a small wicker basket making many around her draw an inward sigh of relief – 'why are we all seeing the dark man in our dreams?'

'Well,' Hari puffed out his chest, raised his belt and looked for a moment as if he was going to launch into his own presentation but then finished lamely: 'He is an energy.'

'That's what they call starting with a bang and ending with a whimper,' Rita chided Hari with a laugh, and walking towards the whiteboard, picking up a fat marker pen. 'Let me take it from here.'

'Yes,' Hari said gratefully. 'But before you start, I must ask you to curtail yourself to ten minutes. I have been trying to impress on this most esteemed gathering of learned ones, that this is not a seminar. We are in a Code Red situation here. Please do not lose sight of the goal.' Hari tried to toughen his stance but could not keep a hint of pure panic from betraying him. 'Our aim is to defuse an energy crisis. It's not to write a Pulitzer Prize-winning paper.'

Kamini noticed that his entreaties for the Code Red situation had been getting more and more plaintive with every passing mention.

Like a leader of crows the man lay in his reclining chair, eyes closed, arms crossed, legs stretched out long, unnaturally long for a human body. The crows gathered around his shut laptop. He smirked as if he were smiling in his sleep, and only his wife knew why.

'Point noted,' Rita said, but so pleased to be centre-stage that it did not look as if she would stop talking soon.

'I'm warning you,' Hari could only threaten her in the mildest of tones. 'You have only ten minutes. We need to move immediately after this to emergency protocol for crash courses, and a three-hour intensive training at the healing camp.'

Hari looked momentarily at Rudra who was staring blankly ahead, and thought – *what do I do about you?*

To which Rudra had already replied. Nothing.

And the leader of crows sneered.

'Tomorrow there will be meetings, one in the Ascended Masters temple, one with the white light workers, and one with the mirror workers.'

'Aye aye, Cap'n,' Rita smiled. ' By the way, you just took away a minute of my time.'

Hari raised his hands in apology and settled back in his chair.

Kamini took the opportunity to get back to the question she was meaning to ask. 'The black man is an energy? What the hell could you possibly mean by that?'

Everybody trained their eyes on Kamini. They were all sliding into thoughtful conference mode again, Hari noticed in despair.

'And the crucial question is –' Mira cued.

'Why are we all seeing him?' came the collective zombie response.

'Because he *knows*,' Hari said, tapping his fingers nervously on the table top. 'The influx of sudden group energies has upset the balance. He – they – know we are planning something –'

'Something not good...' Ali said, then all of a sudden, frantically waved his hands before his face.

Mira looked at him in concern.

'I don't know. It felt like something flapped in front of my eyes, like bird's wings,' Ali said, distraught.

'Not good for them,' Carlos continued.

'Who?' asked Kamini eyes widening. 'The black man?'

'Of course,' Mira said patiently. 'Who else?' She watched Kamini closely to see how she was processing all of this, and seeing her struggle, explained: 'Like in many other 2012 case histories, negative energy build up has happened over time and stages. The first stage was actually caused by the meeting of XX and XY. It flared their karmas to a negative build up. When the force of negative energies crossed the first threshold, it caused 3D or physical separation; when it crossed the second threshold it caused 5D separation in the subtle world. The black man came in between the time frames of 3D and 5D separation. He used their weakening hold on each other as a breach to come in and spin out so much negative energy so as to completely erase any positivity in the situation and therefore prevent any possibility of reunion between XX and XY.'

'But why?' Kamini protested. 'What does he want?'

And the reclining man re-crossed his unnaturally long legs in a gesture so sinuous that Mira blubbered, adlibbing his words, as if under his spell, 'Power, darling, power,' he said.

'Actually,' Mira said regaining her confidence, 'at the level the black man is operating, what might seem like an agenda is just the conscious manifestation of the power of the negative to seek out the positive and nullify it. The entropy of the universe seeks to move towards chaos, the path of least resistance, and the harmony created by UCL is such a high spectrum energy state that entropy seeks it out like a stealth missile. But in the levels we operate this is usually understood as the need for the control of others, or greed, or ego or money.'

'He is the reason we are here,' Mira continued. 'The project exists to neutralize him. We have been manifested by UCL and its precarious need to preserve the balance of extremely high energies. Needless to say, it has not been easy. In the last few years he and his team have channelled such a huge negative energy stockpile, that the cyclone and the riots we thought were months away, are upon us already. It's a question of days now, maybe hours.'

Kamini was silent. To ease her understanding Carlos said, 'It's a "scramble" situation here, to use old military parlance. It seems as if he pre-empts our every move, is always a step ahead of us.'

'He knows,' Kamini whispered.

And the smile on the man's face was not only slow it was sensuous. 'Guns and roses baby,' he whispered in Kamini's head, making her think – this is not love, this is war.

'Think of him like a general in an army. Armies are rallying,' Rita smiled at Kamini and with great gentleness, 'Or didn't you know?'

'What the ...?' Kamini blurted.

'Shush,' Hari warned. 'Family audience.'

'Don't you dare look at me,' said an indignant Ali.

'I'm looking at Rudra,' Hari laughed.

'As you have known from previous presentations –' Rita tried to steer them back to the topic – 'all energies are polar, binary, opposites, like the two digits of one and zero in machine language. Male female, negative positive, dark light, aggressive passive –'

'– Good bad,' Mira helped.

'Very simply put, gross reality is dual in nature. Let's call it double vision –'

'Double vision?' asked Ali.

Mira and Rita spoke one after the other in a call-and-response fashion, making Kamini follow them in absurdly jerking head movements:

'We either see hatred or love, fear or courage, aggression or passivity. Always swinging on the two ends of the seesaw. Never in the fulcrum, the centre –'

'– the zone.'

'– Buddha's Middle Path.'

'– the Golden mean.'

'– Yoga, all spiritual disciplines end with the word Yoga, which, if you notice, also means union of duality.'

'When the binary energies of the dual world are united in Yoga, you immediately create and release a lot of energy, like during the fusion of a Uranium atom. Enough energy for a portal to open into another dimension,' Mira said.

'By dimension, we mean an energy world that is vibrating in a particular frequency,' Rita pointed out.

'Our world is also an energy world. A gross energy world,' Mira said.

Aw, come on! the leader of crows thought, almost asleep in the terrace sun; such a bunch of useless professors.

'Would it then be correct to say that the different orbits of an electron correspond to different dimensions and worlds?' Kamini narrowed her eyes in concentration as if it helped her to follow the train of thought better.

'That would be correct,' Rita looked very pleased with the aptitude of her new student.

'What Hari,' Rita continued, 'was trying to explain,' (rather badly, thought Kamini) 'is that extreme positive energies also attract extreme negative energies. And that the Twin Flame project and our group activities –'

'– vibrating to the tune of the highest and noblest motives, might I add –' said Hari.

'– have alerted the polar opposites, the negative energies so to speak. And since most manifestations first take place in the energy world, we have begun to see them in our dreams.'

And the leader of crows shot up in sitting position, no longer somnolent. He looked around him suspiciously, because a chill was wafting around him, weaving him into a cloud.

'And the reason we are all seeing it together is that the manifestation is a reality strong enough for all of us to sense.' Rita was slowly launching to the full-throttle projection of her seminar voice: 'That also means that the group energy vibrations are working and rising in frequency even as we speak. The bad news is –'

'– the black man is real,' Kamini basking in a new confidence, stemmed Rita's flow.

'Thank you,' Rita said. 'For taking the wind from my sails. But that is correct.'

'Who is he?' Kamini blurted out in compulsive curiosity again. 'And, really, Rita Ma'am, I still find it difficult to believe he is real.'

'Of course, he is real, darling,' Rita's soothing voice was having the opposite effect on Kamini. 'Everything is real in the invisible world. And he has already started manifesting in the visible world.'

'Is he Satan?' Kamini asked point blank.

'Of course, he is. Satan, the devil, Lucifer, Shaitan, Rakshasa, take your pick,' Rita laughed. 'But our black man here would make Satan look like a poor country cousin.'

The crows cawed, all in a flutter. Their leader had left the terrace.

'What are you saying?' Kamini cried out in alarm.

'Don't think he's just a tame old horned toad with a bad complexion,' Ali said enjoying the analogies.

'Nothing that a good surgeon can't fix these days...' Carlos chipped in.

'With terrible teeth,' Hari said.

'The chosen weapon of mass destruction for medieval Satan must have been bad breath...' Carlos added.

'Okay boys,' Rita interjected. 'We are not to confuse the young lady here. Please, if only you would let me finish what I have to say, maybe she will have a clearer idea by the end of the day.'

'Which does not even exist on my priority list, but please go ahead,' Hari said in a friendly tone.

'I shall not even dignify that with a response,' Kamini returned but proceeded to give him a hard pinch above his elbow.

'Ouch,' Hari commented.

Encouraged by the comfortable silence that followed Rita launched into her presentation:

'All of you know my area of interest is Quanti Mytho. What I have been working on is taking up all the mythologies of the world and translating them into the language of Particle Physics. You must understand that these translations may seem esoteric and abstruse because of the nature of refinement of the concepts. But it is important to note that both languages are really talking about the same things. Once you start joining the dots an entire interconnected world springs up to view, much like an X-ray of the lungs against the light. In the experiential level, of course, these concepts are really very simple. They only become complicated when we try to grasp them with the blunt instrument of the intellect.

'Let's start with the theories of Cosmogenesis. The Bible says, in the beginning was the word. Hinduism goes further and says in the beginning was the word and the word was Om. Tibetan Buddhism goes another step forward, or back, depending on which page of Hindu scripture you are flipping, and says that Om is the Cosmic Egg, the golden womb, *hiranyagarbha*, created by the male and female union in the *yab yum* position –'

'The "Big 'Bang" Theory,' Ali said, full of lecherous glee.

'Again the union of polar opposites!' Mira warned,

'Talking of positions –' Ali was warming to the topic.

'– Don't even *go* there,' Kamini threatened.

'Yes, please shut your hormonal trap,' Hari concurred.

Carlos smiled as Ali shut up.

Rita continued valiantly: 'And in the string theory of Quanti Mytho, Om, the word, *hiranyagarbha* or whatever, becomes the first vibration, or pulse –'

'Spanda as spoken in Spanda Karikas of Kashmir Shaivism,' Mira said.

'Ah Kashmir!' somebody said.

'How the valleys must be blooming now,' Ali said.

'You talk as if your grandfather lives there,' Hari mocked.

'He does, actually,' Ali looked at Hari in surprise.

'Oh dear,' was Hari's deep observation.

'A vibration,' Rita said, forcing them to start remembering their school physics curriculum, 'or a pulse, is always the play of contraction and expansion and can be visualized as a wave, with a crest and a trough. Again, two opposites meeting at the middle. Like Om at its centre point.'

She switched on a slide on the projection screen with a diagram and symbols of the wave and wave functions. Looking at all the mathematical notations on the slide Kamini's brain started to shut down when Rita looked at her and literally willed her to understand.

'Look at it, carefully. When the wave rolls back on itself it becomes the infinity symbol Ali was talking about. Its three points are the points of the trinity. Be a little imaginative, picture the mythological Ocean of Nectar and you will see the curling coils of the serpent Shesh Nag on whom Vishnu rests. The centre is also Vishnu's navel where Brahma emerges to create an energy world. Use your imagination and turn the trinity vertically and you get the Om symbol, with Vishnu's umbilical cord rising out from the centre. Go back to the infinity wave roll it up in a sphere and it becomes the Yin Yang ball, the cosmic egg. It is also sometimes visualized as the star of David, two inverted pyramids or the merkaba.

'Okay, now we are done with the pulse, the first vibration. The male female in the yab yum position. The wave. The Shiv Shakti in orgiastic union. The second manifestation of the pulse is sound. The sound Om–'

'– More like a hum,'

'– Sohum, the sound of the breath with the head and tail cut off becomes Om.'

'– It's also Amen.'

'– Allahu.'

'– And in Hebrew –'

'Wow!'

'Well, maybe that too is a derivative of Om. I'll have to check,' Rita said.

Kamini laughed uproariously.

'What?' asked Rita.

'Is there anything that is *not* connected?'

'Nothing,' said Rita, very firm.

'"Only connect" said Aldous Huxley. The chap was quite right even though he didn't know much,' Carlos said.

'It's not that he didn't know much. He didn't know everything,' Hari said.

'What do *you* know of Aldous Huxley?' asked Kamini of Hari, making no attempt to hide her contempt.

'Nothing at all,' Hari said, looking straight ahead.

'Tantra, my dear,' interrupted Mira, 'means web. Web of Connections. The World Wide Web of the internet is the first physical technological manifestation of the etheric communicative web that has manifested in the energy body of the planet. There will be more to follow.'

The crows screamed and clawed in the sky, flapping up a terrible confusion, darkening the air. Their leader's steps down the terrace stairs picked up speed. He wanted to get away from the deep vibration within his own ears – as if it were a well that would erupt, any moment, in apocalyptic sound.

Kamini shook her head in wonder.

'The next manifestation of the pulse,' Rita continued, 'is light. The Bible says – "And God said let there be light and there was light". That is how a world takes birth according to the laws of Cosmogenesis. First the pulse, then light, white light to be precise. White light then breaks up into the various colours of the VIBGYOR. Likewise, the sound Om breaks up into 56 syllables of the Sanskrit language, also Latin.'

And briefly, in a rare moment, the terrace lit up in a fluorescent blue twilight, the kind that happened only occasionally in that part of India, usually during the time of the equinox.

Rita sighed, a bit deeper than usual. 'To simplify a very complicated science, when these vibrational frequencies of light and sound merge or intersect they bring into play energies that create worlds corresponding to that frequency.'

Kamini, Ali and Hari looked at her in stunned silence.

Quietly, compulsively, Mira took out her knitting. 'You must clarify the definition of "world" right now,' she chided quietly.

'Okay,' Rita said. 'By world I mean a space time dimension that is created every discrete instant. It has very little resemblance to the linear, time-objectified world that we perceive as an environment outside us. Which, of course we all know as maya, or illusion. It is a film projected out from the filter of our dirty, conditioned mind, created from the centre of the moment that is neither past, present nor future, but only a play of energies imbued with consciousness.'

Rita couldn't stop now. She had to continue what she had started, in whichever way she could:

'Let me explain. The yantras, geometrical designs, symbols, mandalas that we see in all the different world religions are really descriptions of the energy patterns of different worlds. In Hindu tantra and Buddhism the intricate rituals of mandala worship brings forth into existence – actually create that world. Om is one such symbol. The Maltese Cross –'

'– is another symbol for Radha and Krishna, the union of Yin Yang energies.' Mira's knitting needles had started their clacking.

'The Kabala sephiroths –'

'The Egyptian pyramids –'

Poised between heaven and earth he stood. In extreme balance his arms stretched out. His hands moved in intricate patterns creating geometric designs in the air, like solidifying woodsmoke. There was a faint sound of a lightning crash and the smell of frankinscence.

'The swastikas –'

'The flower of lis symbol –'

'– is the same as the tree of life.'

'All these symbols are found in the texts of alchemy,' Ali added.

Kamini was very quiet. For a brief moment the group quietened, almost as if giving her time to process all this.

'There are fourteen dimensions,' Rita started again. 'Some say eleven, some nine. As I had mentioned earlier, interestingly, a lot of these energies are also imbued with the quality of consciousness – necessitating the need for the existence of energy beings.'

'Whoa,' Kamini exploded. 'You are going too fast.'

'Okay let me try another way,' Rita said. 'As higher energies climb down the spectrum into lower frequencies they create principles with each condensation.'

'Huh?' Kamini said.

'The tattvas,' Hari said.

'If only she could read one alchemy text,' Ali said. 'All the symbologies are there.'

'Don't confuse her,' Hari warned.

'Oh, please,' Ali looked as if he was gearing up for a fight, he had had enough of Hari's protectiveness. 'The five attributes, the panchtattva as Hari calls them are the five creative principles of earth, water, fire, air and ether.'

'And?' Meera prodded, nodding her head in appreciation.

'Because these principles are also imbued with consciousness you will find them in every mythology known to man. Agni, the fire god; Vayu, air; Mercury, Apollo, Mars, Ra the Egyptian Sun God –'

'– Dionysus,' one said,

'–Venus,' another went.

'There are crores of them,' Rita said. 'Almost as many as there are sub-atomic particles in the Quantum mechanical universe.'

'Gods are sub-atomic particles?'

Kamini wondered why she was the only questioning student in the lot. Even Rudra seemed to know more than her, sitting Sphinx-like, his elbows resting on the table.

'What about Shiva, Vishnu and Mahesh? What about Indra and Jupiter, are they the gods of gods? What about Venus, she is the goddess of love, and how the hey can love be a sub-atomic particle?' Kamini fired at Rita, her thoughts running riot.

'Well, right and wrong, yes and no,' Rita went. 'You are right in the sense there is a gradation, a hierarchy of energies. Not all energies are the same. The trinity – Vishnu Mahesh Brahma – are creative principles of the primary act of Cosmogenesis. Indra and Jupiter have been likened to the mind.'

'Oh God, you've thrown in the mind now, as if things were not bad enough.'

'Let me explain,' Rita defended herself. 'Each of the five principles corresponds to a sense organ in a human being. Earth: touch, water: smell, fire: taste, etc., and so the mind is considered not only the sixth sense but also the king of the senses according to the Hindu scriptures which makes Indra the mind. Q.E.D.'

'Phew.'

'You have thoroughly confused her,' Hari decided in his thoughts.

Kamini looked at him in amazement sensing his mind. Hello. Wasn't *I* the one who was condescending *him*?

'Look, it's like this,' Rita sighed. 'When you worship a deity or a patron saint for a particular reason, like Saraswati or Minerva for knowledge, you are really invoking the principle of the matter to reside within you. Because deities are energies –'

'That's how love, sorry, Venus is an energy –' Kamini realized in great wonder.

Rita took a bow. 'The highest, most pure energy of the universe. Equivalent to the energy produced during the fusion of a hydrogen atom. Only this energy creates and heals, it does not destroy –'

'– and that is how you connect it to the invisible world of the atom,' Kamini concluded.

'"The macroscopic mirrors the microscopic,"' Mira said.

'"As is above so is below," Thoth the Egyptian said,' Carlos chipped in.

Rita looked at Hari and Hari shook his head. Rita concluded her talk by saying, 'I have many slides to show how mythological symbols convert to energy patterns, how gods convert into positrons and bosons. How with the catalyst effect of Cupid and Venus, the quantum of energy released by the fusion of a particle with an anti-particle changes the course of space and time. I had wanted to show you what Einstein meant when he said space is curved. Actually, what he was trying to say was simply that matter is the condensation of the space time dimension, the foundational premise of all the para-sciences. I had wanted to show you the play of energies in the great mythological stories of Adam and Eve and the churning of the ocean but I shall quickly wind up by saying that the keys to the portals of all these dimensional worlds are within the human body.

'All the nine chakras in the invisible spinal column from the base to crown correspond to the different colours of VIBGYOR, to different syllables of sound, and because they are imbued with consciousness, to different deities. From Ganesh at the base, to Radha Krishna at the heart centre, to Shiv Shakti at the crown. And the key that opens all the doors to these chakra portals is Time.

'You melt past, present and future in the centre of the moment and vibrate your concentration to the frequency of the syllable sound associated with the chakra and the lock opens.'

'Of Pandora's box,' Kamini laughed.

'That actually is the story of Pandora's box,' Rita said solemnly.

'And many others –' Mira added enigmatically, knit, purl, knit, purl.

'When Prince Charming kisses Sleeping Beauty he awakens the Yin Yang union energies, also the reason why Shiva cuts off Ganesh's head and replaces it with his own. Yin without Yang is incomplete. The seven dwarfs are the chakras. I could go on, but these are stories for another day.'

'Bedtime stories of the New Age,' Carlos grinned.

'I shall end,' Rita said hurriedly because Hari was manically rattling his watch, 'by saying that it is not for nothing that the body is called the City of Nine Gates. And,' she finished with a flourish, 'why the Kingdom of God is within.'

Later, as they moved on to the healing camp on the second floor Kamini tried to keep a distance from the group. Her head was reeling, not only from all the newfangled thoughts that had been thrown at her but also because of an uneasy sensation. She knew that she had somehow gravitated to the centre of the group, that she was the cynosure of their attention. Though she enjoyed her new position, on another level it made her uneasy.

She walked over to Rudra standing by his faithful attendant who watched over him like a trained policeman. Rudra greeted her with a slow smile and gave her his hand. A cool rush washed over Kamini, and she was at peace. How can a non-verbal kid with special needs have such an effect on me? she wondered.

At that precise moment, Mira staggered out of the Ladies' washroom. She stood in front of them shaking, looking uncharacteristically white-faced even as she strove to look unfazed.

'What?' Hari said, instinctively reaching his arm behind his waist, as if for an invisible pistol.

'He is standing behind me,' Mira replied not moving and looking straight ahead.

'Who?' Kamini asked, but knew the answer, for her blood had curdled.

Black man.

'Nobody move,' Hari said looking very grim.

Silence ricocheted off the corridor walls as everybody froze.

Suddenly Kamini's vision was completely obstructed by a violent flapping before her eyes, like a wounded bird's wings.

Terror gripped her throat, choking it.

22.

Three events took place exactly at the same time, just like Rita's trinity at the centre of the moment. Under Dodo's bedroom pillow a mobile phone pinged a muffled announcement that it had received a message; Uma's tear-streaked face turned in the direction of the sound when she heard it; and Indira got up from the dining table realizing that her mobile had been locked up inside when Uma had slammed the door behind her.

The chair shrieked in protest at the force of Indira's realization. It interrupted the trancelike silence around the dining table.

She was at the door in a trice. 'Open the door,' Indira said, as quietly as she could.

'Not a hope in hell,' Uma shot back, and snatched off the pillow uncovering the mobile with the urgency of a life and death situation.

'You are being very childish,' Indira couldn't stop her fists from feverishly thumping the door ahead of her.

It was a Nokia phone. Uma was unfamiliar with its functions. Her fingers shook as she manoeuvred the key pad and she wondered why she was trembling.

'Very,very childish,' Indira menaced.

An sms flashed before Uma. She experienced the completely physical sensation of the blood in her veins cooling instantly. The last time that had happened was when she had watched her son fall an entire flight of stairs.

Wl b unabl to execute if no ring by 2moro, the text said.

'Oh my God,' Uma sat on the bed. I *knew* there was something about the ring.

'Open the door, Didi,' Dodo said, his hand still caked with the rice he was eating. 'Don't make me break down the door of my own house.'

Shivering, Uma flipped screen after screen till she reached the inbox. 'Stay away from this, Dodo. It's not your fight,' she shouted from behind the door and went back, memorized the unsaved number of the sender, and opened the inbox again.

'Neither is it yours,' Indira screamed.

There were three messages from the sender, all about the ring. *Need a valued possession*, said one. *Need it by 2moro*, said another. *Plan getting delayd bcoz no ring*, said the third.

'Uma!' Her mother belted out a full-throated shout.

'What?' was Uma's distracted response.

There were many messages from the sent box to the unidentified person. The most significant was a loaded and telling question. *Hw abt a diamond ring?*

'Open the door,' went a chorus of unidentifiable voices.

'Women!' Giving up, Dodo returned to his now cold lunch.

Uma thrust the pillow back over the mobile and opened the latch to the door. The women streamed in as if to a movie hall going house full. Indira flipped away the pillow, picked up her mobile phone still glowing from all the attention it had received, and turned to confront Uma. 'You little snoop,' she accused.

For some strange reason, Uma opted for nonchalance as self-defence but had no idea, given the array of inscrutable faces, whether she was succeeding.

'You just went through my mobile.'

'I did not.'

'Yes, you did, you nosy-parking so and so,' Indira flipped through her mobile. 'I knew it. The messages are opened.'

In her entire life, Uma had never imagined a day would come when a young cousin would hit her. That changed when she saw the expressions flitting across Indira's face. 'Even if I did,' Uma said, trying to put past them an act so shameful that she did not even remember doing it in school, 'what do you have to hide?'

'See, see,' Indira turned to what she perceived as her remote-controlled mob. 'She accepts her crime.'

'No such thing,' a voice inside Uma's head kept repeating, even as her knees started to shake; defence is the best offence: 'I want to know why you are sending messages to unsaved numbers regarding the diamond ring.'

'None of your business.'

'Too late for that now.'

'By the way, where is the ring?'

'None of your business.'

'Anything to do with my father is my business,' Indira turned to plead with her mob. 'Do I have to be subjected to this now, of all times?'

'But, child,' Uma's mother said. 'To whom are you sending messages about Raj's diamond ring and why?'

'No, no,' she charmed her mob, surreptitiously eyeing the messages she was deleting. 'It's not like that at all. What your utterly malicious daughter is presuming to be the ring is a phone call. Phone call, ring, get it? And the unidentified number is my husband's. His mobile crashed recently.'

'Why haven't you saved his number?' Uma pounced.

'I didn't have time. My father was dying, remember?'

'Don't believe a word this woman says,' Uma pointed at Indira. 'She's a lying cheat.'

'Uma,' her mother warned.

'Yes, Uma,' Ishita agreed.

Dodo thought he should get up to intervene but chose to finish his lunch instead.

'Where is the ring? Give me the ring. You are obsessed with the ring. Give me the ring,' Indira said in one breath.

'Give her the ring,' Uma's mother echoed. 'What belongs to her father belongs to her.'

Beseiged, Uma turned to her belongings to do the mob's bidding but a thought, almost like a physical force, stopped her. The germ of an idea started up from her navel as a point of light and shooting up her throat flashed in her head.

'Okay,' she said. 'But on one condition.'

Indira looked at her suspiciously.

'Only if Raj Mamu says the ring belongs to him.'

'That's fair,' Uma's mother said.

'But he can't speak!' Indira said, exasperated.

'But you said he has begun to gain consciousness for a few hours?' Ishita intervened.

'Has he?' Uma asked, hope rising within her like a lunar tide. Ishita nodded at Uma, finally pitying her sister's situation.

'Isn't anybody listening?' Indira saw her tight rein on the mob loosen. 'He can't speak.'

'He can nod yes and no, can't he?' Uma shot a poisonous dart at Indira.

'That's settled then. Dodo call for a taxi,' her mother said.

'Where are you going now?' He had lost the thread of the argument.

'To the hospital.'

'Oh,' Dodo said, moving to wash his hands in the kitchen sink.

And Indira knew that now the situation was out of her hands.

23.

'You stupid woman,' Raj said to her brooding melancholic presence, sticking to him like a polyester shirt in summer. 'I have not abandoned you. Not because I don't want to, but because I can't.'

And he knew that he would never be rid of her, ever. She was not an irritating puppy that he could shake off his leg, a nagging worry that he could shrug from his shoulders. She would never fade away like a college crush. She was not an orgiastic release he could forget by shutting his *Playboy* magazine. He could not shut her away in the bottom drawer with the Havana cigars in his uncle's bathroom.

She was aqua regia. She was the acid that was dissolving him slowly, inexorably, unforgivingly. She was spreading inside his veins like a golden liquid dissolving his arrogance, his difference, his otherness and any other density that came in her way. She was slowly but surely obliterating him. He got a flash of what was going to happen. How the differences of their bodies would dissolve into their minds, their minds into their individualities, their individualities into the One, till there was only golden light that dissolved and filled every pore of the Calcutta Chowringhee apartment building.

I am a system of duality collapsing into itself, layer by layer, identity by identity, category by category and shall continue to do so till I find her and merge with her in such a way that we can never ever be separated. And *that* is why I can experience so much fear and so much freedom at the same time.

So this is what it is about. What inspires poets, what makes Sufis dance ecstatic. What Tennyson and Gibran were trying to say. This is what aspiring saints mimic in their efforts to manifest true love. This is why songs are written, this is why Romeo and Juliet are not Jack and Jill. This is what they mean by love, and this is what they mean by God, and this is what they mean when they say God *is* Love.

I know, he said to nobody and everybody, and don't ask me how, and don't ask me why. I know the universe is watching, and the world is waiting.

Watching this pain, waiting for it to get worse. If I go to her, he thought, and tell her how I feel, she will look at me in that funny way of hers, her eyes full of knowing, and her face full of pretence, and she will laugh and say something inane like, 'Don't be silly,' or something witty like, 'Yes, sure. And pigs can fly.'

I would die if she did that, he decided, even if I knew she was lying.

That's why I can't see you again. Because your laughter makes me impotent. Because I can't sweep you into my arms and walk away with you. And I will not survive another glimpse of your wedding photograph. I know you are angry because I gave you the money without meeting you but it's better that way. Do you know that it is your face I saw under the veil on the day of my engagement? It was your finger I slipped the diamond solitaire on. Your shoulders I wrap the most expensive pashminas. It's you I shall be marrying next month. Your hennaed hands will be placed in mine. You will go with me to Switzerland for our honeymoon. It will be to cover your perfumed thighs that I shall buy expensive lingerie from Paris.

So don't just sit there in my awareness and sulk like that, though I enjoy that too – nobody can pine for me the way you do. (He knew he derived a perverse pleasure from that, and also knew she hated him for it.)

Once, as his family streamed in through the apartment door after a frenzy of shopping in New Market, he caught her scent by the door and in the melee of consumerist excitement, stopped dead in his tracks. He could smell her, like a hunter on a trail. She had been there, she had stood next to the door. She had strained her ears to catch his sound, heightened her senses to feel his impress in the air. She had been sad and lonely. She had brooded over her jealousy, had felt stifled by the festivities in the air. He saw her, as usual, in a flash, her haunting eyes accusing him for his intolerable cruelty. It thrilled him to the bone, and all his fine hairs rose in their pores.

So he was not alone in his insane pastimes, not that it mattered. As a matter of habit, he had taken to parking his Volkswagen as close to her canary yellow Fiat as possible. Sometimes consciously, but mostly unconsciously, he made a complete circle of her Fiat before reaching or getting away from his car. He would linger only for a fraction of an extra moment near her car, and an overwhelming rush of her would leave him breathless. He would know if she had been to the Kali temple, or visited a friend, or made a quick dash for groceries. Once he spotted, in the humid confines of the car's insides, the wilted, brown paper covering of Waterbury's Compound falling off the corner of the seat and immediately saw, like a short movie reel,the baby's griping pain, her panic-stricken anxiety, her mad rush to the chemist, and the hurry to get back to her baby. And in her wake, like an aftertaste, the lingering of her pain for him, the haze of tears, her longing. Her longing, her longing. For him, for him, always for him. Forever for him.

His eyes filled with tears, and he opened the front door of his Volkswagen to slip behind the steering wheel and weep for her. It was a strange kind of weeping. The more he longed for her the more he filled up, like an emptiness that was full, satisfyingly full.

He knew the universe was conspiring against them, because his one hope of a chance meeting did not happen. There were no accidental encounters on the stairs even though he had made it a point to visit Mr Biswas living above her, more than often. He never saw her car come out of the garage, or her come down the lift. Even Bairah and Jhunu, whom he suspected were carrying on with each other, seemed to have cooled off, as if to stop any vicarious pleasure he could get from them. There were no crossings on the street, no bumping into her while she ate egg rolls at Nizams or bought movie tickets at the Ritz – however popular the film.

Maybe that was the reason why, when he wandered into their connecting terrace, he did not expect to see her at all. How the gods must have laughed! He was unshaven and in his pyjamas. The tingling feeling that he would bump into her had made him clip his moustache to perfection every day till then, and he hadn't even bumped into her maid. Now here he was, caught with his pyjama string dangling to his knees! If he had known he would at least have shampooed his hair.

It had been one of those days; without promise, less than ordinary. His aunt had been prodding Manik to check the seepage that seemed to be coming from the terrace – because she just did not trust Bairah's or her husband's architectural knowledge in seepage matters – and had finally turned to Raj when Manik refused to budge.

'At least come with me, you good-for-nothing, lying there like Marilyn Monroe, flipping through a magazine,' Raj had scolded his cousin.

'Marilyn Monroe yourself! You sound as if you are going to battle.' Manik's ennui was implacable. An argument – which Raj considered the principal occupation of his clan – ensued on what was of greater national importance, the seepage in one of the historical relics of the country or the unmitigated support provided to artists by buying film magazines to keep art and culture thriving. Art and culture won and Raj grumbled his way to the terrace. His grumbling automatically stopped when he saw her standing there, in a crumpled sari, a rose plant in her hand.

It was then that they realized this was why their hearts had started to thud even before they came face to face. They understood then that their bodies responded to and sensed the proximity of each other much before they did. As they stood facing each other their eyes locked in a desperate clasp that immobilized them. She became aware of a slow trickle wetting her thighs and his body started to ache from the strain of staying away from her.

This time there were no excuses between them. The wind was their breath, the earth their flesh, and the water of their bodies the surge of the oceans. Time was their secret conspirator and the two pigeons cooing on the neighbour's roof a message from the gods. She knew from the way he looked at her that he could separate the distance between them in three short steps and touch her. And the thought of it was so overpowering that her knees buckled. She felt herself melting from the heat of his intention. She had often imagined this moment. Sometimes exactly the way it was happening now. But never in her imagination had she expected to experience so much terror. Her body tightly withheld, she turned and walked away to her apartment.

It was only much later that she realized she had been clutching the rose plant for hours.

As for Raj, he stood rooted to the spot till it started to rain, and even much after it stopped. Cold hard rage seemed to have nailed him to the ground. What an utter, utter fool he had been. It was all a lie. None of what he thought was happening was actually happening. He was the victim of his own diseased imagination.

Never again, he swore at her closed terrace door knowing she was shrinking behind it.

Be careful, the rain cautioned, sometimes declarations come true.

Soaked to the bone, shivering but not with the cold, he did not care.

Even though she never saw his wife or received a wedding card she knew when he got married, and when his wife moved in to her husband's apartment. She would walk past their door and know if they had quarrelled or whether she was sulking, or when the household throbbed with quiet domestic harmony. And she also knew that through it all she was in his thoughts, just as he was in hers.

I want to see you before you get married just once, she had pleaded with him after their coincidental meeting on the terrace, but his cold hard resistance had filled her with unforeseen anger too. When she could bear the silence no longer, she steadied her shaking hands to write him a note.

Don't think, she wrote in her convent-educated cursive handwriting, *that I am just a bored housewife. Astrology is my profession. I charge ten rupees extra for future predictions.*

When he saw the chit Raj felt his body blanch in white hot anger. She is trying to tell me that I think she is a bored housewife looking for an easy dalliance. She is not only of impeccable character, she cares two hoots for me. He immediately fished out a hundred-rupee note from his wallet and handed it to Bairah. Bairah was made to race to her apartment with the money and a chit that curtly said, *Keep the change.*

The money came back in ten minutes.

Maybe I should not charge people with futures as dark as yours.

Bairah again raced back with the money and a note: *I suggest you keep the money. I don't see many clients in your future.*

He returned this time with a chit that said, *NEVER DARKEN MY DOORSTEP AGAIN*. Bairah knew enough English to know that when it was written in capitals it carried a fairly dire message, and thought that by now it was safe to pocket the money.

It was only when the apartment building became silent and the guard whistled out the first watch of his nightly guard that she realized that he was not going to reply. Her husband did not notice that she spent the entire night sitting upright on the bed. In the morning during breakfast when she casually chatted about the arrogance of the so-called bluebloods downstairs who were so miserly that they didn't even pay up, he absent-mindedly said, 'Don't fight with the neighbours, dearest.'

She did not notice when her husband went for a month-long sojourn to America. Raj did not notice when he got married. Both were only aware that their fight continued through and across the ceilings and walls and landings and corridors of the apartment building.

I thought you had come to my life to give, she said, *but you too, like everybody else, had come to take.*

Funny, he fought back, *how I thought the same about you.*

And, subliminally, they knew they were playing out the human drama of the ego between them. Not that it changed anything.

Many times, when the apartment was quiet and she couldn't sleep at night, she imagined him knocking at her door. She would be prepared this time, she thought, no crumpled sari. At bedtime she made it a point to brush her hair and wear the fetching negligee her husband had bought her in the early days of their marriage and which she never wore. Raj, too, fantasized about knocking at her door in the middle of the night. Her face would glow in the landing light and this time his pyjama string would be tucked in. In both their fantasies their skin shone like gold.

And then, one day, when he finally knocked on the door and she opened it, and her apartment was empty and the building was still, they looked at each other and wondered whether this was carnal sin or a spiritual practice.

Was what was happening between them sexual attraction or the gravitational pull of two galaxies? Could her eyes burn like this for anybody other than him? Could his? Was there any other on the planet who could make them react like this? Because they did not react in the other's presence, they metamorphosed.

The hall was dark. And all she saw was his burning eyes and his white shirt. They did not speak. When he took her in his arms his skin was cool and she looked up at him and felt that she balanced all of femininity on the point of that one moment. And all of mankind had given to him that night their power to love. There was nothing to do except surrender to it.

They scratched and licked and clutched and sucked. They found pain in pleasure and pleasure in pain. Their surface expanse of flesh rose in trepidation and utter bliss. They clawed and scraped for the other, and found each other in the crook of the elbow, on the balls of the feet, in the roots of the other's hair, in the hollow of the navel.

They made sounds that were not divine. But neither were they human or animal. She lost consciousness many times, and he was relentless, sobbing throughout, unable to bear the sensations filling up his senses, unable to stop.

What happened that night? he wondered, she wondered, for the rest of their lives. Did it happen in this world or another, beyond right and wrong, where all was fair? If what happened was real then they were cursed for they had fallen, because angels do not copulate and maybe that was why the gods had condemned them never to see each other again. But if it had happened in another world, their world of electric lights and heart sounds and ethereal scents, then had they still sinned?

Of course, she turned her tear-streaked face up at him, *because infidelity is in the mind.*

But our world is not of the mind, he whispered to her. *It is of the spirit, and laws of the flesh do not apply there. We have not sinned, we have truly loved.*

No, she agonized. *This is real, we have sinned and are now cursed. Else why is it that we will never meet again?*

Hush, he soothed, stroking her hair in the warm afterglow of their union. *The gods are not cursing us, they are purifying us.*

24.

'There is no such thing as good and evil,' Rita slipped on her TAG Heur shades and tightened her Hermes scarf against the wind rushing in through the car windows that Ali had insisted on lowering even though the Hummer was careening down the road to the airport at breakneck speed. 'At most, the loosest definition we can give to good and evil is whether we are increasing the harmony in the universe, or the chaos. Chaos is the closest definition of evil, the lowest energy state, the path of least resistance, which the universe automatically takes.'

'A lot like Delhi traffic,' Carlos shouted over the gushing wind and screaming tyres. An array of bumper lights and the faint honking of jammed cars on the flyover visible in the distance seemed to concur with their pontifications.

'Now I know why Delhi traffic is evil,' Kamini theorized.

'The Second Law of Thermodynamics states that the universe progresses towards entropy,' Rita said. 'Fear, hatred, bitterness, road rage,' Rita gestured prettily, 'are low-energy states. It requires tremendous amounts of energy to create harmony or balance. Love, ecstasy, bliss are the highest states of energy. Notice again the play of energies, the attraction of the poles necessary to create the high energy state.'

'Is *that* what Hari did so valiantly to save Mira from the throes of danger?' Ali laughed not looking up from the blue psychedelic light of his PS3. 'Zap hatred with a dose of unpolarized ecstasy, cowboy style?'

'Something like that.'

Hari was embarrassed, sensing from the back of his head the admiring gaze of the women sitting in the rear.

'But what *was* that?' Rita gushed, unabashed. 'I have never seen such a deft clearing of negative energies. There were so many of them flying around, attacking us, half of them attached to Mira's aura, sucking her dry. I mean, we all know that vampires exist at the energy level' – and when Kamini jerked her head towards Rita she explained briefly – 'Yes, darling, vampires are energy parasites. Blood is symbolic of vital energy. So you now know what "bloodsucker" really means. A clingy friend is actually a vampire.' And returning to her listening audience streaming through the wind in the powerful vehicle she said, 'They were really powerful, Hari. Mira is not weak, but I have never seen her look so ashen. And you put Harrison Ford to shame.'

'It's an old technique. The five-step silver bullet visualization technique. I'll teach it to you someday. In fact, this is the basic course taught to our Veerbhadra warriors. You do know that Mira's incident scrambled VNP to deploy a large Veerbhadra contingent to the Twin Flame site. So rest assured, wherever we go, reinforcements are already there.'

'You know,' Rita said, tightening the scarf around her. 'In all my years in VNP I never knew there was a VNP mafia.'

'Rita!' Hari exclaimed as if she had just mutinied. 'It's not the mafia. It's a military contingent. And we need it! Haven't you been reading the papers, watching TV? This is 2012. Japan is reeling from earthquakes and nuclear disaster. The Middle East is in foment. We need all the help we can get!' And turning to Kamini's luminous eyes glowing in the dark, he pre-empted her accusation, 'No, not one drop of three-dimensional blood has ever been spilt by VNP – so far.'

The wind howled against their cheeks and the window panes, their hair lashed about their faces, and the group lapsed into a thoughtful silence, until Kamini piped in again: 'Can I ask a stupid question?'

From the front seat Hari gave her a backward glance and sighed, 'It's been a while. Please go ahead.'

'Where are we going?' she asked after a hesitant pause.

'You mean nobody has told her yet?' Hari exploded, his face flushed.

Delhi's wind chill factor does attractive things to his skin, Kamini thought. And she basked in the sweet pandemonium of excuses and counter-excuses that ensued, knowing that, once again, she was the cynosure of their attention.

'We are going to make First Contact,' Hari said by way of apology, his sudden deference to her making her nervous.

'First Contact?' she thoughtfully repeated.

'You already know that we are in Code Red. I've been saying that till I've been blue in the face from the very beginning...'

'And never stopped,' Ali chortled. 'Blue Face Shouting Code Red is his Native American name.'

'An emergency regarding the subjects XX and XY, requiring immediate energy intervention has occurred. As you may have learnt during the crash course in the healing camps, to begin the process of healing or any type of energy intervention we first need to establish a communication channel, like a hyperlink to a website.'

'Okay, okay,' she snapped, not knowing why. 'What's the emergency?'

He was giving her that intent look again, across their bumping ride, deepening a subliminal anxiety just beyond her reach. 'The emergency is that "he" has already made First Contact. And we have just learnt that it was quite a while back.'

'Who?' she said and answered the question herself. 'The black man?'

'VNP is calling him the Green Lyon, an ancient alchemical term, borrowed from one of Ali's ebooks.'

Greening Kamini thought, and remembered patches of Ali's presentation. In spite of the screaming wind the vehicle seemed strangely quiet. She remembered how Ali had prophesied that the subjects were near death, without knowing anything about them. She said so.

'We are going to Kolkata,' Hari finally said to Kamini.

'Is that where the subjects are?' she asked. Both avoided looking at each other.

'Yes,' he said. They had reached the chartered flight. And Hari remembered to say – 'And to pass the time Mira can give her presentation.'

'Pass the time?! Discrimination against old people,' Mira grumbled.

'Totally,' he said, helping her off the Hummer and hugging her.

When they had all settled into the chartered aircraft in perfectly humidified and scented twenty-one degrees temperature, a glass of sparkling wine in their hands and a blanket across their knees, Hari sighed, 'Ah, the perks of the job.' Meera took out her knitting. It was almost complete: the shape of a child's sweater with its multi-coloured Donald Duck motif now decipherable.

'Oh go on. Even *that* can't bother me now,' Hari said, pointing at her knitting. He adjusted his head rest and fidgeted about till he found the perfect position. 'Nothing like a good nodding nap during a VNP presentation,' he said.

'Hari asked me,' Mira began her talk, 'to make a karmic database for XX and XY. Many of you must have concluded by now that XX and XY are soulmates. Well, the jury is in regarding that matter, and what it has to say is,' she stretched out a line of pink wool over the blue one, 'you are right and you are wrong. Right in the sense that yes, they are soulmates in the way you imagine them to be. In fact, looking at their esoteric charts, I know that in one lifetime they were Heer and Ranjha, so there is some karma backing up on them here, and in one lifetime they were Bimbisara and Amrapali –'

'Huh?' Hari involuntarily lifted his eye-patch.

'History was not your strongest subject, was it?' Kamini had found a breach for a malicious jibe. Mira smiled indulgently, letting Kamini score her brownie points. 'Bimbisara was one of the most powerful emperors in ancient India, Buddha time, based in Patna. And though history is confused about Amrapali, legend has it that she was a courtesan he fell in love with. But since she was Nagar badhu, "wife of the city" in Vaishali, technically his enemies, she had some loyalty issues, and he ended up with abandonment issues. She was one of the first women to shave her head and join Buddha's Sangha. I don't think that helped his psychic blocks any.'

Hari was quiet.

'So you see, I know my history,' Kamini said.

Hari pulled down his eye-patch and turned away from her.

'Well, I'm still working out the permutations of that possibility,' Mira intervened. 'What was I saying? Ah, yes, you would be wrong to conclude they are soulmates, in the strict definition of the term. And to clarify that, I have, literally, to go back to the beginning. And by beginning here I really mean the beginning of time. That moment of eternity that Rita has so eloquently described as the source.

'Most people understand the source as God. When God, as the first spark, decided to manifest, he sent out many rays of light. And each ray, out of necessity, divided into two. We are all cells in God's heart. We are all rays of light vibrating to our own signature vibrational frequency. But somewhere in this world your mirror image, our vibrational frequency carrying the opposite charge, exists. That opposite charge is your Twin Flame.'

'Why is that so difficult to believe?' Kamini frowned.

Hari twitched. 'Because the majority of us have never, in all the crores of lifetimes spent on this planet, ever bumped into our Twin Flame.'

'The reason being,' Rita murmured – it was difficult to ascertain whether she was appreciating her delicate sips of wine or making a rhetorical statement – 'the energies released during such a meeting would be powerful enough to destroy not only them but many others around them.'

'By destroy you mean…?' Kamini was captivated,

'Karmically, circumstantially…' Mira's needles clicked. 'The best cases in point are Romeo and Juliet, or Laila and Majnu. See how much death and destruction their exchange caused – for themselves as well as others.'

'That is why,' Carlos offered quietly, staring at the tiny bubbles rising to the surface of his wine, 'they can only meet when they are energetically ready.'

'And they are energetically ready,' Ali recited as if from a poem, 'when they have resolved most of their karmas. By that we mean, learnt most of the lessons their soul wants to learn.'

'That's why you never meet your Twin Flame. *Poof!* You go up in smoke,' Hari gestured, still blindfolded. 'Or die like Romeo and Juliet.'

'So when *do* you meet?' Kamini asked, her eyes round like saucers.

'Usually when you are ready for self-realization. Or in your last, or penultimate, birth in this world. Then your coming together is beneficial not only to you, but to Mankind in general.'

'Of course,' Kamini said. 'Let's not forget Mankind.'

'Now you know why even the lowliest demigod has a consort,' Mira said. 'Look closely and you will notice most saints, man or woman, had a mate tucked away somewhere. Ramakrishna had Sharda Ma, Christ had Magdalene, Aurobindo had the Mother.'

'Vivekanada had Sister Nivedita,' Ali said. 'Gandhi had Miraben,' he added after some thought.

'You are pushing it,' Kamini warned.

'Twin Flames are a necessary tool for enlightenment,' Rita concluded.

'For completion, for closure,' Kamini whispered.

'I want to quote Khalil Gibran here,' Hari raised a finger before his blindfold.

'Hmmm. Khalil Gibran! I worry for you,' Kamini retorted. 'Zorro.'

'When you are in love you should not say God is in my heart, but rather I am in the heart of God.'

'Bravo.'

'Hear, hear.'

'I drink to that.'

'Coming back to Twin Flame Energy Mechanics, let's see what happens after the first division. Imagine the Om, the cosmic egg, the *hiranyagarbha*. Imagine it dividing up into more and more cells. Taking the analogy further, it is crudely like some cells are wired to become the liver, some the kidney, etc. Now, taking the analogy back to the cosmic egg, some cell clusters belong to the same soul group.'

'I am sure I belong to the Urinary Bladder soul group,' Ali complained.

'So,' Mira said, trying not to be distracted, 'every individual person has many soulmates in varying frequencies closer or further from their own, depending on when the division took place. You can have many soulmates. Soulmates are people you have karma with.'

Carlos leaned across his armrest to conspiratorially wink at Rita. 'That's good news, Rita,' he said. 'We may not be Twin Flames, but at least we are soulmates.'

'For sure,' Mira said. 'That is true. In fact, all of us here belong to the same soul group. I know that because I was on the esoteric chart consultation panel when we were choosing the members of the team. But in our soul group XX and XY are the closest, the First Division, the Shiva and Shakti of the group.'

'Really?' Ali snorted, finally resurfacing from his PSP game. 'And what are we? Poor country cousins?'

'That's your viewpoint,' Mira smiled. 'We all have Twin Flames roaming around somewhere in the galaxy but here and now, we are all XX and XY's soulmates. The reason for that is we still have to play out our karmas with them. We have dues; that's obvious. We owe them...'

'I must have been his evil stepmother,' Rita muttered. 'I haven't had a moment's rest since this damn project started.'

And then, like a whiplash, she turned on Mira. For the first time she was the questioner, not the compatriot: 'You *know* all our past-life connections with XX and XY, don't you?'

Meera focused on counting the stitches with extra attention.

'Aw, come on.'

'Tell, tell.'

And bestowing the sweetest smile to her hungry horde Mira winked from behind her glasses: 'Doesn't Miss Marple wait for the end to tell us who the murderer is?'

'Oh God,' Carlos buried his head in his hands. 'I am the one who murdered Bimbisara.'

'Do you want to finish this seminar or not?' Hari remonstrated. 'We are going to land soon.'

'What's there to say?' Mira looked around. 'All of us has a Twin Flame. And even though we belong to the same soul group, when we are ready, and have learnt all the life lessons our soul wants to learn, the Twin Flame shows up.'

'So is it like the perfect romance?' Ali brightened.

'Yes and no,' Mira said. 'The chemistry between them is so volatile that in the beginning the flying passions can blow them away, but soon after the flames are ignited they go through this very painful process of clearing up their remaining karma. That is a little like a weight-loss programme. The last four kilos are the toughest.'

'Why so?'

'You have to transcend the deepest levels of existential delusion, what we call maya. You have to go beyond the limitations of your physical bodies, your self-beliefs, your identities. One must realize that not only are notions of romance and love illusory belief systems but also that space and time are not real.'

'Can Twin Flames be of the same sex?'

'Of course,' Mira said. 'Some of the finest, most sacred love poetry written by Rumi described gay love. Khalil Gibran's Twin Flame was not only many years older, but married. You see, though all of us have taken birth in both genders to realize what the other is like, fundamentally we carry one charge. And our Twin Flame the other.'

'I thought,' Hari finally took off his eye-patch, 'that our souls were beyond gender.'

'Of course, at the level of the source, we are beyond gender. But in its first descent one's soul does produce a charge, and its Twin Flame the opposite. And by the time they descend to the grossest dimension they have lost all idea of who they really are. They are covered in layers and layers of identities and belief systems. And that is why their coming together after millions of lifetimes, of learning and unlearning sometimes terrible and terrifying lessons, their meeting is not only a reunion but a homecoming. That is why the love they generate, the love they feel, is enough to heal any diseased place, animal or thing around them.'

A hushed silence was the satisfying response she received.

'Gods crave for a human birth to experience that kind of love,' Mira finished the last line of the border of her sweater, and looked up at her audience in satisfaction.

'And even though we have never experienced Twin Flame love, we have experienced some notion of it during our first crush, when we married, when we had our first baby. And still do, when we read poetry, or truly listen to a child laugh, or to Beethoven, or watch a child hug his child. We experience what the gods crave.'

And beaming at them she finished, 'So, the next time you are stuck in traffic, think of that.'

25.

Clutching the wilting petals of a marigold in her hand, Uma's mother tried to argue with the hospital doctor. The doctor, looking suitably ridiculous in his green duck shoes and green shower cap, was nevertheless a picture of resolute dignity.

'All I want is to give these to him,' Uma's mother brandished the decomposing flower in front of the doctor's face. 'This flower fell from the puja on my lap during my morning worship.'

'Yes, madam,' the doctor intervened. 'That is all very well, but I do not understand why so many of you want to enter to give him one flower.' He looked pointedly around at Uma, Indira and Dodo. Their aunt had stayed home with Ishita in Dodo's flat.

Dodo clutched the remaining marigolds of the rest of the wilted garland, wearing the slightly petrified expression of a man nudged around too much by the women of his herd.

Their mother pointed at the decomposing flowers Dodo held and exclaimed, 'Because there are so many more flowers.'

The doctor stared at Uma's mother in quiet certainty of her insanity and maintaining as much dignity as his green shower cap would allow, replied, 'I'll just get back to you,' before disappearing behind the double doors of the ICU.

Disenchanted, Uma's mother turned to her brood.

'This is such a waste of time,' Indira said.

'Stop your belly-aching.' Uma had dropped all pretence of civility with Indira.

'But, Ma,' Dodo was exasperated. 'Mamu is conscious. Why didn't you just tell the doctor that you need to ask him a few vital personal questions? What is all this about puja flowers?'

'I agree. He just thinks you are crazy,' Indira said bitterly. 'I don't blame him.' For once nobody refuted her.

'Oh, come on,' Uma's mother flopped onto a vinyl chair. As usual, it vibrated in response to her weight. 'I was thinking of a reasonable excuse. I couldn't tell him we need to ask him a question about a diamond ring. How ill-bred that would be. The doctor would think here the Raja is not even dead yet, and here his sister is, already trying to grab his worldly possessions.'

'Oh, Ma,' Dodo muttered, deciding to eat the kernels of the marigold flowers like he used to when he was in school. He plucked out the petals, littering them all over his trousers and said, 'How silly is that. Nobody knows he is a Raja here.'

'Not unless Indira has distributed pamphlets to the effect to everybody in the lobby. Which she may well have.'

'Okay, this is it,' Indira rose from her chair. 'I'm going home.'

'Home?' Uma's response was sarcastic. 'You mean Dodo's flat? Since when has that become home?'

'Enough,' Uma's mother's indignation made the chair vibrate harder as she closed her eyes in distress. 'Please –'

'"–Well-behaved families do not create the scenes in the public places,"' Uma and Dodo finished for her.

Indira snorted.

Dodo chewed the marigolds with a faraway expression on his face. 'Stop it,' his sister pinched his elbow. And then as an afterthought added: 'Cow.'

Thus they waited for the doctor to decide their fate. Dodo chewed on. In that pleasant state of stupor Uma's phone whistled out its *Kill Bill* caller tune. She looked momentarily at the number and then looked away.

'Aren't you going to answer it?' Indira's question was marked with suspicion.

'No,' Uma lazily replied.

'Why?' demanded Indira.

'Because it's none of your business,' Uma said, staring at an interesting pattern of betel juice spittle on the opposite wall.

'Of course,' Indira fidgeted in her chair. 'Only *my* father's business is *your* business.'

'Probably just a marketing call,' Dodo pacified. 'Like Jhunjhunwala Estates...'

'Standard Chartered Gold Card...'

'Raheja Builders calling for my Orchid Petals flat. "Madam, would you like to rental your Patel property...?"'

'HSBC car loan...'

The brother sister back-and-forth attempted to kill time. After they ran out of ideas there was a silence in which their mother delicately pulled at her nose till it turned the gentle shade of cut watermelon.

'There are no male cows,' Dodo suddenly realized.

'Such a clever boy,' his sister glowed at him. 'Like there are no female peacocks.'

Then why did you call me a cow?' Dodo demanded.

'This family is crazy,' Indira announced.

'Interesting point,' Uma conceded. 'I should have said bull.'

'Ya, bull.' Indira got up from her chair that vibrated in recoil. 'Bullshit to be more exact. Can we please go home now?'

Uma was lost in contemplation for a while. She came out of it with what she presumed was a very important observation. 'The problem with Mamu, like the rest of his generation, was that he never had a job.'

Her eyes shut in great pain, their mother shook her head with so much sorrow that Indira couldn't help let out a giggle. 'The problem with you children is that you know so little of your family history.'

'He had a job?' Dodo's eyebrows disappeared into his receding hairline, at last showing some sign of interest in their dying uncle.

'What do you think the Calcutta flat was *for*?' Their mother shot out of her chair and paced up and down the narrow corridor in indignation. 'It was to prepare for his Indian Forestry exam papers.'

She mistook her audience's dumbfounded expressions for awe and continued, 'It was his dream to work for the conservation of forests. He studied religiously, for years on end.'

Indira was giggling openly now. 'Till Ma realized he was never going to make it. And put up the flat for rent,' she clarified.

'Whatever.' Their mother shook an accusing finger at them. 'Do not ever allude that we were a bunch of good-for-nothings. Because, don't deny it, *that* is the allusion.'

'Come on, Ma,' though Dodo placated his mother, he sounded genuinely stricken. 'Studying for an exam for years on end is not a job.'

'Whatever.' Presuming her dignity restored their mother sat down on the vibrating chair.

After a few more minutes of crushing ennui Dodo whispered to his sister, out of his mother's hearing, 'Indian Forestry? Who studies for *that*? They don't even pay you.'

'Forests? Lodges? An illusion of zamindari? The feeling that one is in one's natural habitat?' Uma whispered back.

Her eyes still shut in extreme pain their mother retorted, 'I heard that!'

There was no other resort but more crushing ennui while they waited for the doctor.

The doctor finally returned without his shower cap, looking quite bald. Uma noted that he actually looked better with the shower cap on – not that she was the fashion police or anything, it was just an interesting observation.

'All four of you can go in but not for more than five minutes,' the doctor announced. 'You can give him the flowers,' he shuddered in mild distaste.

Commie, Uma thought.

'Oh, that won't be necessary,' Indira beamed at the doctor. 'My cousin has already eaten them.'

Still staring at them, shaking his head solemnly, the doctor disappeared through the double doors to attend to more serious business.

The first thing that Uma noticed when they entered the cramped spaces of the ICU was that her uncle's eyes were following her.

He was conscious. Attached to many leads and beeping equipments, but conscious.

Uma pushed Indira ahead of her and presented her to her uncle, like a gift.

'See,' Uma smiled. 'You had been asking for her. Now I've brought her. So get off that bed, now, and get well fast.'

Raj, rendered totally expressionless from his illness, still managed to look confused.

'Oh, Papa,' Indira said, oozing an affection so fake that Uma backed away from her. 'Were you asking for me?'

He slowly shook his head.

'My poor dad,' Indira said quickly. 'It's quite obvious the medicines have taken their toll. It's okay, Papa. The doctors say you will be fine soon. Your vital signs are improving every day.'

'No, they are not,' a white-jacketed intern muttered from the nursing station.

Raj looked bewildered by his daughter's sudden show of affection. But concentrating on it too hard made him tired. He lifted his scrawny neck from the raised hospital bed and clutched at Uma's sleeve, 'They beat me,' he rasped. Uma noticed that in spite of his condition his eyes still shone with an unclouded light.

There was a quick exchange of glances from everybody. Uma's mother sighed.

'Who beat you, Mamu?' Uma tried to sound as natural as she could.

'They,' he whispered, with a furtive glance around.

'Who is *they*?' Indira asked sharply.

'They tie me to the bed and beat me. At night, when everybody is asleep they burn me with hot coals.' His throat was parched. He looked piteous. The shrivelled fingers clutching at Uma's sleeve felt cold and clammy. Everybody took a deep breath and a step back from the bed. Uma looked at the nursing station. Without looking in her direction the eavesdropping attendant shook his head.

'No, nobody beats him. It's ICU psychosis. And even if we did, where would we get hot coals?'

Still Uma's mother pulled her nose suspiciously at him and Uma thought, *But you've been tempted, haven't you?*

'The MRI shows a swelling in the brain. You do know that, don't you?' The attendant defended himself against the hostile pairs of eyes trained on him.

That's when Uma first noticed it. The presence of dark menace in the room, like a pungent stench. The negative energies of a hospital? Uma shook her head, as if it would shake away the thought, but the sensation persisted like a miasma. She looked around her like a dog smelling the air, and felt a hot breath rustle through her hair. There was something swirling around Raj's bed, like a dark cloud, and she noticed her uncle looking at her with that Eureka expression.

Now you know what I mean? she thought she heard him think.

Yes, she thought. *What is it?* She thought he responded with a thought but could not catch what it was.

'Take out the ring already,' Dodo was saying.

Uma fished it out of her pocket and snapping open the Cartier box, held it under Raj's nose. His nose, she noticed, had successfully maintained the typical morphology of their clan. 'Do you recognize this ring, Mamu?'

Her uncle looked first at the diamond ring and then at her. It was the way he held his gaze steady that made her spine prickle. He looked first at his daughter, then rolled his eyes up as if to gesture at what she thought was swirling around him, and then turned back to look at her.

No, he shook his head. Yet to Uma his expression said that there was a man behind the curtain who had a gun trained at him.

'There you go!' was Indira's triumphant response. 'Thank you, Dad. This niece of yours has been insulting and humiliating me for the last few days over a piece of junk she is building a conspiracy theory around.'

Her cousins let her continue her tirade, but all the while, Raj did not once take his eyes off Uma. *You are reading me right,* his eyes said. *This is a cry for help.*

'What a waste of time,' Indira finished.

'Why?' Uma said, not taking her eyes off her uncle. 'Wouldn't you have come to meet your precious dad anyway?'

'I don't need you to tell me when to meet my own father,' Indira snapped back.

That's when Uma felt her throat constrict, as if an unseen hand was throttling her. She knew she had to get out of the room. She turned to leave when her mobile started whistling the *Kill Bill* tune again, bringing up thought forms of Uma Thurman. Gesturing apologetically to the glaring attendants that she would take it outside, she staggered out of the double doors. She could sense her uncle craning his neck to see the last of her as she left.

Indira watched her cousin go through the double doors, listening with rapt attention to the words being spoken into the phone. Then she turned and looked accusingly at her father. Raj cringed, unable to meet her anger. Filled with dread of an inevitable future Indira decided to display it anyway, though knowing somewhere it was not yet time.

Uma knew Indira would walk through the double doors to join her. She turned to face her squarely.

'Who is it?' Indira hissed.

Uma's phone was no longer at her ear, it was cradled in her hand. The deed done, the die cast, Uma looked finally at peace.

'Who was it?' Indira asked again, and the silence that greeted her seemed to be a reply from eternity.

Finally Uma said, 'That was Kamini.'

And when the silence stretched just long enough to reach the borders of a scream, Uma said, with a hint of sarcasm, 'Remember Kamini? Your sister?'

26.

Every passing winter gave Raj and Aparajita the hope that the next season would bring them closer to their fruition. And every season passed like a streetwalking tease. Yet as the years rolled by they did not feel they were growing older, they were simply ripening. Taking another step towards a foregone conclusion.

On Christmas eve, one festive Calcutta December, Aparajita sensed Raj's rush of elation and knew that he had become a father. But she could not locate where he was.

In Bellevue Nursing Home in Bombay, when a swaddle of fine Egyptian cotton was handed into Raj's unsure arms, he took a first look at his daughter's shrivelled face and his eyes welled up because he could see Aparajita smiling at the both of them.

'I'm sorry she's not ours,' he said to Aparajita. And she felt the pang of what could have been, a life that could have been led.

'She was not meant to be,' Aparajita said.

Peering into Indira's puckered face he felt the first parental stirrings and tried to find his lost love in his newborn's eyes.

'Then what was meant to be, my love?' he asked.

And Aparajita pulled a light shawl closer around her and told him the answer to that lay like a growing seed in the womb of time. They would know when they were ready.

And as the planets and galaxies moved around to the roll of kettledrums, they wondered whether they would ever be ready. Because they had not met for too many years and the longing between them had became such a powerful force that it pushed them further apart. Aparajita's family had moved to Delhi because her husband had landed an opportunity to practice in the Supreme Court.

Raj allowed his wife to persuade him to put their flat up for rent and move to the seaside port of Puri, closer to their ancestral home. And when the both of them left they each felt the pull of their heart-strings getting stretched beyond the point of endurance.

A pall of gloom hung over the apartment building, something its inhabitants sensed but did not understand. Aparajita cried all the way to Delhi, so much so that, when she reached the grim, forbidding city her eyes were puffy slits. Her husband and son tried to reassure her all along, telling her she would make new friends.

Some years after they arrived in Puri, on a trip to the seashore, Raj swam out two kilometres from the Puri shoreline before he turned back. His wife laughed and said his daughters and she thought he was going to swim right across the ocean. He stared at two-year-old Kamini as she bounced up and down in the sand singing, 'My bonnie lies over the ocean, my bonnie lies over the sea.'

Guilt cleaved his heart into two and he swung her, squealing, over his shoulder. 'But you are my bonnie and you are right here.'

And as the four of them sat, like a family for once, in the cooling darkening sand, watching the sunset, his wife said, 'Maybe your bonnie does lie over the ocean.'

In her calmness Raj could see storms tumult.

'I thought Singapore was across the ocean,' he joked and seeing his wife delving deeper into turbulence he turned to Indira, 'You are old enough, Indira. You should be able to tell me what lies across the horizon.'

'Treasures,' Indira brightened. 'Islands full of treasures.'

'Sometimes,' Kamini's mother couldn't stop herself, 'I don't know whether you are crazy or I.'

Kiran's attraction was that she carried a strength and delicacy at the same time. She was earthy, she was airy, she was flexible, she was strong. But at that moment, right then, when Raj looked sideways at her, the stray wisps of hair whipping across her face just made her look vulnerable.

And again he felt his heart break. *Is it the part that knows I love another woman? Or the part that does not know who she is?*

Raj's chin sank into his chest, even as he followed his wife's gaze to the sea's end. Kamini's puny dimpled hands scooped out wet sand in measures of no consequence. Indira drew figures of eight around them with a damp stick.

'Every man loves another woman, Kiran,' he said putting his arms around his wife. 'And that woman is his mother.'

She sat stiff and straight against his chest, and he realized that in spite of the birth of their two children their bodies had never really known the other, never relaxed with the other. Because bodies can't lie, Raj thought.

'You have been a dutiful husband,' she said at last, turning to him. 'A good husband; maybe even a faithful one. Maybe that's why I hate you so much.'

He hugged her tighter. 'So it's settled then. You are the one who is crazy.' Raj sensed the depths of his wife's sorrow and he was powerless to do anything about it. If you ever knew, he thought, that my true love is a void, a nothingness, you would truly go crazy.

And, as if to do his wife a favour, to put her out of her misery, to give her something concrete to hate him for, he started having an affair.

She was a schoolteacher who came to their beach home three days a week to give tuitions to Indira. As his cousin Manik would say, she had a figure that would make a Bishop throw stones at stained glass windows. She wore her sari delectably below the navel, and for Raj she became the perfect foil for his tortured fantasies.

The emptiness after their intercourse brought back Aparajita's scent, her smile. It was a guilt-free liaison that provided a much-needed respite to Raj even though he realized he was sinking into complications that would one day come back to bite him. Every time he made love to Aparajita in his fantasies he was guilty for their one night of indiscretion when she had said – infidelity is in the mind.

Every time he loved his wife, he was guilty for not being true to his self. With the schoolteacher there was neither. Raj discovered the under-rated joys of a purely lustful relationship and all was fine for a while.

But soon, when the schoolteacher realized that Raj was not inclined to accord any permanence to their relationship, she started dropping little clues for Kiran to find. Scented handkerchiefs in his drawer, love bites that would not go away, coy smiles, bold references to 'him'. Indira, by this time, was old enough to realize that it was expedient and politically advantageous to create a potential situation of warring parents. A rift between her parents became her first exercise in a prospective political career.

Raj worried about his daughter's malevolence. That Indira was not normal, he had always known She was of a sweetness that was vile. She was loyal to him like a cancer. Yet he could never consider her evil. Her greed was too honest, her duplicity too obvious. There was a spiritual angst in her beastliness, she too was searching, just like him.

Kiran, for several years, chose dignity as a political choice. But each un-confronted year stretched her poise to a point of no return. Finally, when she chanced upon the schoolteacher's cheap underwear under her pillow, years of resentment found its breach.

'How could you?' she wept at Raj, beyond humiliation, beyond insult. 'Have you no shame?'

'I am sorry.' But Raj knew his apology was to Aparajita and not Kiran. And knowing that made him beyond redemption.

For years, their household became a living hell. But strangely, Raj found relief in that hell. At least that hell was something, it was not a nothing. He would never know whether it was relief or a reaction to that relief that drove him to drink, but relief had something definite to do with his alcoholism.

The brain-numbing deadness brought him closer to her, to the nothingness which was her, to the nothingness of time which was also her. To death and decay which was not her, but at least he could hold on to something that was not her. It was relief against the knowledge that he had created only bad things around himself. Anger, bitterness and hatred, and somewhere she was responsible and somewhere he had failed her, because she would have expected beauty and goodness and truth, or would she? Oh fuck it, I need a whisky.

'At least wait for the sun to set,' Kiran said so quietly it could have been a scream.

'The sun has set in Tokyo,' Raj laughed, heading for his bar.

The years fell over Raj in layers, like blankets, and he sensed the darkness gather around him. And if that darkness had a physical manifestation he would say it was his daughter Indira. Something about her frightened him. It was as if she knew; had always known. It was as if she had seen their indiscretion, as if her spirit had watched them across the landing when Aparajita and Raj had first met, and she was punishing them for it.

When Aparajita had first seen Indira the thought that came to her mind was Lucifer, or Icarus, and she did not know why. God's fallen angel.

Tiny seven-year-old Indira had rung her doorbell. It was one of those rare years when both Aparajita and Raj were in the same co-ordinates of space and time, in the apartment building.

Aparajita was in between tenants, and was staying over in the building for a week to finish the repainting of the flat before returning to Delhi. Raj had dropped in with his family and was staying in Manik's flat. Though both had a heightened sensation of physical longing at the proximity of the other, neither was really sure that the other was so close at hand. It was just a hint of suspicion, a feeling, a persistent catch in the throat, a lingering scent in the air.

When Aparajita looked down at the young child she immediately knew that Raj was in his Calcutta apartment and that this was his daughter. Her heart stopped and her knees started to buckle. Tenderness overwhelmed her. She cupped Indira's pugnacious chin in her hand and asked her, 'Are you lost, child?'

Indira belted out a high-pitched screech revealing a gap tooth like an unfathomable abyss and snatched her chin away. Indira's ayah finally huffed up the landing panting and out of breath: 'Ah there you are, you devil child,' the portly Christian ayah said. And in spite of her deep abdominal breathing was unable to stabilize her wobbling stomach.

'I'm so sorry, memsahib,' she said, her portly midriff making strange movements against the constraints of the ankle-length skirt she wore. 'I've been running after this child up and down the building. She's been ringing every doorbell, creating such nuisance. I'm so sorry, madam.'

And to the entirely unrepentant Indira she begged, 'Come on downstairs, Missy baba. Your mother is waiting with your lunch. Stop bothering this good lady here. It is such bad manners.'

Aparajita, still shocked by the unexpectedness of the morning could not reply. So when Indira, now docilely holding her ayah's hand, swivelled her head to train a hostile pair of eyes at Aparajita, she was beyond reaction: 'You stay away from my father, you evil witch.'

Aparajita gasped and a hand flew to her throat.

The ayah gave the child a shake and clapped a hand on the child's mouth. 'Shush, child. Don't speak like that.'

And to pacify Aparajita she said what she had said to every other neighbour in the apartment building, 'Please, memsahib, don't mind it, the child has said this to every woman who has answered the door. She is a bit traumatized, you see.' And with a conspiratorial wink she said from the side of her mouth, 'Her father is having an affair.'

Aparajita did not know how long she had been standing at the door like a marble statue, before the ayah grinned: 'Have you seen the movie *The Exorcist*, madam?'

She did not wait for her dazed listener to respond.

'If you ever saw the movie, you would know that this child is Linda Blair.'

That was the moment Aparajita decided to give in to her husband's insistence that they move to Delhi.

Laying in his hospital bed, Raj knew it was Indira who had called forth the forces of the dark, of fear and evil and mendacity, and would not rest till their love was stamped out.

And he felt fear because even though he was now so weak that he would have gladly obliged, he knew their love could not be obliterated. Their love was Anne Frank, their love was a galaxy or seaweed.

It just refused to die.

27.

Kamini lunged out of the car and stood in the rain right in the middle of the busy Chowringhee Street that had suddenly cleared out because of the downpour.

She stood at the road divider, her shoulders bunched, her hair, her eyelashes, her eyebrows dripping, staring back at a Nandi bull who, unmindful of the rain, continued to chew on the shreds of a Bollywood poster and regard her with keen interest.

Hari, sitting in the driver's seat of the hotel's white Tata Indica with its yellow licence plate, looked very worried. Maybe I didn't handle this right, he bit his nails. Maybe one of the women should have told her.

Karmic peg? Kamini fumed, incredulous. *Karmic peg?* How dare they!

She whirled around, and marched up to his dripping window. Before she could bang on it, he had opened the door and was standing next to her.

Squinting through all the water gushing down she was grateful that at least he couldn't see she was crying.

'All this while my father was dying in an obscure hospital in Calcutta and you *knew*?' She shook her head at the impossibility of such a betrayal, 'And you did not *tell* me?'

'It's not us. It's your family that didn't tell you.' He tried to keep his tone even. Rain was beginning to bead up on his face. Fluid energy making its own patterns, she couldn't help thinking, in a detached-witness kind of way.

That's when she broke. Because what he said was true. And also because he knew what a pathetic life she had. Had always known. How he must pity her.

'Thank you, Hari, for reminding me how dysfunctional my life is. This is such a good time.' She was surprised at how normal she sounded considering the circumstances. She paused, and remembered, 'All along my dad was discussed as a subject. He was XY. You knew. All of you knew.'

Hari did not reply. She sank deeper into her own humiliation remembering the treachery of the past few weeks.

He opened his mouth to say, 'We needed time to prepare you,' but only reached halfway, because she had raised her finger to stop him.

'Don't.'

And because no words came out after that she turned to run away from him and he caught her. And in their struggle she did not know whether she was breaking apart or being put together. All that she did know was that she did all the moving and he was totally immobile. Till she came to be at peace and wept out her life on his already wet shirtfront, while it continued to rain the rain of the Great Deluge and the bull finished the last of the Bollywood poster in the washed-out street where Calcutta watched them from under shop awnings.

Later, in the pristine green and white décor of the Grand Hotel, swathed in soft hotel sheets with a hot mug of chocolate cradled in her hands she sneezed twenty-one times while the team watched her anxiously.

When the last of her sneezes was wrapped up and disposed off in the elegantly understated hotel dustbin, Mira said, 'That should make you feel much better.'

'It does, actually,' Kamini said, even though her nose had immediately clogged up again, and her body felt hot and cold at the same time; she felt light-headed, giggly even.

'We've been giving you healing energies ever since the flight took off. We've been preparing you for this. You will feel good in no time,' Rita said.

'That's an understatement, Rita style,' Hari said, his hair towelled dry but still uncombed. He poured himself a cup from the coffee machine.

'There is a team of healers in VNP whose job description is to give healing energies to karmic pegs. They have been working on us ever since the project began.'

There was silence as everybody stared at him.

'That's how organized VNP is,' Hari shrugged lamely.

'That's pretty inhuman, if you ask me,' Kamini said not looking at anybody, taking a sip of her chocolate.

'That's a compliment, by VNP standards,' Hari smiled at her, for the first time allowing the warmth he felt towards her to show. He was pleased to see the effect it had on her.

'I did not know of your relationship with Raj, if it's any consolation,' Carlos offered. 'All I was told was that Kamini is the karmic peg and needed nurturing.'

'I didn't even know what a karmic peg was,' Ali said, feeling free enough now to put an arm around Kamini's shoulder. 'Actually, I still don't know what a karmic peg is.'

'What the hell *is* a karmic peg?' Kamini finally demanded.

With a cup of coffee in his hand Hari leaned against the bureau and faced Kamini. 'Looks like it's my turn to make a presentation,' he smiled.

Why did I never notice his smile before, Kamini thought. It's lovely.

'As we all know XX and XY are Raj and Aparajita. We shall stop addressing them as subjects now. This is also a good time for all of us to get a little more perspective on the project.'

His audience, sensing this to be an important speech, gathered around him in careful attention.

'We have been talking about Twin Flames and Twin Flame management. We have delved into the natures and dimensions of subtler and more refined universal energies. What we also need to remember – and it is not as if the televisions and newspapers are not successfully reminding us every day – is that we are at the dawn of a new era. A new era called 2012.

'2012 does not really have to start at 2012. Actually, it has already begun. It is under way. Mythologies and all great books have spoken about it since time immemorial.'

Hari took a moment for a sip of coffee and his captive audience broke free:

'The apocalypse!'

'The great deluge!'

'Pralaya in Hindu mythology!'

'The Mayan Predictions!'

Carlos straightened his back and crossed his legs in the lotus posture. 'There is a galactic shift taking place out there, we all know that. The solar storms and realignment of cosmic currents have changed the energy matrix of the planet. The Ice Age is going to finish. The polar axis is already changing.'

'Polar axis?' Kamini frowned.

Hari let out a deep sigh. 'Yes, friends, the polar axis is the fulcrum on which our mythologies hang. Bear with me a minute, while I confuse you with a little more information. Let me mention here, Atlantis, Lemuria, Mu, Egypt, the ancient civilizations.'

Kamini scowled at him. 'Haven't you addled my brain enough?'

He ignored her. And with that their relationship slid back into its old groove.

'Archaeologists have found dolphin bones in the Himalayas and evidence of flourishing civilizations in Antarctica. The engineering feats required to create the Egyptian pyramids could not have taken place in known conditions. The VNP explanation to this is the polar axis, and whenever I think of the polar axis I think of the "cup that brimmeth over".'

'Ah,' Carlos opened his eyes from his meditative pose. 'Interesting take on the cup. Maybe that's what it means.'

'Who knows?' Hari shrugged.

'Cup that brimmeth over? Could you enlightened ones please expound?' Ali was as irritated as Kamini.

'The theory is that the 33 degree angle of the earth's axis changes with every calibrated time change of an era. The earth wobbles a bit on its pole and flips over to the other side.'

'And the cup brimmeth over,' Carlos raised his hand like an Indian classical musician.

'You see,' Hari, too, took to gesturing with his hands. 'The end of each era, or yug, or aeon, ends with each Ice Age. When the earth wobbles to the other side, the ice caps move closer to the sun. Hot and cold, Yang and Yin, resulting in a lot of water, and a lot of energy fireworks. Upsurges of negative energies, wars, pestilence, disease, famine –'

'Do not forget the leitmotif here: floods, deluge,' Rita reminded him, filing her scarlet toenails.

'Water is an energy cleanser, a purge, especially salt water, seawater. We use a lot of that in our healing protocols,' Hari said.

'I can't imagine you as a healer,' Kamini shook her head.

'Believe it, baby,' he said curtly, trying not to show that he had already melted under her admiring gaze.

'Now they say that from the tip of India to Madagascar in Africa and further on till Australia, existed a landmass, an ancient civilization that became submerged in the great deluges marking the end of an epoch.'

'What does all of this have to do with Raj and Aparajita?' Ali looked up irritatedly from his PS3.

'Down, boy,' Hari said grinning and to make it harder, 'Heel. I'm coming to that.'

'Whatever,' Ali said. 'I just scored a 3000.'

'The New Age that is upon us,' Hari became suddenly very solemn, 'is characterized by higher vibrational frequencies. As they were in ancient times, before the dark ages of Kali Yug, which lasted many thousands and thousands of years.'

'Yaay!' Ali squealed, leaving Hari confused about whether his scream of triumph was because of the dawn of a new era or because he had beat his own score.

'A sweeping spiritual revolution has been augured. One that will change each and every aspect of our civilization, raising it to the subtler energies of higher dimensions.' Hari felt a strange elation, a release, even as he spoke.

'This New Age will obviously require a huge amount of energy restructuring to remove gigantic proportions of old negative patterns. That is why the meeting of Twin Flames has been speeded up. A lot of these Twin Flames, created during ancient civilizations, when souls split into two opposite charges, are meeting after maybe a million lifetimes. So one can expect a lot of fireworks in their reunion.'

'Drama, emotion, tears, action,' Ali nodded solemnly.

'A lot of hugging, and a helluva lot of explaining to do,' Rita added, moving on to the next nail.

'Maybe with a couple of villains thrown in,' Ali said, then sheepishly added, 'Sorry about that. I am, after all, the son of a movie star.'

'Never quite the same without a villain, is it?' Rita's concentration was an unbroken stream of consciousness.

'Should we expect a chase to the airport too?' Mira asked, worried. 'I've had enough speeding cars for one project.'

'Villain,' Kamini snapped her fingers, a sudden gleam in her eye. 'Green Lyon – the black man.'

Hari looked at her with immeasurable fondness as the flesh on her arms rose. 'Can I gently, but firmly, steer you back to my presentation?' he said. 'I promise to come back to the black man. He's lurking around here, by the way. Most of us started feeling his presence even before we landed.'

Before Kamini could respond, Hari had returned to what he was saying:

'We need no reminder of the upsurge of negative energy patterns in the last two years. The economic recessions, the market collapses, terrorism, the floods, climate change, the new mutant diseases, the impending war between China and India, the earthquake in Japan, you name it, we got it. The earth is struggling to raise the frequencies of the planet. And for this to fruitfully and painlessly occur, Twin Flame reunions around the world are imperative. The energy released by their reunion has such powerful local effects, collectively and energetically, that the clairvoyants can see Twin

Flame reunions as a network of lights in the earth's aura body. By itself, it can release enough primary energy to raise the threshold frequency by fifty per cent.'

'So love really does save the world,' Kamini concluded.

'Look at it this way, however painful the story of your life may have been, you have a father who, even though he is lying semi-conscious in some Calcutta hospital, is on his way to save the world.'

Kamini turned to Hari. 'I have a feeling you will be talking about karmic pegs next.'

'And right you will be. Like most everything in life, Twin Flame reunions, too, are karmic till they reach the threshold of pure consciousness, when the laws of the universe take over. The VNP Twin Flame project may sound like manual engineering to you but somewhere that is a fact and a falsehood because,' Hari paused dramatically, 'it is also a grand plan of the universe.'

Making sure his point had registered, he continued, 'Somewhere and sometime, when Raj and Aparajita were pure consciousness they had an agreement to descend and learn and experience life's mysteries before returning to each other. But because they were to move so far away and would have collected so many layers and identifications that would obscure their recognizing and meeting the other, they needed karmic situations to catalyse the highly unstable, excitable and therefore explosive process.

'The Twin Flame team is the catalysing and stabilizing ingredient in their union, much like the white dove in Ali's alchemical process. We are the crystal, manifesting and directing their love as they orbit closer to each other. But even a crystal has a seed. You are that seed. You are the black hole into which the earth collapses. You are the root that draws down their karmas to a point in our midst so we can do what we have to do.'

'Aha!' Kamini's smile was twisted. 'I am the bait. I remember my dad's tiger hunts.' And her throat became heavy, her eyes filled with tears. 'They tied a goat to a stake. And everybody waited in the tree machan for the tiger to show up. So taking the analogy further, you guys are the hunters in the machan, my dad and his paramour are the fucking tigers, and yours truly is the goat.'

The room silenced, allowing her space and time for anger. The silence gave permission:

'You know my family broke up because my fucking father was having a fucking affair. After all these years, I was just beginning to forgive him, thinking of it as a moment of weakness, a human foible. Now you tell me that it wasn't even a human weakness, it's a fucking beautiful cosmic opera that is going to fucking save the world. And I am supposed to fucking make it happen. So basically the definition of a karmic peg in this project' – at this point her throat was completely choked – 'is the daughter, whose life became a living hell because her father had an affair, and who must now reunite her father with his cosmic fuck-buddy. Fuck you, fuck you all!'

Kamini got up from her bed in her outsized white hotel dressing-gown. All eyes were downcast, but mostly because an entire breast was showing through the gap in her dressing-gown. Grabbing tissue and spitefully jamming it up her nose she turned to gesticulate to her seemingly penitent audience: 'My dad could have at least had the courtesy to have an affair with the person we thought he had an affair with. But no, he couldn't even do *that*!'

And with that she whirled and, blowing her nose into the tissue, tried to make what she thought was a dramatic exit to the bathroom.

But Hari caught her and holding her shoulders turned her around to present her to the team, like a fait accompli. 'Whoa,' he said gently.

Kamini was suddenly very conscious of his hands on her shoulders and became quiet, even demure.

'We would love to join your pity party, but you see, darling, we don't have the time.' He pushed her gently, sitting her down on the edge of the bed. 'So blow your nose and get over it, fast.'

Hari had taken on a different demeanour. His eyes were boring holes into her. She may even have obeyed him and blown her nose had he not stepped back from her.

'You are not the only karmic peg, love. There are at least two more. One in this team; one more on site.'

'What?' Kamini was going back into the now familiar feeling of total confusion. '*More* karmic pegs?'

'You are the karmic peg for the harnessing of white – that is positive – energies. And the more positive energies we harness, the more negative karmas it manifests because positives also attract negatives. The other karmic peg is the black energy generator. Remember the black man?'

'Yes,' Kamini was interested, curious.

'He is a very complicated manifestation of the other

karmic peg, the centrifugal force of the Twin Flame circle. And that karmic peg is…'

'Is?' Kamini raised her eyebrow.

'Your sister, Indira.'

Kamini exhaled. 'Why am I not surprised?'

'If it's any consolation, I too am a karmic peg. A secondary one, though.'

'Really?' Kamini's eyebrows shot through her hairline. She looked around. 'The more the merrier, I guess. Anybody else?'

'Well, yes, actually.' Hari's smile was secret. 'One more. The strongest manifestation of the black man. My brother.'

'Who is?' Kamini quirked an eyebrow.

'Married to your sister.'

'Excuse me?' Her response was involuntary.

Hari took a moment to respond. 'Remember that Delhi guy she married a year ago? You and your mother weren't invited to the wedding? Well, neither was I. My brother is a master practitioner of the black arts. I guess you could say we have a conflict of interest.'

'So the two of us are the sidekicks of this plot?'

'You could say that.'

'Always the bridesmaid, never the bride. Welcome to the club.'

Crossing his arms, Hari smiled, 'Maybe, but I would like to believe that this sidekick gets the girl.'

Kamini blushed to the roots of her hair. 'Would somebody please get me glass of water?'

'Sure,' Hari said. 'But be quick. You have to make a phone call.'

'To whom?' Her eyes widened.

'Your cousin, Uma.'

28.

Aparajita believed that she had never conceived again because she had sinned. Guilt had locked up her womb, making her recoil at her husband's touch. She was being punished, and justifiably so. She was a fallen woman and the impersonal antagonism of Delhi, the city her husband had chosen to inhabit, remained a constant reminder of her immoral status.

No amount of fasting had helped. There was a Monday fast and a Friday fast. No number of incantations to Goddess Kali and Durga appeased the angry pantheon either.

The worst punishment was that she had continued to wait for Raj, in that pathetic hangdog way she had begun to hate about herself. Her sexual escapades didn't lessen with age as she had hoped and expected they would. They just became worse. She saw the waning of her husband's libido and all the menopausal women around her. But the continuation of her unabashedly carnal longing for Raj, his touch, his hair, his teeth, his navel, his sound, his smell, slowly drove her to the point of insanity that doctors could only confidently point out as being the first stage of Alzheimer's. She understood that the extreme forces that attracted them were the same extreme forces that kept them apart. And there was nothing she could do about it.

Over the years, months, weeks, hours she had sensed her mind strain against her desire for Raj like a stretching elastic band. And later, though she lost most of her memories, she had one very clear one of the moment when her mind snapped. She had been helping her maid wash the dishes after the party in celebration of her husband's appointment to a prestigious Supreme Court panel.

As she bent over the soapsuds, the detergent corroding her hands, her brain had started concentrating in an unearthly focus on the slickness of detergent in the fine hairs of her wrist and she felt something disengage from the secret-most part of her being. Almost in response, the handle of the delicate china cup she was washing broke, as if to manifest the snapping sound that had emanated from the deepest of her depths.

What totally bewildered her was that even as she could see the endless shores that bordered her grief of separation, she was lauded for being the perfect wife, the perfect mother, the perfect daughter-in-law, and very soon, hopefully, if her fasting for her son Gaurav bore fruit, even the perfect grandmother.

She had pasted all these labels on herself like the medals of a war hero and yet did not feel they were penitence enough.

So she had worked harder. She had worried about her husband's cholesterol a little more, had visited obscure homeopathic clinics to prevent Gaurav's hair loss, had neatly wrapped gifts with personal handwritten notes for her daughter-in-law's first visit home to her mother.

When Rudra was born, she realized she had seen his face in her dreams even before he had been conceived. When he stared back at her in the receiving blanket – a blanket that had taken her a month to embroider – she had felt blinded by the light trapped in his eyes. There was wisdom in his eyes, there was knowledge. Oh my God, she had gasped, *He knows!*

And grasping him to her chest she had sat down on a white wooden bench, in the lavender-scented private hospital corridor, clutching the newborn life to her barren heart. Seated there, she had released her hold on the lost decades of no Raj, of the unbearable emptiness that had refused to fill up with her good deeds and repentance, of the impossible longing that had cursed her and blessed her in spiralling movements till there was nothing left inside. She wondered where all those tears were coming from, because she thought that she had stopped existing. *I am crying because this infant is reminding me that I actually have existed, and will continue to do so. That this waiting* is *existence.* You are waiting for something. If that something was not there, you wouldn't be waiting.

A salty drop had fallen from her eyes onto the baby's cheek and even as she wiped it away, the hardness of her thumb encountering the softness of his skin, she understood what he was trying to tell her. *I have come to tell you that you have not waited in vain.*

Later, Aparajita would remember this moment on the bench in the lavender-scented corridor, when she first looked into Rudra's eyes, as the beginning of their conversations.

When she lost most of her memories, when her husband took her home to Calcutta, these conversations were the only ones that stayed with her.

You know, in all this, in this time in the physical universe as I rock you to sleep even as your mother snores, taking perfect advantage of an accommodating mother-in-law, I do not know whether I dreamt him up, whether he is a figment of my imagination. For all you know, if we crossed each other in the street, he would not even remember my name. I would have to remind him that many decades ago he came to my flat to get his astrological chart read, and he would try politely to place me, vaguely remember and say oh! of course I remember, how have you been? And I would not know whether he is still playing games with me or whether he actually does not remember.

Rudra's month-old eyes closed. His small pink mouth opened in a delicate yawn and she heard him say:

You know that is not true. You had bumped into him many years ago at a puja pandal in Calcutta. He was with his entire family and you with yours. My dad was all grown up, a gangly teenager and Raj's girls still so young, so innocent of the clandestine universe Raj carried within him. The two of you were with your respective spouses, maybe that's why you stopped dead in your tracks, spontaneously, at the same moment. There was so much frozen terror in your face that Raj suddenly felt that he was standing on one leg on the spoke that balanced the planet.

Rudra's smile widened in a big toothless grin, and Aparajita laughed out loud at the memory...

'Hello, Mr Ghosh,' Raj had stumbled a bit before extending his hand to Aparajita's husband. 'Shubho Durgo Pujo.'

Though their meeting was brief she had always somehow known that Raj was not comfortable with different dialects. And like an indulgent wife she had found that endearing about him.

'Shubho Durgo Pujo, Mr Singh-Deo,' her husband had said, taking his proffered hand with much warmth. And with that out of the way and nothing else to share besides the fact that they knew each other vaguely as building neighbours, there was a silence uncomfortable enough to start ripping Raj and Aparajita to shreds.

Their children were distracted by the stalls, pulling their parents' hands with an insistence that was oblivious to a world outside their interest.

'I don't think you've met my wife,' Raj quickly offered and Kiran folded her hands in a namaste. She looked so pure in her status as Raj's wife to Aparajita that she felt like a soiled piece of goods beside her.

'And this is my wife, Aparajita.' Mr Ghosh presented his wife like a trophy and Aparajita too folded her hands and felt that the universe was giving her an opportunity to apologize for the utter mess she had created, but she was rendered incapable of looking at anybody.

Indira had turned her second hostile glare on Aparajita and tugged at Raj's pants. 'Papa,' she used the nasal whine that worked best with her father. 'I want that,' she said, pointing at an ice-cream cart.

And just like that, like the ocean from the shore, the two families moved away from each other. Their eyes met only once, very briefly, and the force of it stunned them both into an immobility that made them say after a while to their families, 'You move on. I'll catch up later.'

Across the grassy field of teeming worshippers with the elaborate idol of Durga between them, when Aparajita rose from her plastic chair, she saw Raj on the far side, sitting on a kerb, his head in his hands. And that was the first and only proof she got that they were true. *This* was true. She was not crazy. They were truly the ones for the other. She thanked Goddess Durga for indulging her with the little bit of confirmation she needed.

And at that precise moment, Raj raised his head and looked at her from across the expanse of humanity between them and both had wistfully smiled. And it had felt as if the vast field were empty. There was nobody there except them, and there was no sound except the other's breath, and the humming of the stars in the black sky overhead, and Ma Durga's large watchful eyes.

And Rudra told her as she fed him his first cereal and took his first baby steps towards her that Aparajita and Raj had met to fulfil their intense desire for union with God.

But why the pain, the anguish? It's so unfair. She tickled him and he squealed, his face lighting up with joy.

The pain happens because you are not ready. But every time you experience it you free yourself from it. Remember, he said, clutching her index finger in his puny little hand, *you are attaining freedom, not from love but towards love.*

True love is true renunciation, he said.

Love is the primordial substance of the universe, he said.

You realize it's true love when you sacrifice it, he said.

We are just souls using our bodies to gain knowledge, he said.

The sun is not the centre of the solar system, the heart is, he said.

The key is time, he said. *Use your will to focus past, present and future into the centre of the moment and vibrate your concentration to the frequency of the sound of the universe and the lock opens.*

When Rudra was four and still not talking, panic broke out in their little household. Aparajita begged him to speak but all her cajoling, threats, tears and frustration did not work. And somewhere she knew she was responsible. She had done this to him. She shook Rudra's puny little shoulders. 'You can't do this to me. I forbid you to.'

And Gaurav's mother ran up to them to snatch her son away from her demented mother-in-law's anger.

'There is something wrong somewhere,' Rudra's mother told Gaurav behind the closed bedroom door that night when Rudra was safely asleep in the middle of their bed.

'What do you mean?' Gaurav peeled off his socks and asked in that resigned way husbands have when they know they are headed for an argument.

'You know,' she said, rubbing cream on her hands as casually as she could.'With total respect to your mother, I think she is responsible somewhere for Rudra not talking.'

'And how is that?' Gaurav asked, running a tired hand over a head that had gone bald despite his mother's best efforts.

'It's just a feeling. I can't explain it. It's as if she has pulled him into her own weird unreal world.'

He looked at her in gentle reproach. 'And a child as young as that has the capacity and understanding to get drawn into it?'

'I don't know,' she said, wringing her hands.'Rudra is different.You know that.And I've read up so much on child development. It's amazing how little research there is on the subject.'

Rudra's deliberate silence showed his complete reluctance to dwell on the topic. His wife and he had beaten down the topic of child development so many times between them that the subject was dead for him. He didn't want to go there anymore. It was a swamp.

'And your mother is strange.You know that.'

He slipped between the covers and closed his eyes. 'You know, in another time and place the daughter-in-law would have been accused of producing a child that was mentally challenged. Lucky for you we live in times that immediately think of the mother-in-law as the first culprit,' he said. He felt an explosion of resentment beside him and, fearing that the fight that would ensue would wake up Rudra, he turned his back to her and pretended to sleep.

But with her ear to their door, Aparajita who had been passing by, had heard their conversation and agreed with her daughter-in-law. *The child is carrying my cross. The gods have sent him to purge my sins.*

Gaurav had spoken to the principal before the tense drive to Rudra's first day at play school. It was fine, the principal had reassured him – more so, Gaurav suspected, because he was the CEO of Msoft – for your son to attend play school. Many children are late talkers.

Only conquering suffering can get you freedom, little Rudra had said, as his father had led him away.

He had turned and waved to Aparajita so bravely that she had burst into tears. And Rudra took his first unsure steps into the uncertain world of muteness.

No such thing, Rudra said to her when he came home.

No such thing as what?

No such thing as good and evil.

Then what else is there?

A question.

What question?

Are you using your power to create harmony or chaos in the universe?

Harmony. Trying to, at least.

Then you are not evil. You are good.

Rudra's speech therapist was a middle-aged woman who squinted behind thick spectacles and had deep frown lines. Her office was a sunless room where no hope filtered through. One dirty purple Barney soft toy was the only pretension she had of being child-friendly. Cramped between her desk and window was a wooden high chair with leather straps.

'This child is severely autistic,' she told Rudra's parents and grandparents. 'I will not permit any questions regarding my methods. The attendant is to wait in the lobby till summoned. At no cost must I be disturbed during session.'

She had come very highly recommended.

Even though Aparajita sat in the furthest corner of the lobby, which smelt of mouldy leather, she could not stop hearing Rudra's cries escaping up the hall. After every session he would come out blank-faced, tear streaks down his cheeks the only evidence of what might have happened. Before Aparajita could open her mouth to ask a question, the therapist would turn and leave.

'That woman is a ghoul,' Aparajita said, wondering why there was no anger in her words.

And Rudra turned towards her in the car and looked deep within her soul:

Your extreme desire and extreme resistance to that desire has created a lifetime of suffering. Experience your desire, find its bottom and you will find freedom.

That did it. She turned to him and smiled: *You've finally gotten through.*

After that day she became still. She continued becoming more and more still as the days passed and her illness progressed. *Experiencing the experience destroys it. Shiva is the experience. Shiva is the destroyer. Rudra is the destroyer. Shiva is Rudra.*

Slowly, the veils of her mind fell, one by one, till finally her mind gave way and she started walking towards the hum that had been increasing in pitch over the last few years. That was when she was consigned to the wheelchair. And yet she walked naked to the sun surrounded by blinding light.

Rudra smiled.

Speak, she said.

Not yet, he said. *It's not yet time.*

Aparajita's dreams of Raj became more and more lucid as her illness progressed; their lovemaking more and more real. And yet it felt as if they were getting smudged out in light, their differences dissolving.

They met at twilight in strange settings. In the courtyard of a palace; in balconies overhanging weathered wooden jharokhas; and stone lions watched over them as they embraced. Sometimes she would see shadows around them, people flitting by, whom she did not recognize. Sacred Fibonacci numbers haunted her and ancient symbols she could not decipher.

Where are we, Raj? she asked many times.

This is where I belong. There was no emotion there. It was a statement of fact. *This is where it is going to happen,* he said.

What?

But then their connection broke – like a satellite link. He disappeared into his light, she into hers. And try as she might she could never meet him after that. Could not feel his arms around her, feel his breath against her neck. She could not kiss him anymore. And he did not answer when she called. She could not summon him at will, push her magic button, hold him whenever she wanted. The genie was no longer in the lamp.

She was really alone.

Oh well, she thought. *This is as good a time as any to die.*

That night, after dinner, when she returned her husband's overly considerate questions with a glazed stare, Gaurav saw his father lose his cool for the first time.

'Why are you punishing me?' he shouted. 'However much I try, why do you always escape my grasp?'

'Easy, Baba,' Gaurav said. 'It's the illness.'

'Bloody hell, illness!' Spittle gathered around his father's mouth. 'She is doing this on purpose. She has never given a thought to anybody but herself.'

'Baba!' Gaurav warned. 'How can you say that? She gave her life to us.'

'You don't know anything about your mother. She is the most selfish person I know. She does exactly what she wants.'

That's when he saw his father break down like never before. 'And her love has never included me,' he wept a sea of tears. 'It has *never* included me.'

29.

Kamini was about to press the green button of the Nokia that would connect her to Uma when she remembered. 'What about Rudra?' she asked.

'Interesting that you ask,' Hari smiled. 'Gaurav brought him here yesterday to visit his grandmother. Totally unrelated to the project.'

From the group hovering around her emanated a voice, 'But she's smart enough to know that –'

'–there is no such thing as a coincidence.' Kamini finished, grinning. 'So, somewhere, VNP engineered this?'

'Only by intention,' Hari loomed over her. 'Now can we please call your cousin?'

'But what I want to know,' she stalled, 'is whether Rudra is the other karmic peg. He has to be, since he is Aparajita's grandson. Strange, how I always felt related to him. His big staring eyes. Oh my God, he always knew!'

'A karmic peg,' Hari looked down at her 'has a localizing effect. You, your sister, my brother, your cousin Uma, are karmic pegs varying in intensity and degree. Rudra is a herald. He cleans what you guys localize. Like the detergent Ariel.'

'That's interesting,' Mira smiled her wondrous little girl smile. 'Ariel is also the name of an angel.'

'Rudra is the one who has brought both of them to this point. Without his catalytic effect VNP would not have been able to even manifest the project, leave alone bring us where we are.'

'And you? What are you?'

Taking a deep bow, Hari said, 'I am the conductor of the symphony.' Then he glared at her: 'Quit stalling. Make the call.'

Kamini put the mobile on speakerphone. The sound of the ring tone pierced the hushed silence.

'Hello?' Uma said, warily. It was an unsaved number for her; *probably Raheja Estates,* she thought.

'Hi Uma, this is Kamini.'

For a moment her words hung over two worlds and then the worlds coalesced.

'Oh my God, Kamini,' Uma whispered loudly, moving out of the double doors. 'Where *are* you?'

'Here in Kolkata,' Kamini felt strangely calm, in control.

'Who told you about your dad?' Uma exclaimed.

'Never mind that,' Kamini said hurriedly.

'Not Indira, for sure,' Uma felt guilty indulging in family gossip but couldn't stop.

'Regarding that' – remembering her agenda, Kamini's voice took on an insistent tone – 'do not at any cost let her know that I have called.' But Kamini's own voice echoed back at her, distorted, like an evil man's conjuring trick and the communication broke.

Ping! went the phone. Everybody knew Uma hadn't heard a word that had been said.

'Why did *that* happen?' Kamini asked Hari, as if he was supposed to answer every question.

And it seemed he did know the answer. 'What did you think? It would be that easy? The universe moves towards entropy. And entropy just hit back.'

'Bit you in the ass,' Mira said. And when they all turned to the cursing, knitting grandmother lady, she said defensively, 'To be more precise!'

☯

'Who was that?' Indira asked Uma.

'Your sister, Kamini,' Uma replied.

And there was silence for a few minutes.

'This bullshit has gone on long enough,' Indira whirled around abruptly. 'I'm taking my dad out of here.'

As Indira sped back into the ICU Uma's phone rang again and she snapped it up.

Without preliminaries, Kamini said, 'At no cost must you tell my sister that I am in Kolkata.'

'Already done that,' Uma replied, very apologetic; even though she did not know what was going on, she trusted Kamini completely. Always had. 'Even though I don't know what is going on,' Uma said, 'I trust you completely. Always have.'

'Okay,' Kamini said. 'Listen to me very carefully. Indira is going to try everything not to get Dad back to Vishnupur. Do not at any point let her succeed. She wants him to stay in the hospital. He will die there. She wants him to die. The material cause of that is his vast property but there are other reasons as well.'

'Material cause? Okay, fine. I'm not asking any questions.'

'Don't,' Kamini warmed to her cousin the way she always had. There were so many questions she needed to ask her. How was her husband? How old was Vir? Had she put on weight? Had she lost her sense of humour? 'I don't know how you are going to do this, Uma, but there are three important things we need you to do.'

'We?'

'Never mind.'

'Okay, never minded.'

Kamini laughed, and a little bit of the hysteria showed. At this point Hari could not stop taking her in his arms as she cradled the phone in her hands. She tried not to let her cousin know that she had started to cry. 'One, without Indira's knowledge, you've somehow got to get Dad to Vishnupur.'

'Oh my God, how am I going to do that?'

'Second is the ring. You've still got it, right?'

'How do you know about the ring?' Uma was incredulous.

'You've still got it, right?'

'Yes, I have.'

'Oh, thank God,' all the eavesdroppers said in chorus.

'God seems to be taking a very active part,' Hari said through Kamini's hair. 'It's a good sign.'

'You've got to place it in Aparajita's hands.'

'Aparajita?'

'The Chowringhee neighbour upstairs.'

'Ah!' Uma said, 'I *knew* there was something to her.'

'Third is,' Kamini was now sighing with relief that she had got all that across without a break in communication.

'Third is?' Uma asked, squaring her shoulders.

'Meet me somewhere fast. I owe you a huge explanation.'

'But, child, why are you moving your father to a nursing home? And that too without consulting with the rest of the family? His condition is still very critical.'

As Manik tried to reason with Indira he felt dizzy and disoriented, as if he could not decide what to think or say. Not surprising, the observer in him watched his own confusion, my cousin has led such a strange life; it's difficult to wrap one's head around it. But standing across the billing counter in the lobby of the hospital at that moment it felt most expedient to question his cousin's daughter.

Indira was trying her best not to shift from foot to foot and look over her shoulder. 'Haven't you heard? Papa has made remarkable progress in the last twelve hours.' *That interfering minx of an Uma has done something, I am sure of it.* Indira ground her teeth mentally. And now the proverbial stuff had hit the fan. *The only option now is to take him away. If they can't locate him they will not be able to resurrect him.* Though she sensed the presence of powerful light workers who did not need even his location co-ordinates to heal him, to do their work, at least it would give her time. Time to confuse, distract, deploy resources, create enough shields around him to prevent the light from passing.

A medical resident in a white coat with a stethoscope around his neck was listening in and decided to give his opinion on the subject, as all bystanders in the city of Kolkata are wont to do. 'I've heard,' the doctor solemnly butted in, 'he is one for the case-study books. Within twelve hours, all vital signs are stable, fully awake, with only a mild state of altered consciousness. Except for a slight paresis he is in full command of his faculties and is recovering fast. This morning he was creating a ruckus in the hospital' – Indira was digging her hands deep into her pockets in an effort not to wring them –'asking for shammi kebabs and a shot of tequila, would you believe it?'

'Go cousin, go!' Manik applauded.

Indira looked at her uncle in mild disgust. Grey on temple, paunch on belly, yet goading his sixty-year-old cousin like a schoolboy prodding a cheerleader.

'When I came in the nurse was in tears. You know how Dad can rip people verbally to shreds?'

Manik allowed himself a deep sigh. Of late he had known that only too well.

Indira's eyes searched the lobby as if to find the culprit responsible for her dad's miraculous recovery. Somebody was even giving *her* calming energies, a lot of them. And she could tell the healer was a powerful one. Could it be her silly little cousin? No, this was way beyond her measly capacities. This was going totally out of hand. Even her uncle's mind was resisting the thought forms and auto-suggestions she was inflicting on him. She could sense a protective shield around him, defending him against her effect. *Who is doing this?* She recoiled from her uncle sensing her own vibrations bouncing back on her.

'Nothing short of a miracle,' the doctor said again, shaking his head in awe.

'So, finally the temple prasad I was infusing into his IV fluids worked. And God has listened to my prayers,' Indira sounded so morose that had Uma been there she would have laughed outright at her pathetic subterfuge.

'Still, child, you need to reconsider moving him into a nursing home so fast. At least speak to the rest of the family.' Manik was getting genuinely worried at the hastiness of the decision.

'I will,' she replied curtly and turned to the billing counter. 'I've been waiting half-an-hour for the damn bill,' she snapped.

'And I've been trying to tell you, madam, for the last half hour, and you have not been listening, that your bill has been paid.' The accountant's inscrutable face trotted out a glum response.

'Paid?' asked Indira, not understanding.

'Paid.' The accountant looked back at her with total indifference. 'Your patient has been discharged,' he said with sadistic satisfaction, noticing with interest that his comment had caused some dismay.

Indira whirled back to face her uncle who returned her gaze in complete innocence. *They have even started deploying decoys.* Indira was shocked at the realization. This has got to be serious.

'I have to speak to my husband,' she said and started fumbling in her bag for her mobile.

'But he is in Vishnupur. What can he do?' Manik asked.

From the corner of her eye Indira saw an ambulance slowly pull out of the parking lot in front of the hospital entrance. A fleeting glimpse of Uma in the front seat and in a flash she knew what was going on.

'Bitch!' she yelled, speeding out of the entrance. She finished one flight of stairs and banged into Dodo, who stood like a wall in front of her, hands in his trouser pockets, looking at her in that steady implacable way of his she had resented ever since they were children.

'What's the hurry, Indira?' he said, calm, too calm, way too calm, for Indira's comfort.

'Where are you taking my father?' she asked, all at once evenly in control – as if somebody had pulled her lever by remote. Only her white face betrayed a cold hard anger as she sped past him down the final flight of stairs.

'Vishnupur,' Dodo was puzzled, as he ran behind her. 'Didn't you know?'

'What the hell do you mean, "don't you know". Of course, I didn't know,' she gasped, running out of the hospital and edging on to the middle of the driveway, meaning to stop the van at the gate. 'Who decided this?' she demanded.

'Your dad did,' Dodo was right behind her.

'My dad is not in his senses, you crazy people,' she shouted. 'Why wasn't I consulted?' If she could have bared her fangs at him she would have.

'They told me to inform you about it.'

'Then why didn't you, Dodo?' she asked, laying a lot of stress on the last word.

'Didn't I?' He was so casual that she didn't know what to think. All she could do was look at him with pure hatred. He took a step back, as if hit by a dart. 'Oh,' he said. 'I must have forgotten.'

She ran to the gate wildly waving her arms, signalling the ambulance van to stop. Inside the van, Uma was gesturing to her brother to stop Indira. Before the driver could put his foot on the brake pedal, Uma asked him to pick up speed and the foot that was moving towards the right moved left, towards the accelerator. At that precise moment, Dodo placed his arms around Indira's waist from behind her and physically moved her from the front of the moving car.

'Let me go!' Indira let loose all bounds and allowed herself to scream hysterically.

'Shush! Indira, shush.' Dodo resorted to what he believed to be good experience with hysterical women – 'Let's be rational,' and 'You are overwrought,' and 'Your dad is going to be just fine,' were standard-issue statements that came to his lips with facilitated ease.

Indira suddenly calmed down, dried her tears and turned to Dodo. 'Okay, I'm fine now. Just get me a Coke.'

'Are you sure you are fine?'

'I'm sure I'm fine.'

'I'll get you a Coke.'

'Good. Just get me a Coke.'

'Stay right where you are.' Dodo backed away from her gently, as if she was standing on a landmine.

'I'm right here,' Indira said and sat down quietly on the steps of the hospital entrance. As if to prove to him she would not run away screaming with her hair on fire.

'Good,' he said, continuing to back away slowly from her. 'I'll be right back.'

'Good,' she smiled sweetly at him.

He smiled back, relieved, and thinking it safe now turned his back to her to walk towards the cafeteria.

When she was sure he wouldn't look over his shoulder she sent a text message to her husband:

They are headed towards VNP. *This is serious. Kamini with them. Do something. Stop them now!*

The exchange of passengers took place on the outskirts of Kolkata.

A Grand Hotel taxi with a yellow number plate and the ambulance van pulled over to a side of the bypass, where garbage had collected over such a long period of time that it now seemed like a river of compost. To a man, each last one of the hordes of thin swarthy people who walked past the two vehicles, did not fail to peer inside the van, guided by the irrepressible curiosity of the Kolkatan; but they were indifferent too, guided by the intractable Kolkatan angst at the futility of it all.

Raj lay supine in the ambulance, pleasantly relieved to feel his breath moving without labour, and deeply happy to be reunited with his younger daughter, Kamini.

The VNP group hung about in various postures within and without the vehicles, allowing Kamini her moment with her dad, before she began trying to explain all to Uma and her father, who was now frowning, cross-eyed in concentration.

When Uma's eyes glazed in incomprehension over a lot of what was told to her, she was reassured that in time she would process what was happening, and that the understanding would come at various levels. Incomprehension too, she was told, was a part of the process.

What really convinced her, though, was the look on Raj Mamu's face when he realized that the burden of his crazed secret love was not just his to resolve. There were other people in the know, people who did not need to be convinced that what he had felt for Aparajita all these years was more real than reality; that the force of his love for her was not only reciprocated, but that the heat of it was enough to fuel the love of others.

'All that's fine, but I need to know why you are taking our old wheeze to a village without medical facilities when you can do what you have to do by waving your hands in the air?' Uma demanded.

And Kamini told her that that had been the original plan. That the original plan had been an elaborate one, set up to bring Raj and Aparajita together in a physical setting, but the plan had been aborted because of the shifting time frames. The cyclone build-up and the impending riots in the villages of Orissa that were currently ravaging the country were meant to have occurred a few months later. Indira and her husband, however, had so successfully escalated the negative energy build-up that there really was no time any more. The cyclone was barely a few hours away, and a tsunami of unprecedented proportions would soon follow.

'Why is Indira doing this? And her husband? There were times when I got the distinct impression that she wanted Raj Mama dead!' Uma shook her head at the incredulity of the thought.

'They probably think they are operating out of greed for money and power,' Kamini said. 'Considering that Mother and I have been prohibited entry into Vishnupur and I know the love the people of Vishnupur still have for Dad.' She took a deep breath and continued, 'It is true that Indira was born as Father's nemesis. She, and now her husband are channels of the universe to neutralize the unconditional love generated between these two. Entropy of the universe moves to neutralize UCL.'

'Huh?

'Never mind. Physics was never your strongest subject.'

'Huh? Physics? Aren't you guys healers?'

Kamini took a deep breath. 'Suffice it to know that the reason Dad has to go back to Vishnupur is because that also happens to be the headquarters of the VNP. By the way, VNP stands for Vishnupur. It took me a long time to figure that out.'

And because her voice broke at this point it became the very moment that Hari put his arm around her and she immediately felt a weight lift off her chest. Uma tried to maintain an expression of studious unconcern, but for some unfathomable reason suddenly felt very happy for her young cousin.

'Vishnupur is a sacred site, one of fifty such on the planet. It is a geographical trapdoor to many other dimensions, an established and much respected ley line, like the Stonehenge. Many worldly and other worldly battles like the Mahabharata have already been fought there, and VNP had been previously ordained to be the destination this time as well. By taking Dad to Vishnupur, he gets the power to go back to source and it also gives VNP the chance to move, literally, to the eye of the cyclone and defuse it at the origin.'

'Shouldn't she be with him?' Uma asked uncertainly. 'Wouldn't all that UCL be useful for you?'

'Too dangerous,' Kamini smiled at her cousin's shifting paradigms. 'They will be sitting ducks in VNP. The strategy is to deploy her in Kolkata with the ring and a huge VNP contingent. That way, counter-energies get decentralized from VNP.'

Even though Uma was sitting in a car in the middle of the day in busy Kolkata traffic she began to feel the stillness of the present moment, like a white feather in the silence of free fall. 'Okay, just two questions,' Uma said.

'Shoot.'

'What's with the ring?'

'The ring is of extreme importance,' Kamini declared. 'It is the first and only physical manifestation of physical reunion in the three-dimensional world. The only tenuous link of hard reality between them, and it embodies all the purity of Dad's intention, his UCL. My sister wanted the ring to destroy this link; the minute the ring reaches her hands, her husband and she are safe.'

'Okay,' Uma said, not entirely convinced.

'The original plan,' Kamini explained, 'was something similar. We were working towards union with the stepping down of energies at every level – like a transformer. First their union took place at the causal level, when VNP made an intention for them to come together. Then, the union was supposed to have taken place in the subtle level. With the new plan it will happen with Dad in Vishnupur and with the ring in Aparajita's hands. Inshallah, if all goes according to plan, we will move to the third and final level – physical reunion.'

'Okay,' Uma quickly said. 'I didn't understand any of that, but last question.'

'Shoot, dearly beloved, shoot,' Kamini said with a theatrical flourish.

'To safeguard Aparajita in Kolkata, this huge VNP contingent – who is it going to have?'

Kamini smiled sweetly at her cousin. 'Oh that would be you and me.'

Uma coughed, and somebody ventured a laugh. Soon there was a riffle of nervous laughter in car. And when Uma joined in with the others, she tried not to notice, as did the others, that through all her smiling, Kamini's eyes had misted over with tears that were very real.

They also noticed that Hari was not laughing at all.

'Where we come from, in VNP,' Kamini smiled wistfully through her tears, sensing all their thoughts, 'there is no such thing as parents.'

She couldn't prevent the catch in her voice.

30.

Aparajita sat upright on her wheelchair by her favourite bay window from which the mid-morning sun streamed through to her upturned face. Rudra sat on a chair next to her, staring at the sky over Chowringhee, following the flight of two birds.

What if you walked the ends of the earth for somebody, and the person did not want to see you? she said.

That's known to happen, he said.

He is not going to come, she said.

She had been so certain. So certain. She had felt the certainty of the last few decades. But now she was beginning to despair.

He will come. Rudra was quiet in his own certainty.

There was silence. The only activity was domestic. The peaceful rhythm of the cook chopping onions in the kitchen for the lunchtime meal.

Why did you not take the ring when it was given to you? Rudra complained. *You set the project back by two energy levels.*

It was so sudden, she defended herself. *I couldn't believe the waiting was over. That he had finally come. When there is a sudden cessation of doubt it is kind of scary. Like Sushmita Sen getting the Miss World title.*

Rudra laughed.

The maid in the kitchen heard what seemed to her to be unprovoked mirth and shook her head at the extent of his brain damage.

Rudra looked at his grandmother carefully. Her face shone golden in anticipation. The stiffening muscles had relaxed, her movements were more fluid. Her eyes were long and unwrinkled. It had taken half a year of half of VNP's best distance healing resources to do that.

Walk, Rudra had said.

Talk, she had replied.

And they had both laughed.

The cook was about to wake up the nurse nodding off on a corner stool in the corridor to go and attend on the two cuckoos when the bell rang, and the nurse woke with a start on her own.

There was a waiting silence at the bay window.

Both heard the hushed conversation at the main door.

No, Mr Ghosh and his son were out for the day. They would be back only in the evening. There was nobody here, really, please call and come back in the evening. You want to meet them, I am not sure, they are, you know, not quite... well, okay, if it's okay by you. They are not violent or anything, as long as you are aware...'

There was a brief silence and then a bright voice chimed out to herald the guests: 'Rudra baba and his Thakuma have guests. They are coming in right now,' the nurse sang out, making it sound like a warning, so they could stop anything naughty they might have been doing.

Uma and Kamini walked in and stopped at the end of the room to just look at Rudra and his grandmother.

'Hi, Rudra,' Kamini said across the room. 'It's so good to see you again.'

She thought she saw a hint of a smile. But she couldn't be sure.

The two women walked up to Rudra and Aparajita.

There were many preliminaries that happened. The tea, the searching for words and what to say next, the mindfulness of what was going to happen, the slow waning of light in the room.

Finally, Kamini stood in front of Aparajita in an ultimate face-off and the older woman looked up at her with eyes shining in surrender, willing to accept whatever came from the daughter of her beloved.

Kamini found herself frozen, unable to say anything.

Too many years, too many memories, backed up on her, like a car involuntarily reversing into a lamp-post.

Then Uma took the jewellery case clutched in Kamini's hand gently away from her. This was not how they had planned it. But Aparajita could not take her shining eyes off Kamini. She asked for a notepad and a pen, and even though Aparajita could still talk, the nurse, used to her idiosyncrasies, complied.

Tell her, she wrote, *that I know her from before she was even born. Tell her, that I've loved her like my own. Tell her, whatever happens nothing and nobody can take that away from me.*

Kamini slowly sank to her knees, rested her tired head on the old woman's knees, and wept.

Uma, with shaking hands, snapped open the jewellery case and held it out in front of Aparajita. Aparajita saw the glittering solitaire and an Urdu couplet flashed in front of her:

Diamond, if you want to show me your brightness,
Come and meet me in the dark.
Any piece of glass can sparkle in the day.

And she knew that Raj knew this couplet. Not only because she knew he had always loved Urdu poetry, but because she just knew. The other detail was that she had never heard the couplet before. But, as they say, those were just details.

Uma took out the folded piece of paper concealed in the lining. She opened it. Aparajita gestured. Uma understood the gesture. *Read it.*

And she read in a shaking voice what had been haunting her for the last few weeks:

I told you I would find you.

Let them know.

I am coming to take you.

And with tears streaming down her cheeks, Uma said, 'He left this at your doorstep, before he lost consciousness and slipped into a coma in hospital.'

'That's fine,' Aparajita spoke for the first time in many years. Graciously, as if she were telling an overwrought chef in an expensive restaurant who was sorry they were just out of sour cream: 'It's fine. It's all right.'

She and Rudra were the only ones not crying.

Maybe, Kamini thought, *because they have done enough penitence for all of us.*

31.

It was not that the highway was especially busy at that time of the day. The highway, in fact, was always busy except in the dead of night. The driver, an emaciated but heavily moustachioed man, expertly swerved the ambulance between a speeding SUV, a garishly tasselled truck's rear that declared 'Rinky loves me!', and assorted chickens clucking across the road with one hand, and changed radio stations with the other – all the while complaining about the irregularity of the situation: 'The cities of Cuttack and Bhubaneshwar are on red alert because of the impending cyclone. And you are asking me to drive into the middle of it!'

'Arrey, driver bhaisahib,' Carlos, sitting cramped shoulder to shoulder next to the driver said in his perfectly accented Hindi, learnt in Benares from the most renowned pandits of Sanskrit, 'You know the weather reports are always wrong.'

'Wrong? Well, Cuttack has been evacuated. So has Bhubaneshwar. The whole of Orissa seems to be taking the warnings seriously. Fishermen have come back from the coast. The cyclone has devastated Bangladesh!'

'There is not going to be any cyclone,' Hari said calmly from behind.

'And how do you know?'

'Tchh,' Ali leaned into the driver's ear in a conspiratorial whisper. 'He's omnipotent, omnipresent and omniscient. He knows.'

The driver cracked his knuckles over the steering wheel. 'Jokers.'

In the tail end of the van, Raj was awake, sitting upright on his stretcher, his eyes wide and his knees drawn up to his chin. Rita and Mira stared back at him in silent encouragement.

'She needs to know,' he told them, amazed at how coherent he was, how clear his head felt. 'My wife Kiran needs to know. This is important. We can't hurt Kamini and her anymore. We can't hurt anybody anymore.'

'They know, Raj,' Mira said, compulsively missing her knitting, somehow thinking it would have helped soothe Raj's nerves. 'We know. All of us know.'

But Raj was not convinced. And he needed to talk. The way a person who has not spoken in many years needs to talk: 'You see, we are united in consciousness. We are not lovers anymore. Never were, actually. Even our physical union cannot be called lovemaking.'

'Not that you ever made love,' Rita said, and blushed at her unwarranted intrusion.

'Because there is no gender between us now, no age, no caste, no creed,' Raj ignored her interruption. 'We are beyond even thought and belief.' And then he said by way of introducing something alien: 'They call it unconditional love.' Raj looked apologetic, as if he stood over a devastated site of his own making.

Rita felt the urge to help him out of his misery. 'True union burns all duality. So that, I mean, that, is what unconditional love is.'

None of them noticed when the driver pulled the van to a stop by the roadside for chai. Ali and Carlos climbed out of the front and squeezed into the back of the van to join in the conversation with Raj.

'Do you know the first time I realized what I was feeling was unconditional love?' Raj said.

'When?' Mira prompted.

'When I realized that I did not have an affair with her because I could not bear to see her guilty for hurting her family. And later, when I realized I was actually having an affair to give my wife a good enough reason to hate me.'

They did not register when the burnt tea came, when it got swallowed between hot and cold gulps.

'True union is Yoga. You and I are one,' Carlos butted in like a schoolboy in a locker room. 'That's also what "namaste" means. One day I hope to realize that.' And with that Carlos folded his hands and said, 'Namaste. My name is Carlos.' And everybody else folded their hands too, laughing, 'Namaste'.

When Raj smiled it felt to him as if the last time he had smiled like that was when he was a child. They all crowded in on the stretcher and passed around another round of scalded milk and reheated tea leaves.

With every passing minute his face was clearing up, his eyes becoming long and unlined, like a schoolboy's.

'It's interesting,' Rita decided, sipping her chai only as a gesture of solidarity. 'How all of us have met Raj before at some point in time.' Looking into his eyes staring intently back at hers she said, 'I went to school with your cousin Manik. And I lived for a while in the Chowringhee building.'

'My family owns property in the Chowringhee building,' Mira said. 'I too have lived there. I'm also Kamini's landlady. She's family to me.'

'I don't know whether you remember me,' Ali said. 'I once accompanied my dad for a film shoot to your palace when I was very young. I was very disappointed not to see you sporting a crown and a sword.'

'And I,' Carlos said, 'spent four years as a wandering fakir in and around Vishnupur.'

Raj looked at him intently.

'I had a beard then,' Carlos explained, stroking his clean-shaven chin.

'I remember you,' Raj said. 'The silent monk. I sat in front of you many times under a tree and meditated with you.'

Carlos nodded and blushed at some thought that crossed his mind. 'I cannot say that my journey or predicaments were the same as yours, but they were similar.'

And because the silence in the crowded ambulance was too empathetic – alluding clearly to the fact that his friends always knew but paid homage by never mentioning his journey or predicament – Carlos changed the topic. 'I knew then that we would have a closer encounter. But I didn't know how and I didn't know when.'

Just then the driver came running up to the van in a rush of anxiety and yelled: 'I am not going to Vishnupur.'

'Bhaisahib,' Hari said calmly. 'Don't shout. We have a patient here. This is an ambulance not a taxi cab. By the way,' Hari turned around to introduce himself to Raj. 'My brother is married to your elder daughter, Indira.' *And I plan to marry the younger one,* he finished in his head.

Raj smiled: 'You are not planning to marry the younger one, are you?'

They all laughed. But the driver was very agitated; he was jumping and gesticulating at the same time.

'No laughing matter. No laughing matter. You laugh. Have you seen the TV?' He pointed at the small portable television blaring in the dhaba. 'It says that the eye of the cyclone falls in the Vishnupur district. You want me to drive there? Never! Not even for a crore of US dollars.'

'Oye, chill maro, driver,' Ali said, 'just media sensationalism,' and cajoled the poor driver back behind the wheel.

32.

Why Vishnupur?' asked Uma. Kamini and she had pulled up their chairs by Aparajita and Rudra. The four of them sat in a circle by the waning light of the bay window. A storm was brewing in the middle of the day. Thunder was already darkening the horizon. Yet nobody wanted to switch on the lights.

'Vishnupur is a portal. A trapdoor to the fifth dimension,' Kamini explained. She remembered how stupid she had felt when she had realized that VNP stood for Vishnupur. And not any other Vishnupur, because there would be many invisible villages called Vishnupur in the map of India but the Vishnupur of her family, her childhood. The bloodline of Vishnupur ancestors that ran in her veins.

'I think that it is also not only an ancient battlesite but also a yogbhumi – a place of penance since many millennia. Sages have attained realization here. And in so doing they have shifted the consciousness of humanity.'

'*And in so doing they have shifted the co-ordinates of time and space.*' Raj was having a similar conversation in the congested van.

The cook stopped by the kitchen door as Aparajita spoke in a scratchy voice. Uma and her cousin looked at her. 'She does talk when she wants to,' the cook said, as if to say, Stop looking at me, this is not a miracle, and turned and walked back into the kitchen. The rice was almost done. She hoped the guests would not stay for lunch.

'I see Egypt there,' Aparajita sounded troubled. 'And ancient civilizations before the calibrations of time. I see armies arrayed in terrible battle. As they have been since before time began.'

'And so they have been.' Kamini rose from her chair with an involuntary sense of urgency. 'I have always known that Vishnupur was a historic site. King Ashoka had been there, so had Buddha, but only in VNP did I learn that it goes back to pyramidal times. It is not only a historical site but also a mythological one, from an age when continents were made and dissolved. One of the few ley-lines on the planet, which is a threshold between two interfacing dimensions where ancient and eternal battles are fought.'

She drew the curtains further apart, as if to fight against the dying of the light.

'I am sure, even as we speak, Rita is making analogies of the Churning of the Ocean mythology,' Kamini said.

And so Rita was, as the van swerved to dodge oncoming bullock-carts piled high with people; driving against humanity fleeing from Vishnupur even as they sped towards it. Rita was explaining the analogy exactly the way Kamini was imagining she was:

'About unconditional love. So let us in on the trick. What is the secret?' Mira quizzed Raj in the back of the van like an old, nay, an ancient companion.

'Love has to become pure,' Raj had said and shrugged at the sheer simplicity of it.

'That's what hunchbacked alchemists were trying to do in their extremely unhygienic and badly-ventilated cellars. Because the alchemy of gold is the alchemy of love,' Ali remarked, adding a couple of warts and moles to his eccentric patron saints in his mental vision. 'They were trying to find out how to purify love. That is the secret of alchemy. Alchemy inherently demands the removal of impurities – negativities, matter, beliefs that this world is real – these are all impurities.'

And at the exact moment that Kamini remembered her, Rita started churning her favourite ocean: Mount Meru balanced on the tortoise in the ocean pulled by the serpent Vasuki, the devas pulling from one side and the asuras from the other, for the final reward – the nectar of the gods, ambrosia. And to her jostling audience Rita used her favourite gesture, her fingers for inverted commas: 'When love is no longer "torn" (Vasuki) by the "duality of illusion" (the tug of war between the devas and asuras), it becomes a certainty (Mount Meru) and that's when the blessings, "ambrosia" –'

'– "post-coital bliss" –' Ali mimicked the inverted commas.

'– starts to pour,' Rita finished, glaring at Ali.

Raj looked at Ali thoughtfully, scratching his unshaven hospital stubble. For the first time Ali's team saw Ali actually look a little embarrassed.

'When did our boy become old enough to learn about the birds and bees?' Carlos jibed.

'Sex is an energy,' Ali explained, trying not to look at anybody.

'That would be synergy.' Raj made it sound like a peace offering.

'Sin-energy,' Carlos laughed.

On the highway to Vishnpur, Raj finally came to terms with the process that had unfolded more than three decades before inside his being: 'Sex is pure. When it becomes a karma it becomes a sin, and vice versa.' He stared out at the crowded convoluted road, at the press of people desperate to move away from the cyclone, and felt the need to make his travel companions understand what had happened to him.

'Usually, suffering is karma. The more we suffer, the deeper we entrench ourselves into the karmic cycle. But our – hers and mine – suffering was different. It was an intense desire for union. It brought us closer to our higher consciousness.'

And then he said with a fondness that moistened Mira's eyes: 'It made flowers bloom on her window sill. We didn't realize it, but our suffering had become a purification process, an elaborate esoteric ritual.'

For the first time Ali looked at Raj directly. 'But, sir, then why all the sex?'

'Desire for union.' The answer came straight, as if his experience had been ironed out by time. 'Just consciousness needing to fill the other part of itself.'

'Remember the presentation on Shiva and Shakti, Ali?' Mira reminded him.

'I would imagine Shiva and Shakti know a few tricks the shop-owners of Amsterdam would give their eye-teeth for.' Ali grinned lecherously and squared his shoulders, feeling his old self again.

'At it hammer and tongs, I tell you,' Mira giggled. 'An old couple as ancient as them. Shameful.'

The van turned off into a dust track from a board that said Vishnupur, and the vehicle kicked up a fine golden dust in its wake. They were flanked on both sides by emerald rice fields. The crop was in.

The van trundled up to the giant stone gates of the palace. And then they were being signalled down by a man who stood in the middle of the road.

He stood alone, dressed completely in black. They all saw him in the same instance and the chatter died. From behind the man looming large in the middle of the dusty driveway, hundreds of crows flew off in a simultaneity that momentarily darkened the horizon. The light changed.

Inside the car, the team started mentally rehearsing all the lectures given them by visiting VNP symbologists, energy-specialists, mirror-workers and Black Hole warriors. It was time to put it all to practice. They had been told that the ley-lines of Vishnupur set it as an ideal arena. Seeing the man standing resolutely immobile before them, they saw why.

One human life was equal to one pulse vibration, like that of a tuning fork, so they had been taught.

When the vibration ended, like the dying out of a note, the life of that person ended. Tonight, they knew, was the night that many vibrations would clash, resonate, cancel out, die.

Death did not take you to a far-off place. It happened in the here and now. They were prepared. It was time.

So this was Armageddon.

The only sound was of the whirring of the van's beat-up engine. Even the driver had stopped his whining litany. For one last time they thought of Raj and Aparajita. How they had lived, how they had maintained in a state of conflict for such a long time. He with the dark. She with the light. It had been imperative. That is why the forces needed to move to VNP. All of them were points in a network. The unearthing of one cable pulled out all the others. But they were prepared. It was time. They had tuned in to the one vibration already.

'Uh huh,' Carlos commented quiet as a whisper. 'I declare the games open.'

Ali took a deep breath.

Because in that moment, Carlos seemed like Caesar, and the Vishnupur palace driveway took on the look and feel of the middle of the Coliseum.

And the man standing like a monolith in front of the car, the personification of their nemesis.

33.

Tears streamed down Aparajita's face and fell on her hands that lay folded in her lap. 'We can't harm our families any more,' she whispered. 'We can't be unfaithful any longer.'

Kamini reached out and took the liberty of holding the older woman's hand.

Aparajita looked at her, still needing absolution, ceaselessly imploring: 'For many years now it was enough that we were wandering somewhere in the same time. Where we are now, even that is not necessary. Where we are there is no space or time.'

'You were never unfaithful.'

Aparajita opened her eyes and looked at Kamini through her tears. 'Technically, no. But truthfully, yes. Because there was destruction around us. In my definition, destruction is evidence of infidelity. Love creates, it does not destroy.'

Kamini stepped back from the enormity of her statement. 'So you are saying that love is sacrifice?'

Aparajita smiled wanly, 'Don't put words into my mouth.'

'I'm holding you to this one,' Kamini said.

'Well, let me see. Yes, if you insist. Sacrifice is giving. But true sacrifice gives to get. To get the treasures of the universe. Sacrifice that gives without getting is self-destruction. What do you think Christ got from his crucifixion? He got resurrection. He got an elevated mass consciousness. Sacrifice is misunderstood,' Aparajita said, sitting strong and straight on her wheelchair. 'It's the most politically incorrect word I know. Because my understanding of it is that sacrifice is selfish – truly, deeply, ultimately, selfish.'

And seeing the incredulous expression on Uma and Kamini's face her laughter rang out, tinkling and suddenly joyous in the darkening drawing room: 'Let's not talk about it. Let it go.'

'The path of true love never did run smooth, somebody said.' Uma, wanting to contribute, suddenly remembering her school ICSC syllabus. 'I think it was Shakespeare,' she said, involuntarily visualizing a multiple choice question. 'Love is never convenient.' Uma was feeling a bit drunk. 'Definitely, never convenient...'

But Kamini wasn't listening. She was staring at Aparajita who had turned pale. 'What's happening?' she said to her in alarm.

Aparajita held the Cartier box to her chest. 'He's weakening. His strength is ebbing away.'

And so it was. Raj's knees buckled as he got off the vehicle.

Maybe it was a bad idea not getting a doctor along, Hari was panicking. Even though he was fairly confident of the reiki and healing energy protocol the team had been using on Raj, he should not have underestimated the negative strength of his brother.

'This is such an unwise decision, Hari,' Vinay, Raj's son-in-law and Hari's brother, spoke solicitously, assisting his father-in-law with a great show of politeness as he struggled to stand: 'To rush a comatose man here, to the back of beyond. I am surprised the hospital gave you permission.'

Vinay put his hands insouciantly in his trouser pockets. He was altogether too casual, too suave, too quiet, too unhurried. His hands released a force. His magnetism started drawing the crowd in. They struggled against its dark gravitational pull.

Hari too put his hands in his pockets. 'We didn't, actually.'

Vinay's face darkened like the horizon around him, 'Indira told me you were coming,' he said, taking Raj's elbow, with a show of much deference. Raj jerked it off. Unfazed, Vinay continued, 'I took the liberty of arranging the guest rooms in the west wing.'

'The furthest away from me, I notice,' Raj said.

Vinay ignored him and led his guests in. 'Let me show you the spots. If you notice the steeple up there...'

Vinay's proprietary air was what irritated and distracted Mira and she involuntarily looked up even as the others were mindful not to. The minute she glanced at the steeple a hundred gargoyles flew off it. Hari raised two fingers discreetly, pretending to pat his hair, and they vanished in a cloudburst.

As they walked into the numerous courtyards of the main wing of the palace, they became aware that the statues and awnings were clogged heavy with spirits, rising like fumes to envelop them.

'Those steps are too steep for you, sir,' Hari expertly steered Raj away from an invisible mandala meant to trap vital energies. Carlos and Hari were mentally scanning the entire palace and locating all the tantric spots to be avoided and annihilated as soon as they got the chance. Where they could, they swiftly removed the black patterns with white light energies even as they walked and made small talk.

'Why don't you wash up and then let's all meet for dinner at the Banquet Hall,' Vinay suggested when they reached the central hall of the palace.

But his guests promptly said that they were too tired to be hungry and would rather turn in early. Under no conditions would they allow the manipulated energies of the palace's food and water inside their systems. Carlos insisted on sleeping in Raj's bedroom, citing reasons of Raj's delicate health. Vinay argued, but on Raj's stubborn insistence, gave in. And they all retired to their bedrooms to prepare for the countdown of the moment that they had prepared for, for months.

The diamond twinkled in the jewellery case.

'It's so expensive.' Aparajita was speaking to Raj. *'You shouldn't have.'*

'The cost of the ring was nothing,' Raj said, slipping so easily back into their connection again that he didn't even realize it. *'It's getting you to hold it the way you are holding it now that was the price that took the mickey out of me.'*

'What is with the ring?' Uma asked, polishing off the left-over kheer in Aparajita's fridge. As the cook feared, the guests had not only stayed for lunch and dinner but looked like they were planning on spending the night.

Gaurav and Mr Ghosh had got stuck in Park Street in the downpour that had unleashed on Kolkata in the afternoon. A worried Gaurav had called the apartment to let the nurse know that there was no way they would make it home in the floods and wondered how she would be able to handle Ma and Rudra without them. The nurse had reassured him saying there was no problem, some kind building neighbours were giving them company and had offered to stay the night. What a relief, Gaurav thought, and that dealt with, wondered whether he could nip into the Saturday Club for a tot.

'The ring is crucial.' Kamini said. 'The ring is the first and only physical manifestation of a love that has not yet descended from the subtle energy realm to the third dimension. It is the nucleus, the seed crystal that is anchoring in and drawing down the Twin Flame union energy to the physical world. It has taken years of purificatory suffering for them, and much expenditure of VNP project energy to put Raj's ring into her hands.' Kamini paused to take a breath. 'It is also the nucleus that will draw into its field Raj and Aparajita's first physical encounter in their present condition. Your next question will be why is Aparajita not in Vishnupur. The answer is the same. Like a transformer, the charges have to be stepped down gradually before they reach the third, the gross dimension. First the ring, for their reconnection in the subtle world, then their subtle encounter in Vishnupur. If that is successful, only then can they meet in the physical world. You and I will have to sleep here tonight and ensure that nothing goes wrong. So you see, the ring is all important,' Kamini said. 'Indira would kill for that ring right now. She has to stop their union somehow. That's what she was born for.'

Uma said, 'She will soon figure out where we are.'

And so she had.

Indira had found out from Vinay's scan where Kamini was. A little interrogative grilling of her uncle Manik had also helped. But by the time she had reached the Chowringhee apartment the basement had flooded, jamming the lift.

Indira took the stairs. They seemed very familiar. It was in the landing of Aparajita's apartment that she felt unable to move forward. An invisible wall had risen before her and she was unable to manoeuvre around it.

Damn, she thought. *Kamini's team is protecting Aparajita.*

She took a deep breath to prevent herself from cursing Kamini because she knew that cursing would only deplete her resources. The doorbell was barely a few feet away. If she rang it somebody would answer and once she was face to face with Kamini she knew she had the strength to make her succumb. But she was unable to move towards it.

She decided to wait for the resistant force to weaken and for Vinay to send reinforcements. She sat down on a landing stair. It would be a long wait.

The members of the VNP group were building similar defences in the Vishnupur palace. Doors and windows were being sealed with mantras and incantations, counter mandalas were being visualized to deconstruct the prevailing ones, and opposing forces were made to forcefully disintegrate. And even though the team had been scattered in different bedrooms they managed to align their group energies in their meditations and reinstate the intention of their mission.

Meera and Rita, both in the same bedroom, were grateful for the clean sheets and the dust-free environment. They had even been prepared to camp out in the open. The soft pillows and eiderdown covers were a good sign. Still, both were deeply revulsed, not with spiders and cobwebs, but with the denizens of the netherworld that continued to seek an entrance through their marked boundaries.

'Centaurs, gargoyles, succubi, incubi, plant spirits, animal spirits, they've got them all.'

'Disgusting,' Rita shuddered. 'The place is virtually crawling with them. And it doesn't help that the Vishnupur royal lineage has been a fairly cruel one. Vinay and Indira have successfully managed to harness a lot of angry and discontented spirits against Raj here.'

'By the way,' Mira massaged foot cream in the cracks of her soles. 'Stay away from the artefacts. There are some discontented rajas here too. And they are sticking like limpets to all the expensive vases.'.

Just then Ali knocked and entered to hand them their lucid-dreaming pellets.

'Looks like it's going to be a long night,' he said.

Wisps of white cloudy smoke lashed across the sky and started wrapping around the palace, like a bandage to a fist. All of a sudden, bright drops of rain as large as pumpkins started hailing down on Vishnupur. The sky turned a brilliant lilac. A shooting star streaked across the sky.

And, just as suddenly, the rain stopped.

In their room, Raj turned to Carlos who was arranging his drinking water by the bedside table and said, 'You've been meaning to ask me a question for a while. Why don't you just ask it?'

Carlos smiled in apology. He smiled because what Raj had said was true, and in apology, because of the nature of the question. 'How does one *know*?' Carlos asked. 'How did you know?'

Raj walked up to the balcony window that had turned purple with the intensity of light. 'When you pine for her too much, does it start to rain?' he asked

'Um, no,' Carlos said.

'Then you'll have to wait,' Raj said. 'Maybe it's not yet time.' And then, with gentleness, 'She came to teach you about courage and commitment. And you learnt your lessons well.'

Carlos nodded his thanks.

Outside, the birds confused by a universe that was no longer familiar screeched their anguish, swinging around in despair, carpeting the courtyards with feathers, like in some archaic ritual.

Just before they turned out the lights, both men put their lucid-dreaming pellets into their mouths under their tongues. And when all the lights went out only a few storm lanterns burned in the outer courtyards.

And battle raged.

Lancers stretched out to eternity in a perfectly straight line. Conches were blown. Bugles were sounded. And dream worlds moved towards each other like bubbles trying to equalize surface tension. They merged and coalesced in microcosmic sighs as movement began its slow flurry. Everybody came out into the central courtyard in thought forms of their own choice and making.

Rita was young and clad in red flowing robes. Mira was slender and tensile. Carlos flew. Ali was a knight annihilating armies with a single gesture. Hari and Vinay met in a mid-air collision and circled each other like the ancient adversaries that they, in fact, were. Indira found Kamini in the palace gardens. But this time Kamini was different. She did not cower as she had done as a child. She bared her teeth like a cat and stunned Indira for a moment. Uma was surprisingly swift and succeeded in instinctively helping her cousin when she needed her.

Rudra rowed out with his grandmother across a wispy boat on silver waters, keeping his eyes on the pink moon. But, Aparajita, who sat in the boat could not find Raj. They searched for him over valleys, climbing mountains, crossing galaxies and star systems, but he was not there.

The sound of thunder shook the three worlds, and lightning cut across the inner skies like Thor's weapon of choice. Raj emerged from wormhole to wormhole but there was no sign of Aparajita.

There was a display of heroism, of courage, of resilience, of strength, but the fury of conflict did not abate.

'Oh, but we have to forgive,' Rudra said, dressed all in white, serenely steering his course through still waters.

'*Forgive, forgive forgive,*' ran the whisper through the rustling of seaweeds in turbulent waters and the shivering of leaves in the storm.

The thunder cracked in agreement.

Dogs howled to change the night watch and the wolves from the Vishnupur forest took over, as if on cue.

'We are weakening,' Rita said.

'*Forgive, forgive, forgive,*' the palace wall drums beat out like the clock of all time. *Forgive* tick, *forgive* tock. *Forgive* drum *forgive* roll. *Forgive* Om. *Forgive* Om. Om *forgive*. Om *forgive* Om.

'Of course!' Ali shouted across to Mira on the golden shore where she had just lanced Indira through the shoulder. 'That is right. They are powerless against forgiveness.'

'He is right. Only forgiveness will release their grip.'

'The forgiveness prayer now.' Carlos sent out a clarion call. 'All regroup for the forgiveness protocol NOW!'

And they blessed and they blessed. *Bless, bless, bless, bless.*

Hari, his brother; Kamini, her sister; Aparajita, her family; Raj, his; Rudra, his grandmother; Uma, her uncle.

Bless, forgive. Bless, forgive.

And, slowly, ancient cords were cut. And old pernicious bonds were broken.

They say in the scriptures, Raj said, that old enemies are born as your children.

Kamini laughed. I forgive you, but I shall never forget that you forgot my seventh birthday.

Laughter reached them like far-off bells, as gradually the clashing of swords grew less clamorous.

☯

Raj found Aparajita in a green meadow under a tree of pink cherry blossoms in full bloom.

Raj touched her hand. She looked up at him.

'Are we in China?' she asked. 'As far as I know there are no cherry blossoms in India.'

Raj, flummoxed for a moment by her clinical response, gathered himself and picked up a flower. 'You are right,' he mumbled, studying the flower. 'I've never seen that colour on a cherry blossom before.'

And the surrounding sound said like a voice-over in a movie: 'Will somebody remind these jokers that they are the lead actors in the play. Act appropriately!'

Raj and Aparajita thought they would never stop laughing.

34.

When Hari returned with the chocolate sundaes to the corner table of Café Coffee Day in the Kolkata mall he found Kamini staring out thoughtfully from the window.

'I thought I was the spare wheel of the project, the joker of the pack,' she said after a long silence.

'You were the ace of spades,' Hari put the two orders on the shiny rosewood table.

'If I had not forgiven them what would have happened?'

'Think of it this way,' Hari said, slipping into his chair and cleaning a wet slick with his paper napkin. 'Your forgiveness saved the world.'

She rested her chin on her hand and looked more deeply out the window. 'You know, you and I, we have probably raped each other, murdered each other, pillaged each other, and lord knows what else, in past lives to learn our life lessons. But what I take away from this project is an opportunity to try and learn about love.'

Then he had lost her again, somewhere through the portal of the café window.

'I was there when they met, you know.'

'I presume that went well.' He tried not to look too interested.

'"Why didn't you tell me you loved me," she asked him.' Hari noticed that she said 'him' and not 'dad'.

'What did he say?'

Kamini laughed. 'He said, "You never asked."'

Half a sundae later, Kamini had tears in her eyes. This time Hari didn't even bother to prompt her.

'You know, they smiled at the same time, at the same pace. There was so much secret laughter between them.'

Hari thought it safe to help himself to her sundae.

'He picked her up from the wheelchair and walked out of the apartment with her, you know. "Can you walk?" he asked, looking at her with so much tenderness it seemed they were dissolving into each other. "With you," she said, "to the ends of the earth." She smiled so sweetly.' Kamini started to cry.

'I'm a little confused,' Hari said. 'You are crying because?'

'Because love like that can't cause any harm.'

'No,' he said. 'Not any more. It can't. And you are forgetting one thing.'

'What?'

'Love like that can also cause miracles.'

After a while she said: 'Interesting how there is love and there is true love. True love is only associated with soulmates and Twin Flames. A mother and child can be pure love. But only soulmates are true love.'

And he replied, 'Your forgiveness is complete. That officially draws this project to a close.' And it dawned on him then that so were the stringent rules of propriety forced on him as the Keeper of the Flame.

'And Rudra,' she smiled, remembering the small boy. 'Under the cherry blossoms. When I couldn't look at them anymore and turned away, he came running across a meadow and hugged me. He told me that I had done well. He looked older, and so handsome! That's when I figured he was the VNP chief.'

The café had faded out around them. Nothing existed. No billing counter, no chrome and steel tables, no franchise logos, just her words, hanging in the air.

'How do you know he is the VNP chief?'

'It's simple. Like the Dalai Lama reincarnations are not deciphered through gross intellectual categories like background, age and nationality, so it makes imminent sense that the VNP chief is somebody who is only operating in the subtle realm. It precludes the possibility of hierarchical systems and efficiency being dragged down to the gross. To receive an instruction from the chief you need to be tuned in to subtle frequencies. That's it. Period.'

'Would you like another sundae,' Hari said after a long pause, as if assimilating this. 'I would like a brownie.'

The café was slowly coming back into focus again. The red and black glare of their sensex listed brand, the smoothness of the floor beneath them.

She turned to smile at him. 'I don't believe it,' she grinned, staring, closing in. Hari's shiftiness had given him away. And Kamini was prodding him, like a slightly inept predator who had at last found an easy prey.

'What?' Hari rapped his knuckles on the table, squinting at the menu pasted above the waiter's head. 'I think I'll have a sundae.'

'Hari?'

'What?' he fidgeted.

'You didn't know who the VNP chief was.'

'Did too,' he said, stubborn, not laughing.

'All these years in VNP and you didn't know?'

'Did too.'

She doubled over, thumping her fist on the table.

'No, you didn't. Not till I told you,' she whooped.

'Did too.'

And somewhere laughter found a breach in his misery and he joined her, laugh for laugh, squeal for squeal, guffaw for guffaw. And they knew then that they may not be under the cherry blossoms but some of Raj and Aparajita's joy was theirs to share.

35.

There were no definitions left behind any more. No identities. Not even attraction, or love or emotion. Or romance or the creations of romance. Raj and Aparajita were just two energies united by a single consciousness. And when that happened they realized that all their stories had resulted from the pain of separation. A pain they would never experience again. Because they had reached the point where division was no longer possible. Because the other no longer existed. A column of light had opened up in their bodies like a dark secret room where a series of lights had switched on. And their columns had merged, twisting around each other like a helix, like a winding stairway to heaven.

And with that Raj and Aparajita realized they were permanently blessed in love. Not only with themselves and each other, but the whole world. Because they *were* the whole world.

She took him first to Jagannath Puri, and showed him the finger imprints of the saint Chaitanya Mahaprabhu, where his hand had sunk into stone like butter at the sight of the Lord. He had transmuted into energy here. They visited other holy places like Mansarovar and Amarnath. In the Amarnath caves two white doves flew out to meet them. They smiled at the similarity of processes but finally settled to choose the Madhuban gardens of Vrindavan near Delhi as their point of departure.

☯

Kamini, Hari and the entire Twin Flame project team drove them up to the garden. It was dusk when they arrived. The gates would shut by the time darkness fell.

It was said that whoever remained behind in the Madhuban gardens after dusk either died or lost their minds. *Why?* Kamini as a child had once asked her mother. Because, when Lord Krishna cavorted with the goddess Radha at night nobody could withstand the force of their attraction to each other. It was said that every morning they found broken bangles and half-eaten sweets offered in Radha's temple in the garden the evening before. At eight at night, all houses and buildings would shut the windows that faced the garden for fear of turning into stone at the sight of Radha and Krishna's love play.

The monkeys and birds had already started leaving the area. There was that strange but familiar hush in the air. Raj and Aparajita refused to let anybody say anything in farewell.

'There are no goodbyes.' Aparajita said. 'Never were. And never will be.'

Neither of their spouses had come to drop them off, though one last meeting had taken place. Separately, away from the other, even though they knew separation was no longer necessary.

'Should I say sorry?' Raj had asked his wife; Aparajita her husband.

'No,' they both had said.

'Why?'

'Because you sustained.'

And later, they added: 'This is better than losing you in an obscure hospital.'

'Maybe. But I wish you had told me.'

'What?'

'That you always knew.'

'What good would that have done?'

There had been acceptance, fond, quiet, all-encompassing. There had been gratitude. And there had been closure.

Raj and Aparajita walked into the garden holding hands. The tulsi trees opened out before them many winding paths. Their canopies had a thick heavy shade and the sky soon darkened above them. They spontaneously took a path through the trees and slowly the humming of bees started out from a horizon they could not yet see. The strains of a flute wafted up to them like a perfume. When the sound of anklets drew close – so close – Aparjita moved closer to Raj and reached for his hand.

To look at each other, shamelessly, for the first and last time. To hold each other like there was nothing between them, for the first and last time. The tulsi branches started curling into and away from them, and the sky moved into the branches – merging into spiralling curlicues.

The air blanched in increasing light and the world started speeding away from them.

They gasped.

As the VNP team took the turn towards the highway, the vicinity of the Madhuban garden lit up briefly in a flash of blinding white light.

Soon a gentle rain began to fall.

It touched everything beneath like a compassionate tap on the shoulder.

All clichés are true. It seemed to say. Love does save the world.

Lightning flashed.

If you can't love, at least forgive.

Epilogue

Rudra swung his long, thirteen-year-old legs off the psychiatrist's couch and asked the doctor for permission to leave. He was late for soccer practice but he had enjoyed the session because he liked the doctor. He found the doctor compassionate; he listened without prejudice.

'Is there anything else you want to tell me?' The doctor, forty, greying at the temples with no attempt to hide it, wore his reading glasses and skimmed through Rudra's file one last time.

'Like what?' Rudra picked up his duffel bag with the NBA logo and Kareem Abdul Jabbar's signature emblazoned across.

'Dreams, nightmares, fears, ideas? '

'Well, I do have a crush on my class teacher.'

'How bad is it?'

'Pretty bad.'

The doctor contemplated him over his reading glasses for a moment. 'Get out of here, you Freudian nightmare.' They both laughed. 'Send your father in. Oh, just one more thing. I forgot this school report you wrote.'

Rudra stopped. The doctor read out the handwritten page:

'"How to create a pink elephant with purple polka dots."'

'Oh that.'

'Let me finish,' the doctor interrupted and continued reading the untidy scrawl: '"You take a pink elephant and you take a normal elephant with purple polka dots. Then you merge them, but it has to be done very carefully. First you do it in the consciousness level, then the psychic level, then the emotional level of feeling, then in the language level of mind and intellect, then the level of the five elements of matter. If you have followed all the steps correctly you will hear a poof sound. And then with a whoosh the two elephants will merge and hey presto! You have a pink elephant with purple polka dots. Now your next question will be where to keep it. To which my answer would be, ask your mother. If you encounter further problems contact me."'

The doctor paused. Rudra waited.

'There is a teacher's comment with this piece.'

'Let me guess.' Rudra put a finger to his lips in a thinking pose. 'That this was written not in a creative writing class but a physics class?'

'Exactly.' The doctor looked a bit worried. 'Don't tell me, Rudra, that all our work has been in vain?'

'Ask me the next question.' Rudra tightened the strap of his duffel bag as if readying for a quizzing buzzer round.

'The question the school wants me to ask you is this: if you had to label this written piece with a genre how would you do it?'

'That's easy,' Rudra clicked his fingers.

'And?' The doctor realized he was holding his breath. Not very professional, he chided himself.

'Scientific imagination.'

The doctor's exhalation was a sigh of relief. 'Good. Get

out. Send your dad.' As he opened the door the doctor's voice sounded like a plea. 'You don't believe all this do you?'

'Of course,' Rudra laughed. 'And pigs can fly.'

☯

When Gaurav came in they spent some time settling into a friendly conversation around the neutral watering-hole of the worsening traffic situation and the impending government elections. After Gaurav was at ease, the doctor informed him that there was nothing to worry about, the routine psychiatric school check-up was fine, Rudra was growing like a normal teenager.

Gaurav was relieved.

'Was there any childhood trauma?' the doctor asked.

'Not really,' Gaurav said, then remembered. 'Oh yes, when he was very young there was a brief autism scare, but that passed, thank God.'

The doctor pored over the file. 'It's there in his papers. A glitch, most likely.'

'Most likely,' Gaurav agreed.

'He seems to miss his grandmother a lot. He talks very fondly of her.'

"My mother was an extraordinary woman. My deepest regret is that I couldn't be with her in her last moments,' Gaurav said.

'How did she go?' the doctor asked gently.

'In a hospital in Kolkata. So my father says. I could only reach after the cremation.'

'That must have hurt.'

'It still does.' Gaurav ran a hand across his forehead. 'It's like she disappeared. I don't know where she went. There was

just no closure. Because I didn't see her at the last it feels as if she exists but doesn't exist. It's weird, you know.?'

The doctor nodded.

'It's like there's no proof, because I wasn't there at the cremation. It's as if, if I called home, logically, she should just pick up the phone.'

'Logically,' the doctor agreed and to draw Gaurav out of his sudden anxiety said something that seemed like a change of topic:

'You know, there is some new and very interesting research that says that historical time is notional time. It says that our histories change according to our notions. So we can cook up an entirely different past according to the notions we hold in the present. For example, if I have a notion of being a successful doctor I'll create an entire history of memories to corroborate that, topping my exams, etc. Likewise, I could change my entire past memories to corroborate the notion that I am a lousy doctor, sibling rivalry, bad toilet-training, et al.'

'Interesting,' Gaurav said, though still blinking, still thinking of his mother.

'So if we can change our pasts why can't we change the history of the world? And if we can change the history of the world, why not the history of Time, and if Time why not creation, or Cosmogenesis?'

Gaurav was thoughtful.

'By change you mean create. You are saying the world is a reflection of us? We created it?'

'I guess.'

'The possibilities are infinite. If we can create all this we can also create…'

A picture of a pink elephant with purple polka dots popped up in the doctor's mind.

'Never mind,' he said.

'Sorry?'

'I have some of your son's jottings. Would you like to listen to them?'

'Sure.'

'"We on earth are gods on masochistic trips."'

'Oh, well,' Gaurav laughed.

'"Each sound produces a form in the invisible world."'

Both were quiet. Finally Gaurav broke the silence. 'Hmm,' he noted.

'"Love is the energy of creation."'

'Whatever my son means by that, I only hope it's legal, Ha ha.'

'"E=mc² is the tip of the iceberg."'

'Oh, okay.'

'"I come from the realms of No Time. I am the creator of what comes into being. I produced myself from primeval matter that I made."'

'The next thing he'll say is that he is self-realized.'

The doctor laughed.

'How's your son, somebody asks. "Oh, he's not doing much. Just self-realized." What a conversation stopper.'

'Well, Rudra is slightly delusional, but that's normal at his age, or any age for that matter. I wouldn't worry if I were you.'

'No worries.'

'There's another one.'

'Yes?'

'"My mission is not yet over."'

'What was that you said about delusion?

The doctor smiled. 'Oh, just one last thing.'

'Yes?'

'What's VNP*?'*

'VNP*?'*

'He mentioned it a couple of times. I presumed it was an abbreviation of something.'

'I have no clue.'

The doctor shot a look of suspicion at Gaurav. His training told him he was lying. His recent lessons taught him that truth and falsehood were two chimeras that laugh at you from the edges of reality.

And reality was? The doctor chose not to finish the thought and sighed: I wonder.